HANNAH AND THE HITMAN

VANESSA VALE

1

JACK

"Flying commercial is bullshit," Jorge grumbled, eyeing the row numbers along the overhead bins.

Jorge was also known as *El Cejas*, or Eyebrows. He was built like a keg of beer, all barrel-chested and squat and had a dark, furry caterpillar for a unibrow. I'd spent years dealing with guys like him–and his partner, Joe, who followed me–and pretty much ignored them. Today it wasn't so easy to do. Not on the packed commuter flight to Denver.

"Isn't this the plane type that crashes?" Joe asked.

I sighed and rolled my eyes. His nickname? Joey Brains. Not because he was smart, but because he wasn't the sharpest tool in the shed.

I wasn't too thrilled about this flight either, but complaining or saying a trigger word like *crash* or *bomb* or *peanut allergy* wasn't going to get the private jet we were supposed to be on fixed.

"It's your boss who wanted you to go to Denver with me," I reminded Joey Brains. "Would you rather still be in the desert sweating your balls off?"

He grunted in what seemed like agreement about the sweaty balls, although I didn't want to think about his. Or if they were sweaty.

Me? I'm Jack Hollister. My job? Hitman.

I just finished a hit for their boss, Sal Reggiano, the mafia head in Vegas. I'd taken out Tony the Tuna Shemansky. Who came up with those nicknames? Besides skimming a few mil off the top of their racing venture, he liked to dope the horses in ways I didn't like. I didn't give a shit out about the debt, but he got a bullet to the brain because of his animal cruelty.

Since this had been my first job for Sal Reggiano, I wasn't going to argue when he wanted two of his men flying back with me to start working with his son, Paul. Maybe Paul was tired of sweaty fucking balls because he moved to Colorado to spread their business into new territory. Since I was also from Denver, I did a bunch of jobs for him on a consistent basis. He was a decent guy, all things considered.

We'd be flying Sal's private plane right now except it broke down. Now I was flying in coach with them. My name wasn't Joey Brains. I knew when to keep my mouth shut and deal.

Did I like any of this? Fuck no. But Tony the Tuna was dead, I got paid a shit ton and as soon as we were back in Denver, I'd be rid of Eyebrows and Joey Brains. Tomorrow night, I'd be on to my next job. The hitman business was booming.

When Eyebrows found his row, he dropped into the aisle seat. After glancing at my ticket to confirm, I settled into the other aisle seat in the same row. With a wince, I shifted my ass and moved the seat belt, then sighed. The thirty-something Black man in the middle seat beside me gave me a chin lift, then went back to a game on his phone.

"I'm in C. You have A. I'm not sitting at the window," Eyebrows said. "You are."

"No fucking way," Joey Brains countered. "You take it."

"Why doesn't *he* take it?"

Eyebrows meant me.

I frowned. Annoyed as fuck. I took in the line of people waiting behind Joey Brains, more and more impatiently by the second.

"You're holding everyone up," I snapped at the two of them. "Sit your ass down. It's a two-hour flight."

Eyebrows stood to let him in, grinning like a sibling who got to ride shotgun instead of being stuck in the backseat.

"Getting capped in the knee would be less painful than this," Joey Brains grumbled as he slid over to the window, accidentally pulling on a woman's hair in the row in front of him as he went.

If I'd had my gun on me instead of having to put it in my checked bag, I'd have shot him myself to find out if he was right. This was flight 265. I couldn't even kill a guy with my bare hands with this many witnesses. Especially not Eyebrows or Joey Brains.

Boring.

The sooner we got back to Denver, the sooner they'd be out of my hair. I felt like a babysitter. I closed my eyes, thinking a nap would make the flight go faster.

"Excuse me, I think that's my seat."

My eyes popped open at the soft voice. All that filled my vision–thank fuck for a narrow aisle–was a perfect ass. Right there in my face. Jean clad. Round. Full. The perfect peach. Wide hips that itched to be gripped hard while... holy fuck. What the hell was wrong with me, getting a semi on a plane for another passenger? Not *any* passenger, this passenger specifically, who it seemed had the middle seat between Eyebrows and Joey Brains.

"Sure, doll," Eyebrows told her.

She moved back so he could stand. Unfortunately, all that did was bring his crotch right in my face.

The chub was gone.

"Can you put this in the overhead for me, please?" I heard her ask.

"Sure, doll," Eyebrows said again, making me wonder if he knew how to talk to the ladies.

He stepped back to make room for the bag, but the woman started hefting it herself. "Oh, um... it's not as hard as I thought. That's weird. Nevermind."

I took in her ass once more–as amazing as the first time–as she stretched and set the wheeled suitcase into the overhead. Eyebrows put his hand on it and helped her shove it the last few inches into place.

She slid into her seat and Eyebrows followed.

The woman–who I could now see had dark hair and a pert nose, leaned forward and shoved a backpack under the seat in front of her. Over her stooped back, I couldn't miss how the guys were eyeing the sliver of skin above her jeans where her t-shirt rode up.

While they couldn't kill anyone on the flight, I wouldn't put it past them to bother the woman wedged in the center seat between them. As amusement. I watched as they crowded her as she settled in, took away both her armrests and had their elbows pressing into her on each side as she set a book in her lap.

"Oh, um. You two are big," she commented, glancing between them warily. "Can I maybe, um... armrest? No? Okay."

She sneezed.

The assholes grinned.

Yeah, no innocent woman belonged stuck between two Reggiano goons. She *was* innocent, that was for sure. It was statistically impossible for her to *also* be a killer, right?

She squirmed, then reached to pull the seatbelt from beneath her, which forced her to shift and her tits–fuck were they high and full beneath her t-shirt that read *My TBR is Bigger Than Yours,* whatever the hell that meant— pressed unintentionally into Eyebrows' arm.

He leered and reached down to adjust his dick in his pants. I growled, loud enough that her gaze skirted around Eyebrows' barrel chest to meet mine across the aisle. At our continued staring, her cheeks turned pink. Her lips were plump and kissable. Hair a little wild. Freckles across her nose. If she had on more than shiny lip gloss, then it was really fucking subtle. She didn't need it. She was the girl next door and every one of my darkest fantasies settled uncomfortably in seat 7B.

Yeah, she was innocent. Sweet. I didn't do sweet and

innocent when it came to women, or at least one who looked like she baked cookies with her grandmother and went to brunch with girlfriends after yoga on Saturday mornings. Hell, I didn't have much time for *any* kind of woman. Or relationship. Sure, I was employed. Owned my own place. Had a very hefty savings account. I was thirty-three and had all my hair.

On paper, I was a catch.

But I killed people for a living.

Not many women were down for that.

This woman? She had no clue that she was seated between two bad men. While I'd probably racked up more kills than Eyebrows and Joey Brains, I only killed bad guys. Those who very much deserved to die. I was discriminate. I had a code.

Those two fuckers Eyebrows and Joey Brains? Zero code. Zero morals.

I popped my seat belt. Stood. A teenager with a hoodie and huge headphones took one look at me on his way down the aisle, then scurried past.

"Move," I growled at Eyebrows, adding a jerk of my thumb.

He looked up. "What the fuck?"

I leaned in. "There's a kid in the row behind you. Watch it with the swearing." See? I had morals. "And the woman next to you did actually pay for an armrest."

"What the f–heck crawled up your ass and died?" Eyebrows asked, standing, his unibrow arching across his forehead. I was taller and broader than him, but he played dirty, which meant I didn't trust him as far as I could throw him, which wasn't even a foot on a plane like this. Man, I hated flying commercial, too.

The answer to Eyebrows' question was easy. Being stuck with these two meatheads and knowing this one knew what the woman's tits felt like. If anyone was going to know, it was me.

"You. Here." I pointed to my now-empty seat.

Eyebrows settled into my spot with a huff.

For the first time, the woman's eyes met mine. It was like an electric current sizzled between us, even though she looked up at me wide eyed, completely confused.

It was strange as fuck.

She blinked.

"Hop up for a second and let the other one out," I told her.

"Me?" she asked, pointing at herself, as if she couldn't believe I was talking to her.

I nodded. "Please."

She blinked again, then sneezed. "Um, okay." She slid out of the row and stood, clutching a book to her chest in some subconscious survival mode. My ego liked a hell of a lot that she obeyed me. I had to tug her to me to let Joey Brains into the aisle from the window seat.

"Oh," she breathed. When static electricity zapped us, her eyes lifted to mine, wide with surprise.

I felt the spark, too, but hell, I was focused on how soft and plush and perfect her tits were pressed against me. Once Joey Brains was in the aisle and out of the way, I took her upper arm, bare below the short sleeve of her tee, and guided her into the window seat. "You first."

After giving both fuckers a glare, I slid into the middle

beside her, reached down by my feet and moved her small backpack to the spot beneath the seat in front of her. Joey Brains settled into the aisle seat, and I elbowed him hard to claim the armrest, all the while my attention was on the prettiest woman I'd seen in a long time.

"Better?" I asked.

She offered me a small smile, then nodded. "Thanks."

"I wasn't letting you be stuck between those two."

I studied her face close up now. So guileless. No hidden agenda. No... sinister thoughts to shoot me in the back. I picked up a citrusy scent. Definitely hers. Joey Brains, beside me, smelled more like stale cigarette smoke and body odor. No wonder she'd been sneezing.

"I'll even let you have the armrest." I winked.

She blushed a pretty shade of pink that matched her t-shirt, then flipped open her paperback to a bookmarked page.

While the flight attendant began the canned safety announcement, the plane pulled away from the gate and started to taxi toward the runway. By the time we were in the air, I was bored. While I didn't have something to read, my seatmate did, and I could read every word because she was that fucking close.

Her back arched as I filled her up. "Yes! Harder!" she gasped as I filled her in ways she'd never known possible. This pussy was mine, claiming it and molding it to my big–

Holy hell. This innocent little thing was reading... sex. Perhaps she wasn't so sweet after all.

Did I mention how much I loved flying commercial?

2

HANNAH

Breathe, Hannah! Read your book and breathe!

Except breathing meant I got lungfuls of the bossy hot guy's scent because he was *right there*. As in inches away. It was as if the hero from the romance book I was reading had morphed into reality.

Solid, sexy body. Check.

Dark hair, smoldering good looks. Check.

Potent stare. Check.

Growly and–oddly–protective. Check.

Dare I say chivalrous, rearranging seats? Check.

Because of him, I wasn't squeezed between the two creepy guys. *Thank God.* They'd oozed over the armrests and pretty much taken up all my space. How I would fly two hours wedged between them, I hadn't been sure, especially since one smelled sharply like his deodorant quit, the other of a potent, toxic cologne which made me sneeze. I'd considered ringing the call bell and asking for a new seat assignment because besides being cramped, they made me weirdly uncomfortable. I knew one stared at my boobs, even though they were modestly covered in the t-shirt I got the day before at the huge romance book signing where I spent all weekend. The other widened his legs intentionally so his thigh pressed against mine. It was as if they were toying with me, a mouse stuck between two mean tomcats wanting to play with their food before they pounced and killed it.

I'd been stuck until the guy in a crisp black suit from across the aisle stood and ordered the men to move. He'd either noticed my discomfort or that the men were being kind of jerks. They had to be traveling together but it didn't seem like they got along. Based on the suits they sported–one better than others–they were probably work colleagues. You didn't have to like the people you worked with. Heck, I was more than aware you didn't even have to like your family.

Whatever their relationship, after an accompanying growl and glare, they did the seat shuffle. So had I. Moved... and obeyed. Obviously, since I was settled into the window seat.

With my book open, I tried to read. Except my eyes darted to the crisp line of the man's dress pants, how they were taut over impressive thighs. Or his hand, resting on the armrest, veiny and large. I couldn't miss the sliver of a tattoo that peeked out of the hem of his suit jacket and the thin line of his white dress shirt.

We weren't looking at each other, but I could *feel* him beside me. The hair on my forearms stood on end. And that zap of static when we'd touched in the aisle? I could still feel it humming beneath my skin. It was so strange, this attraction. There was a pull to this guy, and we couldn't be closer.

I swallowed and tried to focus on my book, *To Have And To Puck*. Based on the catchy title, it was obviously–right?–a spicy hockey romance.

I gripped her hips, knowing there would be small bruises. Marks she'd see for days knowing she was well and truly claimed. By me.

Yup. Spicy. The hero was a six-four defensive player who was the team enforcer. A man who knew what he wanted and took it–with consent, cunnilingus, and a condom.

Except the dominant hockey hottie I had imagined at the start of the book had morphed into the businessman beside me. Distractedly, I wondered what he did for a living. A billionaire CEO saving me from creepy guys? My stomach swooped at the possibility of that trope happening in real life… to me, then realized it wasn't excitement at the possibility, but that the plane dipped with a bout of turbulence.

I mentally shook my head. My fantasy was only that. Not real. No billionaire flew in row seven of a commercial flight out of Vegas. He wouldn't sit in the middle with a kid behind him kicking his seat back every few minutes, especially to help me. I was surprised he even noticed me. Or… what was that smell? God, who farted?

The man raised his hand and subtly pinched his nose. Yeah, he picked up on that unpleasantness, too. He might've saved me from the men earlier, but he couldn't save me from someone else's intestinal problems.

I swallowed hard, then reached up and twisted the air vent. He looked my way, grinned, as if we were in this travel adventure together. I always wondered about lots of things I read in books. One of them? Five o'clock shadows. They sounded too... scruffy. Rough. Oddly intentional. Like, shave sooner, maybe? Or is it a beard or not?

This guy had stubble across his square jaw, and it was a work of art. A touch darker than the hair on his head. If I had to bet it would be soft and would feel amazing against my inner thighs.

Shit. No! No sexy thoughts about my seat mate! Thankfully, cool air spread across my heated cheeks. Maybe he didn't notice the blush from thinking of him going down on me.

Yes, please.

No! This was a random Sunday in September. He was a stranger on a plane. I knew I should take my best friend Brittany's advice and get back out there and get fucked out of my mind–her words not mine–but I doubted she meant Mr. Hot Middle Seat.

I couldn't keep staring at him for the whole flight like an idiot, so I broke the post-fart stare and went back to my reading. It was a book from my library, one of my favorite authors. She, along with over a hundred other authors, had participated in LoveNLust Romance Con. It was a weekend-long convention of fun games, author and reader panels, and book signings. It had been amazing. While I'd gotten a signed special edition with gorgeous foil and sprayed edges of the book, there was no way I was going to crack the spine or mess it up. It was going on my shelf with all my other favorites. I was reading a well-used paperback copy. I was on chapter two and already hooked.

The hero was hot. Rough around the edges and had that *touch-her-and-die* vibe going when it came to the heroine. Sure, he wasn't perfect, but who wanted a man who was? No, a woman wanted a man who saw her and only her. A man like the guy beside me who treated her like a queen but most likely fucked her like a–

I cleared my throat. Gah! My brain was wandering into even naughtier territory. No thinking about how Mr. Sexy Stubble fucked. Read, woman! So I did, getting lost in the story for most of the flight, my eyes flying over the words, especially since the author got to the good parts–the sex scenes–in the fifth chapter.

"You're a good girl, Mia, taking me so well. I–" I flipped the page desperate to read what the hero said next.

"Wait," the man beside me murmured, interrupting my sex reading. I blinked, turned his way. "You're reading too fast. I can't keep up."

If he said the plane was crashing, I would have been less stunned. Or panicked. I slammed the book shut and closed my eyes. As if I did, I'd become invisible. I wouldn't be stuck in the window seat of a plane besides Mr. Hottie who knew I loved reading smut.

"Don't stop now. We're getting to the good part," he added, making my nipples instantly hard, wishing he'd say that to me when we were somewhere else. Like a bed.

"That's what she said," I muttered, then slapped my hand over my mouth. Had I actually said that? Oh my God.

He chuckled, somehow not finding me dorky.

"What I meant was, I need to know how Colin's going to get Mia to believe that she's more than just the woman who bought him at a charity auction. I think he has to tell her that he's her brother's new teammate, right?"

I wasn't sure if it was a smart move, but I opened my eyes, glanced his way. A glint of amusement brightened his dark eyes, but it didn't seem like he was making fun of me. He didn't poke fun at how I loved to read "those books" as my mother called them. Or that I was living in sin as my brother Perry spouted.

As if. I was an official good girl. Breaking the rules made me sweat.

"Wow, you've been reading along for a while," I said, more mortified than ever. My gaze drifted towards his eyes, although I couldn't meet them directly yet. I noticed a spot of blood on the collar of his white shirt. Had he cut himself shaving? I imagined him in a snug pair of boxer briefs, leaning against his sink and running a razor up his neck and–

GAH! Fine. I acted like a good girl, but my mind was very bad.

He shrugged in the casual way of a man who had a heck of a lot of confidence. "It's a good book."

I flipped it over so he could see the cover.

"It's for work," I said, not admitting I loved to read spicy romance. My family made enough fun of me. I didn't need this hot stranger to do so, too.

His lips quirked. "Based on the book, I'm really curious what your job is."

"I'm a librarian. In Colorado." I had no idea why I told

him the state thing. It wasn't like a librarian was different in... say, Miami.

"Ah."

"Yeah, not that exciting," I admitted, glancing down at the book in my lap. Not many people saw books as being exciting, as an escape or a way to visit different worlds. Or fall in love with a character, because book boyfriends were the best kind. They loved your life goals, found your cellulite sexy, growled at any man who looked at you twice, and wanted to rail you against any available surface.

My ex hadn't done any of those things.

"Sometimes exciting's overrated," he murmured. "If those are the books on the shelves in your library these days, I might need to stop in."

Stop in. STOP IN!

I cleared my throat. "So not much of a reader then?"

"Don't have much time."

"What do you do?" I wondered. Should I be talking this guy up? He *had* been reading over my shoulder. My inner Brittany–my best friend–said "hell yes."

"I'm not a romance book hero, that's for sure," he said, self-deprecatingly.

I wasn't so sure about that. He pretty much checked off every requirement.

"So you're not a pro-hockey player auctioned off in a charity event?" I asked, referring to the plot of the book I– *we*–were reading.

The corner of his mouth quirked. "No."

"Rodeo champ headed to the Stock Show?"

He shook his head. "That's a romance book hero?"

I nodded. "Yup. So hot."

He made a funny sound, like a chest rumble, as if he didn't like the idea of me finding a rodeo champ hot. Any conscious woman–unless she didn't like a man in snug Wranglers or was allergic to horses–would toss their panties at one.

"Try again," he prodded.

I tapped my chin, considering all the possible romance hero options. I couldn't believe we were having this conversation. "Alpha leader of a werewolf shifter pack."

His eyebrows winged up. "Um... what?"

The plane hopped over a bit more turbulence, then settled.

My lips twitched with amusement. "Trust me. Those books are good."

"Got one in that bag of yours we can read in the next–" He peeked at the watch on his wrist. The really nice, fancy one. "–thirty minutes?"

I shook my head. "Sorry. You never mentioned what you did." I really wanted to know.

"Hitman." He said it with a straight face, and it had me laughing, my eyes raking over him wedged in the middle seat. I thought I heard the guy on the aisle grunt. Maybe he was the farter and was having more stomach problems. At least he wasn't the other one with the bad cologne that made me sneeze. "What?"

"Sorry. Hitman? That's definitely a romance book hero. You, though? Can't see it."

He set his hand on his chest as if offended. "Now you've hurt my feelings. Maybe I want to be a romance hero after all. You're saying you wouldn't go for a hitman?"

"As long as you're not a petty, cheating, self-absorbed loser like my ex, I wouldn't care what your profession is."

"A man cheated on *you*?" His eyes narrowed and his jaw clenched. "What's his name?"

I frowned. "Why? You going to kill him?"

He didn't answer and for a second I was a little worried he took my little joke seriously. Although, there were moments in the past few months that I wanted to kill Kevin, my ex, because of what he did.

"Okay. No self-absorbed losers," he practically growled. "What would you go for then?"

I blushed, because his voice went quieter, but it also went deeper. More intimate, if that was possible on a crowded plane. Was it my imagination or had he leaned an inch closer?

I swallowed hard as the plane went over another bump of air. The playful banter seemed to have morphed into something else. "Um... what?"

He tipped his head toward the closed book with the sexy hockey player on the cover. "A guy like that in bed?"

I swallowed and his eyes dropped to watch my throat work. We were practically whispering; our heads were that close together.

"You want me to tell you what I want in a guy I have sex with?"

"Fuck," he murmured very softly, the word raising goosebumps on my skin. I looked around, but there was nothing to see but him. The side of the plane, the seat in front of me and... him. "What we were reading in that book was definitely fucking."

"I can't tell you that," I practically hissed, tucking my

hair back. The only experiences I had with sex were the one time with Craig Chlebek freshman year in college and Kevin. Based on what I read in romance books and what Brittany kept saying, neither guy was remotely proficient in bed. They pretty much sucked in the sack since they hadn't been able to satisfy me, which meant I'd only had good sex with my vibrator and vicariously through what I read in romance books.

"Why not?" he prodded, cocking his head. "We have thirty minutes, and we'll never see each other again."

True. I bit my lip. My heart pounded for some reason. Because this was totally insane. But what happened on a plane from Vegas, stayed on a plane from Vegas, right? I'd never see him again. "Fine, but you go first."

He studied me for a moment, his eyes raking over my face. I didn't know what he was searching for, but I felt seen. Like there wasn't anyone else on this plane but the two of us. "Think you can handle my answers?"

Could I? I wasn't so sure, because a guy like him–smolderingly gorgeous and seemingly nice–probably had potent tastes and needs. I wanted to know anyway, or because of that. Definitely.

So, I nodded and let him tell me exactly what he wanted in a woman he fucked.

3

JACK

"He out of the shitter yet?" Dax asked, casually leaning against the low wall that surrounded the roof and kept him from plummeting thirty-six stories. He was using his knife to clean his fingernails.

I stood beside him, tucked beside an HVAC unit, rifle in hand. We were on the roof of a downtown Denver high-rise. I glanced at my wristwatch. "He should be done any minute."

It was the perfect night for a hit like this. No wind. Calm skies. All I had to do was wait for the fucker's very consistent bowels to be emptied and come out onto the balcony of his penthouse for his usual before-bed dip in his hot tub. A man with a routine like his made for an easy target.

That was why Dax came along for the ride. A fun Saturday night with a murder thrown in for fun. We'd been business partners for years, if one could call what we did a business. We weren't software engineers or tennis instructors. I did the hits; he did the fixing.

If I were a girl, I'd call him my BFF. He was my business partner. A fixer, not a hitman. The difference? I took the jobs that killed people who were a problem and Dax fixed other people's problems. An example: *My son was arrested with two male prostitutes and is in jail in Omaha. Make it go away.* Which Dax did. Sometimes people died, but not usually. My jobs had a 100% dead body count.

Dax was extroverted and liked people. I didn't, which helped with the whole killing thing. Besides Dax, I was a loner. Ever since my deadbeat dad skipped out on me and my mom and she had to buckle down and work three jobs to make ends meet before dying at forty-three, I didn't trust others all that much.

We'd been in the same fourth grade class at Pinnacle Hills Elementary. When Vinnie Mancuso, a vindictive little shit with a wicked overbite, stole Mabel Delmar's lunch, we decided to make him pay by giving him a swirlie in the boys' bathroom by the cafeteria.

We ended up in the principal's office and since I had no dad and my mother had been working, Dax's dad, Big Mike, came in to claim us both. He was a tough as nails guy who ran a rough and sweaty fighter gym with a side gig. While he didn't have a title like hitman or fixer, he did a little of both. He took care of the bad guys around town, the ones who deserved to be dealt with and the police couldn't touch for whatever reason.

Dax and I bonded during our three-day suspension, our punishment to clean the place top to bottom. When it smelled more like pine cleaner than dirty jockstraps, he patted us on our backs and told us he was proud of us taking care of the trash. That some people deserved to be taken out, even if that meant using their head for a toilet bowl brush. From then on, he showed us everything we knew, and we learned that everything was black and white. Good guys and bad guys.

No one fucked with either of us at school after that day. Mabel offered to share her lunch with me for a few years, then offered her virginity when we were sixteen.

Dax and I upgraded our technique with boxing, MMA and other, more deadly lessons. As for Big Mike, he retired to Florida a few years back and let us handle things.

I glanced at my watch. It was ten-thirty at night, the same time my target took a shit, like clockwork. Yeah, I researched it. All in a day's work as a hitman.

"Got those new bullets finally," Dax said casually, switching hands with his knife to clean the rest of his fingernails. His hair was lighter. So was his body. So was his fucking mood in comparison to mine. Women pretty much tossed their panties when he smiled, which was often.

"Figured we can test them out."

"I'm down."

This was what two killers did for fun. No beer and a ball game. No recreational softball team. We shot watermelons with hollow tip bullets. And we could write off on our taxes the cost of ammo and the mileage to Wyoming where we had free rein to shoot targets.

"Can't believe you had to fly commercial yesterday," he said, keeping the conversation moving. He shook his head in either commiseration or sorrow. "Must've been hell."

"Definitely not hell."

I thought of the woman who'd been in the seat beside me. I didn't even know her name. But I knew her ass was a fucking work of art, she had a dimple in her right cheek and underneath that prim, good girl exterior lived a naughty vixen who was down for some sweaty, dirty fun. Her taste in reading had been the first obvious sign, but what she told me as we made our final descent into Denver was another.

Every guy thinks a woman wants flowers and moonlight when in fact every woman actually wants to get railed by a dirty talker. You've heard of a lady on the streets but a whore in the sheets? Well, we want a gentleman on the streets who's down for a pound. I have a list and I want to do all of it.

My dick had been hard the entire time–really fucking uncomfortable in economy but thankful that the tray table could hide it–and I almost choked on a sip of my four-dollar ginger ale when she shared.

"What was wrong with Reggiano's jet again?" he asked, pulling me out of my thoughts of Pound Town with Miss Librarian.

"O Ring or something. Eyebrows and Joey Brains were like hangry toddlers."

Leaning down, I peeked through the rifle scope once more into the target's apartment in the other building. The lights throughout the penthouse were on. Someone had good taste in interior design.

"Sal Reggiano must've liked my work because he messaged. He's got another job for me. Next week. Some-one's coming in for the Rockies game. Wants him taken out while he's here."

"Who wants to watch the Rockies?" Dax asked, stunned.

He had me there. The major league baseball team was mediocre, at best, these days and wasn't making any news headlines. Why someone would come to Denver to see them stumped both of us.

"Some guy named Turkleman. He's from Texas. Guess he's got a thing to make it to every major league park or something."

"You're not going to make the hit at the stadium, are you?"

I looked up from my scope, glanced his way. As if I'd be that stupid. I didn't need ten thousand witnesses.

"That's what I thought. Lemme know if you need any help."

"Will do," I replied.

Three jobs this week and another one next had me craving boredom. I wanted to sleep late, read the paper. Go to the corner coffee shop and meet friends. Run. Play racquetball. Whatever normal people did. Not spend a Monday night on a skyscraper rooftop waiting for a sex trafficker to finish taking a shit so I could blow the back of his head out.

Normal, like the woman on the plane. What would it be like to be normal, to not see everyone and everything as good and bad.

"Ever read a romance book?" I asked, then movement out of the corner of my eye had me turning, peered into the scope again. "He's out."

The bedroom door opened and out came the target in a white robe with the sash about his waist loose enough that a large swath of his broad chest and heavy paunch stuck out. He was talking to someone on his cell. Had he talked on the phone while having a shit?

Dax turned, folded his knife and tucked it into his pants pocket, then crossed his arms over his chest. He wore a suit minus the jacket, the sleeves of his dress shirt rolled up.

Roger Thorndyke, the target, was as douchy as his name. Insider trading. Corporate greed. That meant he was an asshole, but not enough for me to kill the guy. But when my client wanted him dead for also being the head of a trafficking ring that kidnapped his niece and took her over the border to a brothel in Tijuana, I took the contract.

Say goodbye, fucker.

"Did you just ask me if I read *romance*?" Dax asked.

I continued to stare through the scope as I answered. "Yeah. It's actually pretty good. Way better than any porn I've seen."

Dax was quiet long enough that I lifted my eye from the target and glanced up at him.

"What?" I asked.

"When did you start reading *romance*?"

"On the flight from Vegas over a woman's shoulder."

A slow smile spread across his face. "I'd think a woman who reads kinky shit's gotta be down for some fun."

I thought of the mysterious and sexy librarian and wasn't thrilled with Dax talking about her that way. Even if he was probably right. Fuck, was she really a *whore in the sheets?*

Right now, I had to think with the right head and not the one in my pants. I watched Thorndyke move around his kitchen. The fridge door opened. Closed. He was milling around, bottle of water in hand, while he talked. After another thirty seconds, he dropped his cell on the counter, scratched his balls, then headed toward the balcony.

"Two mil for this guy?" Dax asked.

"Yup."

"Steep. What'd he do?"

"Trafficking."

Dax's chest emitted a dark rumble. He felt the same as me when it came to that shit.

This was one bad fucker, and hard to access. He had bodyguards and serious security measures. Bulletproof glass on his penthouse windows. But there was no security watching him when he took a nightly dip in his hot tub.

This was the narrow window I needed, lasting at most, a few minutes. With one squeeze of the trigger, the world would have one less bad guy in it, and I'd be a few mil richer. I didn't need the money. I was flush with cash because all I did was work. Same went for Dax. Except, if we didn't work, what else would we do? Take up doubles tennis?

The idea made my mouth quirk as I eyed Thorndyke through the scope.

We weren't "made" like Sal Reggiano–or the King of England–where the only way to get out of the job was death. We could quit and walk away from the life. But "hitman" on a resume wouldn't get me any jobs besides pest and vermin control and I didn't look good in coveralls. Besides that, what would I do? Learn floral arranging? Take up golf? Go on a bike tour of Tuscany?

We were both vigilantes because we wanted all the bad

guys dealt with. Me? I wanted them dead. Ones who deserved to be removed from the earth. Pedophiles. Warlords. Rapists. Murderers. Crooked politicians. Maybe even Little Miss Librarian's cheating, self-absorbed ex.

My constant thought since she told me about that was who the fuck would cheat on her? If she were mine, I'd cut off anyone's hands who touched her. And I'd talk dirty and give her the pounding she craved. Knowing her pussy wasn't getting the attention it deserved was a fucking shame. While I'd take care of her every desire, I wasn't boyfriend material. I didn't date. Didn't do relationships. And my sexy seatmate screamed long-term.

She had a job, a consistent paycheck from Coal Springs Public Library. That was what the barcode sticker on the front of the book we'd been reading had said. Coal Springs was nestled in the mountains above Denver, which meant she was also a small town girl. She probably had a house with a picket fence. A dog she rescued from the pound. A mother who probably made meatloaf and lived down the street.

She also had a very naughty mind. I felt a smile tug as I remembered the look on her face when she found out I knew what she was reading. Or the answers she gave me about how she would want a guy to fuck her.

I love how Colin is focused on Mia. He's into her and is obsessed. He can't keep his hands off her. It's something on my sex list.

"Shit," I muttered. My dick pressed against my pants as I remembered.

"What?"

I focused back through the scope, saw that the target

was beside the hot tub with the interior lights were enough for me to see him.

I wasn't going to tell him about my hard-on, especially during a job.

"Thorndyke dropped the robe," I said instead as explanation.

I glanced away from his low-hanging balls and hairy ass to save my eyes, letting the guy climb in without an audience. My hard-on was long gone. "Kill me if I ever get a gut because I doubt he can even see his micro-dick."

Thorndyke closed his eyes and dropped his head back against the edge of the tub, savoring the hot water and the last seconds of his life.

Dax grunted. "Good thing I can't see that far in the dark."

I focused through the scope, settled into the task. Took a deep breath, exhaled. Pulled the trigger.

I stood and started to disassemble my rifle.

He pushed off the wall, tucked his hands in his pockets. "I'm starved. Pancakes?"

"Yeah." When my gun was back in its case and we were headed across the roof for the stairwell, I asked Dax, "Do you know what a TBR is?"

4

⚡

HANNAH

"If you had any doubt before, I am officially your bestest of best friends," Brittany huffed, eyeing me over the top of a heavy box of books we were carrying up the three flights of stairs from the lobby of our building to my apartment. "There is no way this is less than fifty pounds."

Regardless of box hauling, Brittany *was* my best friend, ever since I moved in across the hall two years ago. She was a year older, a Leo and wore heels every day. That–the heels–wasn't the reason we were struggling with this box. The box was well over the airline regulation checked bag weight. And I was a total weakling.

"It's seventy-seven pounds." I swiped my cheek against my shoulder, trying to get my hair out of my eyes without any luck. Sweat trickled down my back and I was puffing like a magic dragon. "I gave the gate agent twenty bucks to let it through. Another one's," –I awkwardly adjusted my palms again– "coming in the mail. I had to ship it."

"Wow, look at you breaking the rules and being a rebel. Might have to take that good girl tiara away." Her teasing was softened by a wink and a sly smile.

Both boxes were filled with all my precious book finds at the romance convention. Where Brittany spent money on fancy shoes, I bought books. Heavy ones.

The problem? I wasn't strong enough to get my new stash upstairs to my apartment by myself. There was no elevator in this old building.

We were struggling together under the heavy load. She hadn't been home the day before when I got back from the trip, which meant I had to leave the box tucked in the corner of the lobby. She'd recently gotten home from work, dressed in cute pants and a sleeveless blouse. I was in yoga pants and a green t-shirt, having already changed into comfy clothes after my day at the library.

"I couldn't bribe Raul, the rideshare driver, to carry it beyond the lobby," I told her, breathing hard. "Otherwise, he'd be in your bestie spot."

"Raul," she muttered, stumbling on a step, tipping me off balance for a moment. "I could take him. Jesus, this is heavy."

I couldn't help but laugh, then groaned when the box slipped, digging into my hip. When I righted it, I took the bulk of the weight. All of a sudden, it wasn't that bad. It wasn't hurting my back. It felt... *not* heavy, which made no sense.

"Um, you got it?" Brittany asked, eyeing me carefully

and having her hands out in case I needed her again. I felt like a kid learning to ride a bike.

Growing up in Texas, Brittany was raised to never leave the house without her face on or her hair done, her momma telling her she never knew when she'd meet Mr. Right.

I'd grown up the barely remembered middle-child between two overachievers. My family didn't notice what I wore, so I set my own standard of making sure I always had nice underwear on, never knowing when I might be in an accident and medical personnel got to see it.

Not that I didn't pull myself together when I left the house. I wore cute clothes—or at least I thought so—and makeup. I couldn't keep up with Brittany. She was gorgeous—with amazing teeth. All tall and skinny with the most gorgeous mocha skin. I had to wear those little overnight acne patches and I burned an unattractive shade of pink without sunscreen.

She didn't *need* makeup. Or a push-up bra. Or exercise. Or extra protein powder in her smoothie. I sure as hell did, to all of it, not that I did a ton of exercise. Or had reason for a little extra cleavage. I had plenty.

Fumbling with the box, I got it settled better in my arms. It wasn't so bad, which was ridiculous because I'd needed a hotel cart to get it to the taxi in Vegas, then pushed it like a bobsled across the drop-off area from the taxi to the curbside check in.

"Look at me go," I huffed with a surprising grin. "I actually have it. And it's in the best friend handbook. They carry heavy boxes together. Even though you're not actually carrying it any longer."

Going solo, I turned to face up the stairs instead of sideways as we had been. Brittany was beside me every step of the way as a pseudo-spotter. "I think you have the wrong handbook. Best friends get mani/pedis together. They get drinks together."

"I have wine in my fridge," I offered as we turned at the next landing. "The fancy box kind."

Her eyes lit up and she snapped her fingers. "Put some back into it, girlfriend."

Said the woman not carrying the box.

Ten minutes later, our glasses of wine were full and the box half empty on my cheap IKEA coffee table.

"I'm not sure why you needed my help. You did it just fine," she said, comfortably settled on my couch. Even after helping the first flight, her short hair was perfect with the tight curls, and her clothes weren't even wrinkled. "Good thing you're going back to the gym and lifting weights. I didn't go to dental school to be a mover."

She was a dentist and had a small practice in town she shared with a guy patients called Dr. Todd. With a last name of Aszkielowicz, he didn't have much choice.

"I thought you went to dental school to get me free toothbrushes." I stood beside the open box, pulling the books out one at a time.

She took a big sip of her wine and rolled her eyes.

"No way have I gone back to the gym. I went with you last year, remember? That thirty-day free trial where I did all the classes with you? I actually gained weight." I took another book from the box, petted it lovingly, then set it on the shelf in its new home.

She assessed me over her glass of wine. "Huh."

"Yeah, huh. I forgot, but I even hefted my carry-on into the overhead on the plane by myself. I'm not sure what's up."

That made me think of the hot guy who saved me from those two smelly, crowding jerks. Actually, I hadn't *stopped* thinking about him.

"You're strong as fuck in your own way, Wonder Woman. You're not having any more headaches, are you?" she asked, concern in her dark eyes.

I shook my head. She'd been by my side through my radiation back in May and recovery. "No. I mean, I did in Vegas because the event was crowded and the casino I had to cut through to get to my room was loud."

She seemed relieved as one of the side effects for me was headaches.

"I don't know how anyone works in a place like that. Rowdy, drunk gamblers."

"You put your fingers in peoples' dirty mouths after you give them laughing gas," I countered. "What's the difference? And those drills, don't tell me those aren't slowly making you deaf."

She only rolled her eyes again and changed the subject. "Tell me about your trip. Please say you gambled or went to that sexy male stripper revue or hooked up with a hottie or something."

I gave her a look right back. "I was at a romance convention where it's like ninety-five percent women. Besides, this is me, boring Hannah Highcliff."

She tipped her glass toward me, then took a healthy swallow. "They have models there. I've seen the photos. And you're not boring."

I wasn't going to argue with her on the boring part because it was a known fact I'd rather have my nose stuck in a book than do most other things.

"What gorgeous male model is going to be interested in me?" I asked, setting another book on my shelf, my back to her.

"A smart one," she replied fiercely, making me look her way. "I've lived across the hall from you for two years. I see the way men look at you."

I laughed because I was nothing special. Forgettable. "Please, if we're standing side by side, they're looking at you. And my track record with guys is total crap."

With a sigh, she set her glass on the coffee table. "We've got to work on this self-image of yours. And don't even mention Kevin. You're a total catch and he's a dipshit. He should've been run over with a snowplow for how he dumped you."

What she meant was I told him I had a brain tumor and he told me he was done.

"And cheated on me," I reminded. Obviously, I wasn't a woman who kept a man's attention or interest. Per Kevin, I was defective sexually. And physically. Totally not a catch.

She growled. "Don't remind me. I want to go pull all his teeth. He showed his true colors. Not worth your time or energy. You've got a new lease on life, and it should be with someone amazing."

"I'll take amazing." That sounded good, but not very realistic. I grew up in this small town. Knew all the guys. The pickings were slim. And Kevin lived here and probably told his friends about me, although I didn't want to date any of his friends.

I was twenty-six. A weak, slightly overweight librarian with medical debts who was supposedly bad in bed. Not much of a catch.

She grabbed the bag of chips and set it on her lap, ripping the top open. "Fine, so Vegas. No jackpot, no male model, only books?"

She was more invested in my social life than I was.

"It was so great," I said. I couldn't help but smile because I'd been in my happy place surrounded by books and others in the industry. "So many authors whose books I want to put in my store."

My dream was to open a romance bookstore in this little shop space on Main Street here in Coal Springs. I had the space picked out, the business plan written and money to get started. It had almost come about. If I put my pointer finger and my thumb close together, I was right there. Then my radiation bumped my plans out months... or years because of medical bills.

Brittany reached out, took my hand and gave it a squeeze and a sympathetic smile. "It's happening and it's going to be amazing."

I swallowed hard because I tried to compartmentalize the disappointment I felt about my dream being stalled, but it was hard. The only reason I'd been able to go to the book signing in Vegas was because I'd paid for it all–registration, hotel, and airfare–before radiation. It wasn't just the tangible problems, like bills. It was mental gymnastics, too. To be told by a doctor that I had a brain tumor had been devastating, even when she said it was completely treatable with a special kind of radiation procedure. It had been a "do or die" situation and I hadn't wanted to die.

They zapped that tumor with radiation. They *got it*. I was still slowly coming to terms with the possibilities of death, that it could've happened to me this year instead of at ninety. Of surviving. Of being lucky, when I felt anything but.

"There was this guy on the plane," I admitted. I didn't have a Pollyanna-like well of hope and rays of sunshine like Brittany when it came to a happily ever after–and I was the book lover–because I was too realistic about things these days. Yet, it was fun seeing Brittany that way.

Her eyes widened and she set her glass down, practically clapping her hands in glee. She was so much more invested in my love life than I was. "Tell!"

I shrugged, remembering how out of place he seemed. "Tall, dark, and handsome. Had that square jaw and scruff thing going. Dark eyes. Hair that you wanted to run your fingers through. Suit, definitely not off the rack." No way that material or cut was from a chain store at the mall. "He was like a billionaire who got lost and ended up in Economy beside me. Not the kind of billionaire who gets manicures and has four assistants, but the one who secretly wrestles bears and BASE jumps."

Brittany fanned her face. I could only imagine what she was picturing. She was single and wasn't interested in a relationship, more than willing to have a one-night stand to get the orgasms she wanted without all the hassle.

I liked the concept, but I couldn't handle the execution. I was a long-term kind of girl, holding out for Mr. Right, not Mr. Right Now.

"He was reading over my shoulder, B." When she

continued to stare, not understanding the depth of the mortification I'd felt, I added, "*To Have And To Puck.*"

Her mouth dropped open. Then closed. Then open again. "Tell me it wasn't a sex scene."

Sheepishly, I nodded. "He read probably fifteen chapters."

She shoved a chip in her mouth and crunched away. "Shut the front door!"

I put my hand over my face, remembering how mortified I'd felt. Brittany would have probably unbuckled her seatbelt, straddled his lap and did everything in the book.

"And..." She twirled her greasy fingers in a circle to get me to continue.

"And he told me to not flip the page because he couldn't keep up. He wanted to know what happened." I felt the hair on the back of my neck rise just thinking about him. How he looked at me after I finally got enough nerve to meet his dark eyes.

She set her hot pink fingertips over her lips, smothering a smile.

"It was so embarrassing!" I said, tossing my arms up. "The heroine got railed by a hockey player so hard she didn't remember her name and couldn't walk right for a week."

"If you can remember your name or walk right after a good *pucking,* then you're not doing it right."

I couldn't argue, because my fingers or my vibrator delivered guaranteed orgasms, but a man-made one was much better. Or so I heard. Kevin never delivered. The guy from college had zero skills since we were each other's firsts.

God, I would love to be able to not walk right from being fucked too well. I couldn't even imagine.

"You struck up a conversation, and now you're in love, getting married and having his babies." *Now* she was a romance enthusiast.

I dropped onto the far end of the couch. My cozy corner where I snuggled in to read or watch TV. Also known as *my spot.* "We talked." I wasn't telling her *what* we talked about, how I told him what I wanted in bed with a guy. Getting bossed around. Railed. That would push her over the edge into contacting the FAA to find out his name and address. "Then after the plane landed, he got off with these two smelly guys who were traveling with him and left."

I shrugged as if I hadn't been thinking about him since he disappeared in the crowded terminal. Out of sight, out of mind. Not.

"Oh." She reached for her wine and took a healthy swig.

I crossed my legs and pulled a throw pillow onto my lap. "I know I'm the one who's a librarian, reads romance and wants to open a romance bookstore—"

"Will open," she clarified.

"*Will* open," I repeated, knowing she was my biggest champion. "Will open a romance bookstore, but in real life, no hero sits beside me on an airplane and saves me."

She nodded. "That's right."

I frowned, confused. "Huh?"

She reached across the couch, patted my knee. Static electricity had her pulling her hand back. She met my eyes with her serious ones. "You're going to save yourself. You don't need a man to do anything for you. Except fuck you good and hard like in your books. The right man can give you some really good D." She thought for a moment, even tapped her finger to her lips. "That should be on a t-shirt."

"The guy on the plane could give me some D," I said, without thinking. "No question."

"Too bad you won't see him again."

Yeah, too bad.

5

JACK

"You're going where?" Dax asked, his voice coming through my SUVs hands-free calling.

The week before over pancakes, after taking out Thorndyke the fucking Trafficker, we looked up what "TBR" meant. We quickly ruled out Total Bed Rest and Total Business Return for To Be Read. The t-shirt made perfect sense, but because of the randomness of the search, I'd had to tell Dax the full story about the flight. About the woman. About her shirt. The sexy book. All of it. Not *all* of it. I left out the way her tits had stretched the letters on her shirt. Or how she blushed when she learned I'd been reading over her shoulder. Or how she told me her fantasy was to get railed.

Yeah, railed.

I'd imagined that every day since and my obsession

wasn't getting any better. My dick got hard every time I thought of her, and it was sick of my hand. Maybe it was because the life of a hitman was boring. Or that my life wasn't all people imagined. A sweet glimpse of innocence and filth in one lush, feminine package and I wanted more.

I wanted my hands on her. I wanted my dick in her.

I gripped the steering wheel with one hand as my dick got hard... again, then shifted gears with the other as I blinkered and slowed down onto the highway's off-ramp. "Coal Springs."

I was pulling into the small town an hour from Denver, nestled quaintly in the mountains. Based on the cars with various license plates, tourists seemed to have flocked to the picturesque Main Street for overpriced, handmade ice cream, chainsaw-carved bears, and views of the Rockies. The banners on every ornamental light post pronounced this was the "Quaintest Town on Earth." Vibrant flowers overflowed from hanging baskets and... was that a crossing guard at the intersection?

It was like I fell into a Disney movie set that got a shit ton of snow in the winter.

The crime rate had to be nil, and I was probably the only murderer in town.

"Coal Springs? Why?" Dax prodded.

I followed the directions from my SUV's display onto a side street.

If a woman said to him, *I want to get railed,* he'd volunteer for the task. *This* specific woman who'd said that to me was different. She was so far out of my league. Like Mary Poppins, except she read graphic sex scenes.

Disney plus librarian did not equal a hitman's girl. Or fling. Or anything.

Yet, I was still on my way to the library.

"Wait... it sounds like you're already there. Hell, you're going to visit the librarian you told me about last week, aren't you? The one from the plane. Miss TBR. Do you even have time for this? Aren't you supposed to be turkey hunting this week?"

Shit. Yes. He meant Turkleman from Texas. "Yes," I muttered. "And yes, I'm in Coal Springs for Miss TBR."

"Did you at least have Nitro look into her?"

Nitro was our go-to IT guy. His home office looked like a command center for NASA with more monitors than I could count, multiple keyboards, and a high-tech chair. Dax and I had been to his place once. I leaned against his desk, hitting some button that probably took down the Federal Reserve, and we weren't welcomed back. Ever. Now we did business over phone calls and encrypted emails.

Nitro could find anyone, change anyone's grades on a transcript, resolve any IRS debt, and from what I heard, he took over the tracking of Santa from NORAD last December.

I didn't know his real name. I knew better than to ask.

"I don't need him to look her up on FAA flight records," I told Dax. "There's one library in Coal Springs. I figured that out myself." Unlike Turkleman, whose info I got back from Nitro, one quick internet search was all that was needed to find the Coal Springs Public Library. Based on the sign out front and the GPS voice from my dash, I'd arrived. I pulled over across the street from the entrance and parallel parked.

The library was an old brick building. Two cottonwood trees flanked the front entry along with a bike rack and a bulletin board with town notices and community flyers.

"It should be easy to find the hot librarian now that I'm at the library." I checked the time. A little after five, which was when the place closed. Hopefully, I hadn't missed her.

I wanted to see her face again. To see the dark color of her eyes. Watch how I could make her blush. Breathe in her soft scent without Joey Brains' farts killing us.

"Have you heard yourself lately?" he asked.

My eyes roved over the entrance. All was quiet. "What?"

"Call up the service, tell them about your new hot librarian fetish and get it out of your system."

I had zero interest in anything he just said, and I hadn't made use of the exclusive agency of escorts in recent months even though they took care of me without questions, entanglements, or expectations.

I didn't have a *fetish*. I had a hard-on that wouldn't quit for one woman who just happened to be hot and a librarian.

I wanted *her*. Whatever her name was. I wasn't going to remind Dax of that fact because he'd be even more hellbent on steering me away.

I hadn't stopped thinking about her since the plane. About the book we'd read together, whether she'd finished it–of course she had–and touched herself imagining the character Colin fucking her like he had the heroine in the book. Maybe she moved on to that werewolf storyline she mentioned.

I wasn't telling Dax that I looked up romance book plot

lines this morning over coffee. That the shifters she mentioned had big bites and bigger dicks. If my librarian wanted a real dick, not fiction, I volunteered. I'd bite, too, if that was her thing.

"I'm not into roleplay," I told him, looking into my side mirror as a slow-moving minivan passed. Were they scoping out my librarian? Did I have to follow them and kill them? Fuck. Wait. This was Coal Springs, and the speed limit was twenty-five. There were no bad guys around here. I saw the stick figure stickers on the back window that indicated that whoever was driving had too many kids. And a dog. Was that a turtle, too?

"I want the real thing."

"What? A date? So you're going to... what? Walk into the library and ask to sign up for a library card? You don't think she's going to freak the fuck out when a guy from a flight she was on tracked her down to her place of work? A guy who read over her shoulder? There's a term for that. Stalking."

"I'm not stalking her," I muttered, feeling called out.

The library door swung open and out came an older woman. Gray hair, pink pants, floral shirt. Then *she* followed. Dark hair, long like I remembered. The jeans and t-shirt from the plane were replaced with a blue dress that fell to her knees. There was some kind of pattern on it and the cut was loose, probably meant for comfort and keeping cool, not for ogling her gorgeous tits or perfect peach of an ass.

Sitting across the street and checking her out, I was totally stalking her.

Dax grunted as I watched her turn toward the door and lock it. "She's a librarian from Coal Springs, the town that has the annual North Pole parade in December with candy canes and dreidels decorating the lampposts. You sure she's the one you want?" He had a valid point, but I didn't have to like it. I couldn't help an obsession, especially seeing her again now in person.

I had no idea why *this* woman got me all crazy and made my dick hard. It would be simpler otherwise, but no. I wanted her.

"Yes," I gritted out through clenched teeth. My hand itched to open my door and go to her, except she wasn't alone as I imagined.

"Fine, say she doesn't care that you're a stalker. What are you going to do on your first date when she asks what you do for a living? Lie?"

She turned around and her gaze cut across the street and toward my SUV.

Shit! I ducked so she couldn't see me. Slumped low in my seat, my heart pounded. *What the hell was wrong with you?* I asked myself as I stared at the trident emblem steering wheel, angry at myself. *You drove all this way! You came to see her and now you're hiding like a fucking coward.* Dax's words were fucking with me.

"I told her the truth on the plane," I muttered, trying to come up with an excuse to validate why it was okay that I was in Coal Springs and also sitting here hiding. This position was not comfortable. The bottom of the steering wheel was wedged in my chest.

I was met with silence and for a second I thought the car's hands-free system had cut out.

"You told her you were a hitman."

"Yes."

"You said, I'm a hitman."

"Pretty much."

"And she believed you?"

I frowned. "No. We were talking about romance novel tropes."

"What the fuck?" He was laughing at me. I could hear it.

"You heard me." I clenched my teeth. I was not repeating myself. I peeked out the side window. She and the older woman were walking toward the small parking lot on the side of the building where two cars were parked. The other woman went up to a new mini-SUV while my obsession unlocked a small, older model sedan. White. That was a terrible choice for Coal Springs. Not four-wheel drive and with the snow in the winter? No one would be able to see it. It was a four-wheel death trap. She'd need a new vehicle before it snowed.

I could follow her home. See where she lived. Make sure her place was safe.

If not, she'd need a car *and* a new house.

"Do you even know if she's married?" Dax asked, nudging me from my thoughts.

She waved to the other woman–fuck, her smile was pretty–then climbed into her car. "She mentioned a cheating ex."

It still made no sense, anyone cheating on her. I wasn't sure if I should kill him or send him a fucking fruit basket for being a dumbass. Definitely the first option.

"I gotta go make popcorn."

The other woman drove off first. Then my girl followed,

looking both ways as she came out of the lot, then turned toward me. I ducked again until I heard her car drive past. "For what?"

"For when you call me later and tell me what happened. Either you're going to get kneed in the balls or arrested. Or both. If you need to get bailed out, can you make sure it happens before six because I have plans tonight."

"Fucker." I ended the call. Was I as dumb as Dax thought? Probably. We didn't date everyday women. Hell, we didn't date. Period. I had tons of enemies; friends and relatives of those I've killed. If they knew who I was, where I lived, I most likely would be dead. Anyone I cared about would also be dead.

I was dangerous in more ways than one. For a woman in my life, or bed, a service that was more transactional than anything else was the safest way to go. No one who wanted me dead would kill an escort solely because I spent a few hours with her.

Was I being selfish coming here? Hell, yes. But I couldn't help it. This feeling was insane. Irrational.

A craving.

Except I was a total pussy, hiding from her. What if she saw me and wanted nothing to do with me? Fuck, I sounded like a seventh grader in the cafeteria at school. I needed to get my shit together. I didn't come to Coal Springs to be like this. I knew firsthand that wasn't the kind of guy she craved.

I needed to spin this shit around. I took a deep breath.

"I want her," I said to myself in the quiet confines of my SUV, which meant I was going insane. I *never* talked to myself. "I'm going to have her. Find out her name. Make her smile. Make her come. Once I get my fucking balls back."

Because I could kill a man and sleep like a baby afterward, but it seemed I couldn't stalk a woman without acting like an idiot.

6

HANNAH

I walked out of the library with Mrs. Metcalf as she told me all about the community nature walk she was going on tonight. Organized by the city, the group was headed to Mallory Cave to watch the bats fly out at sunset to eat their weight in mosquitos and do whatever the heck bats did at night.

"You sure you don't want to go?" she asked, pulling her sunglasses from her purse. It was a bright, cloudless day. "It's open to all ages."

I locked the main library door, then turned. "No thanks." I went once as a kid with my family, but we'd been asked to leave since Briana tried climbing into the cave and Perry wouldn't stop talking. "Mosquitos love me. I'd be covered in bug bites in five minutes. Plus, I've got a new book."

She didn't put up a fight about me wanting to spend the

evening reading, or the mosquitos. As a fellow librarian, she understood the power of a cozy couch, sweats, snacks, and an amazing story. I read fast and would be finished before I went to sleep, no matter how late the hour.

"What's the title?"

Turning from the building, I tucked my library keys inside the little pocket in my purse as we went down the walk. "*Alien's Runaway Bride.*"

I glanced up and across the street. Squinting against the sun's glare, I saw a fancy SUV with... I blinked. What? No. For a second, I thought it was the man from the plane last week, but there wasn't anyone in the car.

"–only imagine that plot." I hadn't heard half of what Mrs. Metcalf had said. "I'm more of a cozy mystery reader myself, as you know, but you'll have to let me know how it is. I might borrow it."

Thinking I saw the middle seat-sitting fake billionaire romance reader set my heart to racing. Suddenly, it was very warm out.

"Hannah?"

I blinked, then pasted on a smile when I realized I'd pretty much frozen in place. "Sorry, I can't wait to dive into that book." My voice was high and strained with fake enthusiasm. My reaction to a random parked car was really sad. For a second, I had been blissfully hopeful it had been the guy from the plane. That he'd come through with saying he'd stop into the library, which I knew he'd only said as polite conversation.

If he *had* shown up, I wasn't sure if I should be flattered or scared. This wasn't a romance book, it was real life. Mr. Middle Seat wasn't going to show up in Coal Springs any more than I was going to be matched to a doubly-endowed alien and sent to space and have all kinds of hot sex.

I sighed. Brittany and the box of wine last week only got me stewing on thoughts that weren't true. I needed to get my head out of the clouds and back to reality. Sometimes, life sucked. Boyfriends cheated and dumped you when you had a serious health issue. Medical bills stole savings and derailed dreams of opening a bookstore.

I had to keep moving forward. Healthy, but very single. No men from airplanes, only living vicariously through a heroine sent to space where she'd be a perfect match for a possessive and sexually-talented alien. She'd have no health issues other than walking funny after being double penetrated all night long. Debt? What was that? Who needed money in space?

7

JACK

"What happened with the librarian?" Dax asked later that night, after the elevator doors closed behind him. I had my own private one and it opened right into my apartment. His mouth was turned up with amusement. He was enjoying my misery, the fucker. He was in black suit with black dress shirt beneath, the typical uniform of a fixer due to the fact that the color hid blood. Which meant he either just came from a job or was on his way to one.

I was sprawled on my leather couch, my cat on my chest. I'd found Pancake–named after my favorite food– behind a shady bar's dumpster downtown. I'd finished a guy and when he fell to the ground, the body startled the cat out from his hiding spot. He'd jumped onto my shoulder, and I couldn't get him off because his claws had dug into my Gucci suit.

The vet I took him to said he was a Siberian, whatever

that meant. He was a mix of black, brown, and white fur, as if he'd gone to a fancy hair salon and got foils. His ears were pointy and his eyes golden. Since I was the one who gave the vet permission to snip off his balls, I figured he'd be an asshole to me when I brought him home.

Turned out, I was wrong. He liked the high life. Literally. He liked my penthouse, the fancy cat food my housekeeper bought for him, and hanging out with me. He'd scored the ultimate cat life.

"Nothing," I muttered.

"Nothing? What'd you do, chicken out?" When I said nothing, he laughed and shook his head. He kept his hair buzzed fairly short and he ran a hand over it. "Holy shit, you did. You chickened out."

"She's a fucking librarian and I blew a guy's head off last night." I'd flown to LA and gotten rid of a drug lord. Another hard day on the job. "Guess which one's intimidating."

I couldn't believe I admitted that aloud. I hadn't been scared of anything since my dad left when I was eight. That was the last time I felt vulnerable, and I vowed then I wasn't going to feel that way again. I learned to fight, learned to kill, even so I could be strong. Then I *look* at one specific woman and I'm in big fucking trouble.

"You're intimidated by a *librarian?*" His eyebrows winged up. "Holy shit, you really do like her."

Dax unbuttoned his suit jacket then dropped across from me on the matching leather sofa, the glass coffee table between us. My apartment was modern male, all dark wood, gleaming metal, and big windows. Compared to Thorndyke's place I'd seen through my rifle's scope, mine was better. I made more money. I wasn't an asshole. Not that the last made a difference when it came to penthouses. But I didn't need bulletproof glass to keep me safe because I wasn't a bad guy. No one was out to kill me.

I grabbed Pancake, placed him on the floor as I sat up. He raised his snooty face in the air and trotted off, fluffy tail twitching back and forth.

"I'm going back tomorrow," I said, telling him as much as I was telling myself. I *was* intimidated by her. She was too good for me. Smart. I had street smarts but that wasn't the same thing.

"Good for you," Dax said. "Fuck her and get her out of your system."

"It's not like that." With a few flicks of my wrist, I brushed cat hair off my clothes.

"You don't want to fuck her?"

"Of course, I want to fuck her!" He'd riled me up on purpose and I'd taken the bait. A sigh accompanied my next words. "She's different though."

"Magical pussy?"

"Watch it," I warned with an accompanying glare. I didn't like his tone or what he was insinuating. Although I had a suspicion it was true. Perhaps one of the reasons I'd ducked earlier in my SUV was that I knew she was going to fuck up my entire life.

He held up his hands. "Let me know where you want me to send the wedding present."

I glared some more.

"I thought you had plans," I muttered, wondering why he'd stopped by.

"I do. I figured you'd crash and burn and want to go with me."

"So your pep talk was all bullshit."

He clapped his hands and stood. Grinned, even. He was too fucking perky. "Absolutely."

"Asshole."

Except I had crashed and burned. No, I'd chickened out, which was worse. I was wallowing on the couch over a girl, which probably only made Dax more amused.

"Let's go." I grabbed my gun and my keys and followed Dax out of the apartment.

I knew the kind of man the librarian was interested in. She'd told me outright on the plane. I was that guy.

Except for earlier when I'd been a pussy.

I was going back to Coal Springs, going into that library and making that woman mine.

8

HANNAH

"Don't forget your potato salad tonight," my mother said when I answered her call the next day.

I was at work, in the back room behind the circulation desk. It was a small room with a large work area beneath a glass window so I could see if anyone came to the counter. The remainder of the space was shelving and storage for the most used supplies. I'd just made myself a late afternoon cup of coffee in my favorite mug. It said *Love the smell of books in the morning.*

"We're having hamburgers."

"For what?" I asked her, going to the basket beneath the book drop off door. The exterior wall paralleled the alley so patrons could make drive-thru returns. There were a few items–books, and two DVDs–so I reached in and grabbed them with my free hand.

"Dinner."

Holding the items to my chest, I frowned. "What dinner?"

She sighed. I was all too familiar with that sound. It was a mixture of disappointment, annoyance and the audible version of eye rolling. "The dinner I told you about last weekend."

"I didn't talk to you last weekend." Or this one either, although I didn't remind her of that. "I was at the book signing."

"Right, that silly event in Las Vegas."

She didn't admit to not calling me, only spinning it around so I was at fault for doing something she didn't like.

"It wasn't a *silly* event," I countered. "There were over a thousand readers there, plus authors and–"

"Not this again." She sighed heavily, as if *I* was the burden among her children. "Your brother has that many every Sunday and he doesn't have to lure them in with sex."

I hated when she did this. She didn't like my job as a librarian–too quaint and dull which was ironic since she accused me of hanging out with a bunch of sex fiends. She didn't like my plan for opening a romance bookstore–too embarrassing for her and a poor business decision. She didn't seem to like... me in comparison to Perry and Briana.

Silently angry, I clenched my mug and the handle snapped. Shit! Bobbling it, I set it on the nearest desk without making too much of a mess. Grabbing tissues, I sopped up the small spill and tossed them in the trash. How had that broken? Too many times in the microwave?

My mother was a CPA–talk about dull job. She wasn't forgetful. No one wanted someone doing their taxes who didn't remember things, like adding, subtracting, and tax codes. But she pretty much forgot about me. Not only the dinner she didn't remember to tell me about, but oh, me in general. She left me at the grocery store once when she asked me to pick out a jar of peanut butter, checking out and driving home without her middle child or the crunchy spread.

I was used to her behavior, because I was the quiet one with my head perpetually stuck in a book, but that didn't mean I liked it. I glanced at the clock on the wall. Dinner was in two hours, always at six.

Tipping my head back, I stared at the ceiling, looking for patience. All I found were three pencils wedged, tip first, into the tiles. When had they gotten up there? I was the only full-time employee. Mrs. Metcalf, who was seventy-four, worked part-time and was currently somewhere reshelving. Then there were the variety of high school volunteers who helped out as part of their community service requirement for graduation. I assumed it was one of them, not Mrs. Metcalf, who'd been fooling around.

"What's this about dinner?" I went to one of the tall cabinets and pulled out a broom, getting a zap of static electricity at the contact. I wondered what the deal was with all the static lately as I raised it in the air to swipe at the nearest stuck pencil. Maybe I needed to use more conditioner in my hair.

"Perry is in from the Springs."

Perry was my older brother. He was a mega church pastor with over-the-top ideas and didn't leave his devoted flock too often, but it was a Tuesday. We never saw him on Sunday. We weren't a religious family so how he became so devoted to a divine power, I had no idea. My parents, however, were thrilled. Their first born, a leader of his own church. Looking back, it made sense since he used to stand on an empty milk crate by the mailbox and tell everyone who came down the sidewalk his latest thoughts.

It still amazed me he had followers who actually listened to his sermons. I was skeptical of anything that came out of his mouth because, well... he was my brother. I lived through his stinky adolescent phase. Knew about his stash of *Playboys* under his bed from when he was twelve. Heard from his prom date–my friend Sandy McClure–how he'd been a one pump chump. All of it? Gross. It was a hard leap for me to see him as anyone's spiritual leader instead of an annoying sibling.

My family was weird. Crazy, even. Brittany thought they were nuts and has consistently believed I was adopted. Whether they were my bio-family or not didn't matter. I hadn't figured out how to escape them yet. Leaving Coal Springs wasn't something I wanted to do. I loved my home-town and wanted to stay. Wanted to open my bookstore on Main Street. There was no way I could avoid them even if I skipped dinners and blocked their calls. I worked at the library. I shopped at the same grocery store. My apartment was a mile away.

If I told my mom I was busy and had to miss a family dinner I hadn't been told of, she'd only add on more passive aggressiveness to the conversation and extend it into future ones... *if* she remembered me.

The thing about being born between two loud, needy siblings was that I was invisible. I'd been content to read. I'd been quiet and fairly self-sufficient. I didn't take up space, and strangely enough, they didn't like when someone wasn't loud or needy.

Because that meant my parents weren't needed.

I sighed, batted at the pencil and stepped back when it dropped to the carpeted floor.

"I'll be there, but no potato salad since I'm at work for another hour." The one thing she did remember was that I made a good batch of potato salad with a hint of pickle relish.

"Pick some up at the store on your way."

Squatting down, I grabbed the pencil. Another zap of static. I wiggled my fingers as I stood. Blinked, then freaked.

"Holy shit," I muttered, staring through the glass window.

"What was that?" My mom didn't like hearing me swear, my soul in danger of being further tarnished. By further I meant by reading and wanting to sell *those* books and not atoning by attending Perry's services.

There, staring at me from the far side of the check-out counter was the guy from the plane in another crisp, deliciously dark suit. He was staring at me with a vigorous, dark intensity I remembered. He may have had a haircut, the sides trimmed close with the top longer showing off a hint of dark curl.

I swallowed, my throat suddenly dry. He wasn't here for a library card. He was here for me.

9

JACK

She looked better than I remembered, even with the blatant panic on her face.

It wasn't the look I wanted to see, especially directed at me, but what had I expected? For her to fling her clothes off and climb up on the circulation desk for me to fuck her like I've imagined since I got off the plane?

Shit, that thought got me hard, which was bad since a mother with two small children walked by, heading for the exit with bags full of books. Yeah, no fucking on the counter.

The interior was brightly lit with multiple book display islands. To the left was the hold section and DVDs. To the right was a separate room, the kids' section, based on the size of the tables and chairs and a large dinosaur painted on the wall. In the back and up a flight of stairs, were rows of books.

When she kept right on staring, her mouth open, her cell to her ear and her eyes as wide as saucers, I raised my hand and offered her a little finger wave.

Coming out of her stupor–that was a good sign, right?–she disconnected her call, set her phone down and came out of the back room.

Tentatively, she approached the desk as if I was delivering bad news or was a stalker from a plane flight we shared the week before and was nervous about getting too close.

I didn't like the idea of her being afraid of me, even though she probably should be. If it wasn't me but some other guy she sat beside on the plane who showed up at her work, I'd be the first to tell her to run the other way.

But this was me. Hitman? Yes. Stalker? Yes. Yet, completely safe.

"Hello," I said.

She blushed a hot pink and had a hard time meeting my eyes. Nerves or fear, I wasn't sure which. "Um... hi."

Her body was lush and curvy, and I wanted to grab and squeeze and cup and caress every soft inch of her. In a pretty black skirt and white V-neck tee–which only accentuated her more-than-a-handful tits–she looked business casual and cool enough for the summer heat. She looked sweet and innocent.

I knew that wasn't completely true. It was that contradiction that made me so intrigued.

I stared.

She stared.

I stared some more. Took in how her dark hair was half pulled back, tendrils falling loose to frame her round face.

Her brown eyes. The way her eyebrows had a pretty arch to them. Her pert nose. Full lips that would look amazing wrapped around my dick.

"Um... what are you doing here?" she asked, finally finding her voice.

"Isn't it obvious?" I asked.

She blinked, bit her lip. Obviously, it was not. "A... book?"

Squeaky wheels announced the arrival of a cart pushed by the older woman who I'd seen leaving the day before. She stopped right beside the counter. "I finished the self-help section, Hannah. I–" She stopped talking when she noticed me. "I'm sorry. I didn't realize you had a patron."

Hannah.

Her name was Hannah.

It suited her.

A cell rang from the back room.

"Do you need to get that?" the older woman asked.

Hannah shook her head. "No, Mrs. Metcalf. I'm sure it's my mother. I hung up on her a minute ago."

"I can help this young man if you need to call back." Dressed in khaki pants that stopped at her ankles, a pale pink blouse and white sneakers–which were as bright as her short hair, Mrs. Metcalf looked like a catalog model for an octogenarian clothing store. The way she was eyeing me had me wonder how she planned to *help* me.

Why wasn't Hannah eyeing me like I was a piece of meat, and she was a tiger who hadn't had a meal in a while? I'd gladly let her objectify me. Use me. Hannah, not Mrs. Metcalf.

Hannah shook her head, her gaze still on mine as if

looking away might make me disappear. "I definitely don't want to call her back."

I stared.

Hannah stared.

Mrs. Metcalf stared. "Aren't you going to ask what he wants?" she prodded.

Hannah shook her head, as if coming out of a trance and cleared her throat. "How may I help you?"

"Go out with me."

Hannah sputtered. Mrs. Metcalf grinned and clapped.

"I don't *know* you," Hannah said.

"I didn't know Mr. Metcalf when he asked me on a date and we're going on forty-eight years."

Hannah looked to the woman as if she were crazy. Maybe she was, although she seemed to be on my side. "You want me to go off with a stranger? This is how women get murdered."

Mrs. Metcalf waved her hand through the air. "That only happens in the Mystery section."

Hannah couldn't seem to help herself and laughed. "No, it doesn't!" She thumbed my way. "He could be a murderer."

Not *could*.

Mrs. Metcalf eyed me shrewdly. "Are you a murderer?" she asked, point blank. I imagined she could shoot a weapon with wicked precision. She probably had a gun in her purse like the one tucked into the back of my pants, hidden beneath my suit jacket. Although, hers was probably pink or had a pearl handle.

I set my hand on my chest. "I would never hurt Hannah

in any way. If someone so much as looked at her funny, I'd ensure they never did so again."

Both women blinked. Then both women fanned themselves.

"Oh my," Mrs. Metcalf murmured, then looked at Hannah. "If you don't go out with him, I will."

I'd have to tell Dax that Mrs. Metcalf was taking his spot as my wingman. Although if Hannah turned me down, I may have to take Mrs. Metcalf to dinner.

Hannah set her hands on her hips and looked feisty as fuck. "He might be all growly and look hot in a suit and say protective and sexy things, but I don't know the man."

I wasn't sure about the growly part, but her saying I looked hot and said sexy things boded well. The fact that she didn't know me was something I planned to change. That was why I was here.

"He seems to know you," Mrs. Metcalf countered, then looked my way. Her gray eyes held mine. I had a feeling if she was the gatekeeper to Hannah. If she didn't like me, this wasn't happening. "How *do* you know Hannah?"

"We met on an airplane."

Hannah studied me, finally getting over her surprise of having me appear at her work. "How did you find me? I didn't even tell you my name." She looked to Mrs. Metcalf, tilted her head down and gave her a serious librarian stare. "That says stalker and not from any book in the Mystery section."

"Stalker? Not in that suit," Mrs. Metcalf said, giving me another onceover.

"I didn't know your name until Mrs. Metcalf said it a few minutes ago. I knew you worked here because you said you were a librarian in Colorado and the sticker on the book you were reading was from this location."

Her eyes widened again, probably realizing she may have drawn a dangerous person right to her with a simple library book.

"You live here in Coal Springs?" Mrs. Metcalf asked. "I would have *certainly* remembered you."

I shook my head. "No, ma'am. Denver."

"He came all this way for you," Mrs. Metcalf said. Clearly, she was on my team.

"I don't even know *his* name!"

Mrs. Metcalf turned her beady gaze on me. "She does have a point, young man."

"Jack Hollister." I took a step closer to the circulation desk and rested my hands on it. Only a few feet away, the air shimmered with potency between us. It was like on the plane, the draw I felt toward her. It was almost... electrifying. "I do not wish to harm you, Hannah. I came here to take you to dinner. Tonight."

She shook her head. "I can't. I have plans."

"What plans?" I asked at the same time Mrs. Metcalf did.

"Dinner at my parents."

I wasn't sure if she was making that up, but it didn't matter. Being with her mother and father weren't what I had in mind, but murderers couldn't be choosers.

"Then I shall go with you."

10

The day couldn't get any weirder. I broke my favorite mug. I was going to a dreaded dinner. Glancing in the rearview mirror, I saw Jack park his ridiculously expensive SUV behind mine at the curb. It was definitely the car I'd seen across the street from the library the day before. He had been stalking me!

Shifting my gaze, I looked at myself.

"He drives a fancy car," I said aloud. "Not fancy, it's a fucking *Maserati*. He wears a suit. On a plane. In the library. He's hot as fuck. And he wants to join a family dinner. *WHY?*"

I wasn't date ready! With bent elbows, I flapped my arms like a bird, trying to air out my armpits.

Before we left the library and while Mrs. Metcalf had very happily kept him company, I'd dashed into the employee bathroom and touched up my makeup–which meant adding colored lip gloss and ensuring none of my mascara had flaked off since this morning.

My outfit was cute, but it in no way matched Jack in a suit. I was the dumpy small town girl and he was the urban Maserati driver.

Jack. JACK. OH MY GOD.

"The guy from the plane is parked behind me," I said aloud. I squealed, trying not to panic. No one should take my blood pressure right about now. *It was the guy from the plane.* I still couldn't believe he'd come up into the mountains from Denver to see me. ME. "WHY?"

I wasn't exciting, at least not in the good way. Hell, this year had been pretty shitty. No guy wanted to take on my crazy baggage. Proof was Kevin, who bailed when the going got tough. He'd never once come to a family dinner even though he knew my mother through her work. Looking back, I was glad that he hadn't. It would have been awful.

Tonight, might be awful, too. Jack was going to walk in my parents' house, learn how bizarre my genes were and run right back to Denver.

A knock on my car window made me jump. There was Jack, squatting down and staring in. The corner of his mouth was tipped up as if my little pep talk amused him. I couldn't help but stare because he was just that attractive. Dark hair that was cut short on the sides, longer on the top. Piercing gaze. Strong jaw with romance hero stubble. He was rugged, but the suit tamed him. Barely. The combination was... perfect.

And made my nipples hard. And my panties wet.

He was waiting for me.

I opened the door a few inches.

"Coming out?" he asked, his voice deep and rumbly.

I sighed, rolled my eyes. Nodded.

He stood, then backed up so I could open my door.

"Are you sure you want to do this?" I asked in a rush when I was in front of him, adjusting my purse on my shoulder. It was better to come clean and give him the chance right now. No one inside expected him. I was doing him a favor. "I mean, I'm not sure what your family's like, but mine is really weird. My best friend thinks I'm adopted."

On the plane, we sat side-by-side. Now, he stood before me, and our height difference was noticeable. I came up to his nose. I wasn't small. Hell, I was big boned. Or sturdy. Or, per Kevin, overweight. That was only accentuated by the fact that I wasn't tall.

Jack was over six feet, broad shouldered, and he filled out a suit better than any man I'd ever seen. It was definitely custom made. He even smelled good.

"My dad bolted when I was a kid and my mom died a long time ago," he told me.

"Oh. I'm... um, sorry to hear that." Instinctively, I set my hand on his arm. A zap of static electricity had me pulling my hand back. Jack's gaze dropped to where I touched him.

He tipped his head toward the house. "They can't be that bad. I mean, it's Coal Springs. People shit glitter here, right? I bet you have a pet unicorn in the backyard."

My lips twitched because Coal Springs was nothing like Denver. Small, safe, quaint. "Yeah. Everyone here shits glitter. But no unicorn. Sorry."

"Do you live here with your parents?"

I couldn't help but laugh. "No way. I have my own apartment about a mile from here."

I didn't move from the curb and wondered what his fresh eyes thought of the place. If his suits and car were any indication, he wasn't hurting for money. My parents' house was a two-story wood clapboard and stone house. White paint. Black front door. Huge blue spruce to the side of the driveway.

"We going in?" He tipped his chin up. Sniffed the air. "Is that burgers I smell? I admit, I haven't had a home cooked meal in... forever."

I grabbed his elbow, ignoring his question about burgers, even though his nose was right. I was having second and third thoughts. Freaking out that he was here. *Here.* "Jack. This is crazy. I can't believe you showed up at the library after seeing the bar code sticker."

"If my eyesight was good enough to read about Colin and Mia doing anal for the first time, I could see the name of the library on the front."

I felt my cheeks heat. He brought up *anal* and the fact that we read a scene with it together. Could I disappear if my eyes were closed? I cleared my throat. "It's not that."

"What?"

He looked at me with those dark eyes. Perplexed. He wanted to see me and came to Coal Springs to do so. He made it seem so simple. But it wasn't.

"I get that you wouldn't drive all the way up here from Denver if you wanted to chain a woman in your basement as your sex slave or turn her skin into a suit. You'd find someone much closer to home. Say the real reason is that you do want to go out with me. Just... why me?" I cocked my head and squinted, the sun slightly behind his head.

His eyes narrowed. "I do want you as my sex slave, but

I'd use one of my ties to keep you in my bed because it would be much more comfortable for both of us. Also, I live in an apartment. No basement."

I had to laugh and felt a little heated. Him tying me to his bed? "Jack."

Two boys on bikes whizzed by along the sidewalk, one of them flicking a bell as they went.

"What? I have a lot of ties." He shrugged, then raked his gaze down my body. "I also have a lot of suits and your skin is perfect right where it is."

"I saw your car yesterday." I glanced back at it, the expensive SUV at the curb that cost more than I made in a year. Probably twice as much. "Across the street from the library."

He looked away and I could have sworn he blushed beneath his five o'clock shadow. Raised his hand to rub the back of his neck.

"That was your car." I prodded an answer from him even though I was pretty sure of the answer. A Maserati wasn't subtle.

He nodded.

"You are a stalker." I wasn't sure if I should climb back in my car and lock the doors, my family having to fend for themselves, or hug him because he'd come to Coal Springs for me not once, but twice.

"I'm *your* stalker," he clarified, tipping his head down so he was closer. The air was heavy and charged around us. "You should meet my friend Dax. You two would get along great with calling what I'm doing here a stalker thing. As to why I want to go out with you?" His eyes left mine and raked down my body in a *very* blatant review. "You're sexy and fun. Cute and you have this whole innocent look about you, but I know for a fact you're dying to get railed over the back of your couch. A good girl *and* a bad girl."

My face flamed hotter than the grill in the backyard. "Oh my God," I whispered, glancing around to make sure no one in my family was in earshot. Or any of the neighbors.

He leaned in even more. "I want to be the one who rails you."

I was all for him doing the railing. ALL. But... "If you only want sex–"

"If I only wanted sex, do you think I'd invite myself to a woman's parents' house for dinner?"

He had a point. I could picture having sex with him–I'd pictured it a lot over the past week–but the chances of it happening after this dinner were slim to none. It was going to be that bad. Not the sex, the dinner.

"Why me?" I asked again.

He met my gaze, held it. "You, Hannah, intrigue me and I haven't been intrigued in a long time."

That made no sense, but I had to admit, I was intrigued by him, too. He was totally out of my league, but he was standing here.

I believed him.

I took a fortifying breath. "Fine. But I should tell you some things about my family before we go inside."

"They can't be that bad," he countered, swiping his hand through the air as if what was to come was no big deal. "I think I can handle your family."

We were already halfway up the walk so I couldn't ask him if he was being cocky or clueless.

All of a sudden, Jack froze. Stared at the roof of the house. Blinked.

"Um... I think I saw a woman fly." He pointed. "There."

I looked up. Nothing. Then a woman rose up high in the air, then dropped and disappeared.

"Oh, that's my sister, Briana. She does trampolining."

11

JACK

If a woman mentioned that her family was really weird, believe her. Women were known to exaggerate. Not Hannah. I'd never met a bigger bunch of nutjobs before. The fact that they were related to Hannah made it scary. And made me mad because they were all self-absorbed losers. And I knew a lot of them. Hell, killing them was what I did for a living.

Her mother met us at the door. Instead of wondering after the strange man who was with her, she asked, "Where's the potato salad?"

"Sorry, I forgot," Hannah replied.

The answering look on the woman's face was more realistic if Hannah told her she forgot to put on pants and took a stroll down Main Street. "Forgot? We talked two hours ago."

Hannah's cheeks flushed and not in the way that I liked.

She was angry at her mother's shame-laced words. Hell, *I* was upset from the scolding.

Hannah glanced up at me. "I was distracted."

I'd take it as a win that I made her forget to pick up a side dish, but not if it made her head and shoulders droop like they were now.

"Banana! How's my girl?" A burly man came down the hall, a potent cloud of alcohol swirled around him and the full highball glass he held. In it was several fingers deep of a dark liquid and several ice cubes. Probably scotch.

"Hi, Dad," Hannah said, giving him a little wave.

Didn't families hug in this Hallmark commercial of a town? When her dad took a swig of his drink instead of wrapping her in his arms, I had my answer. "I've got a pitcher of cocktails if you want to join me."

His voice was overly loud, and her mother shushed him. Over her shoulder, I noticed a stuffed animal mounted on the wall. Not a kid's plush toy, but an actual dead, taxidermied creature. It was some kind of antelope head. Or a deer. Either way, I had to wonder who in the house bagged it. I'd have to be careful since they were hunted from a distance. It was a lot easier to shoot someone in a room with four walls.

"I'm good," Hannah replied.

We weren't even in the door yet and liquor was looking like a good option to handle these people. Hannah had warned me. I'd volunteered for this dinner. If Hannah was making it through this sober, then I was, too.

"I'm Jack," I said. "Hannah's date. Thanks for having me."

Her mother studied me but spoke to Hannah. "You brought a date and forgot the potato salad?"

I knew where I stood with her, well below a side dish. "Should I go and pick some up?" I asked, thumbing over my shoulder.

"No!" Hannah practically shouted.

"Yes," her mother said at the same time.

"Don't scare him away, Marcia," her dad scolded. "You know this may be the only time she lands a man after Kevin."

What the hell kind of bullshit was that? I hadn't had a father growing up, but even I knew it was a dick thing to say. I assumed Kevin was her ex, a cheating one, too. So why was he bringing him up?

"Dad!" Hannah looked mortified.

"What?" he countered, as if her upset was the problem. Man, her mom and dad were a pair of gaslighters. "You always have your head in a book."

I didn't know why that was a turnoff, especially since I knew exactly what was within those pages.

Her mother cleared her throat. "I'm Marcia and this is Bob. You can call us Mr. and Mrs. Highcliff."

"Mom!" Hannah shouted. "Oh my God. He will not. He's at least thirty years old, not seven."

She stormed past them, yanking my hand and tugging me into the house. My gaze bounced around taking in the place Hannah grew up but caught on a bunch more dead animals on the walls. A raccoon. A squirrel. And... was that a groundhog or a woodchuck?

We made it down a hallway lined with photos–the area too narrow for dead animal heads to stick out–into the kitchen before she stopped suddenly. I almost bumped into her and knocked her over. I set my hands on her hips–which I didn't mind at all–and looked over her shoulder.

"Living in sin, Hannah?"

Who the hell was this holier-than-thou guy?

Probably a brother, maybe a few years older, although they looked nothing alike. He had blond hair, cut and styled like a politician's. On his slim frame was a tan button-up and tan khakis. Tan leather shoes. I didn't see a pocket protector, but perhaps he left it in another tan shirt. I had to wonder if he was color blind and if going mono-chromatic kept him from worse fashion disasters than what he was sporting now.

The only way I'd wear a tan-on-tan ensemble was if I was in prison. And that wasn't happening.

"I ran into Sandy McClure at the grocery store the other day," Hannah countered. "She says hi."

I didn't know who Sandy McClure was, but the way the guy's lips pursed so thinly that they pretty much disap-peared, he'd committed some kind of sin with her.

"Jack," I said, sticking my hand out around Hannah. If I was going to punch a guy in the face, I wanted to at least know his name first.

"My brother Perry," Hannah said without much affec-tion in her tone. "He runs a mega church in the Springs. Perhaps you've heard of it? Paragons of the Divine?"

Perry shook my hand. Limply.

"Can't say I have," I replied because it sounded like a cult. If he was going to be so righteous, then I'd play along. "You know what John 1:8 says, 'If we claim to be without sin, we deceive ourselves.' I'd rather lean into the concept."

Hannah stared over her shoulder at me owl eyed. Yeah, no one expected me to spout Bible verses, but Dax's dad had made us copy them hundreds of times as one form of punishment, and we got in trouble a lot. The guy used to kill and maim people for a living; he was far from a pew warmer. To him, there was nothing more painful to write over and over. I had to agree.

"We all die someday," I added.

Perry and Sandra McClure had to have done more sinning than me and Hannah since we hadn't even sinned. Was stalking a sin? Sure, a crime, but I didn't remember a Bible verse against it.

"Yes, but some go to heaven," Perry countered. Probably he told his flock this after drinking some Kool-Aid.

I shrugged, knowing full well where I was headed, and it wasn't heaven. At least I wouldn't be stuck for eternity with Perry the Prude. "I think some rock musicians had a debate on this. If there's a stairway to heaven and a highway to hell, I guess we know which place more people would rather go."

The back door flew open before Perry could respond. In stormed the woman I saw flying through the air. She was carrying a full platter of meat. In leggings and a skin-tight tank top, she was dressed for a yoga class, although they were a neon pink so bright it hurt my eyes. It was probably so birds and small airplanes didn't hit her when she was up in the air over the backyard like a drone. "Dad, you forgot the burgers on the grill. Hope everyone likes them well done." She paused, eyed me up and down like she was going to skip the meat on the platter and take a bite out of me. "Hey, Hannah, who's the hottie? When he's done with you, can I have him?" She laughed, then winked at me. "Just kidding. Not."

"My sister, Briana," Hannah muttered.

"Oh good. Dinner's ready!" Bob called, the ice in his glass tinkling as merrily as he sounded.

"If it can be called dinner without potato salad," Marcia added, for fun or spite, I wasn't sure.

Hannah was definitely adopted.

12

HANNAH

I had no idea why Jack hadn't bolted for the door yet. Not only was my family being their finest, obnoxious selves, but the burgers were so well done they were practically hockey pucks.

We were in the dining room and settled around a checkered cloth covered table. On it were hamburgers, corn, baked beans, pickles, and chips. On my left was Jack. Across from me was Briana. Beside her, Perry. Flanking the ends of the table were my parents.

In the ten minutes I'd been nudging the food around on my plate, we'd been subjected to Briana's and Perry's endless chatter. Jack's attention shifted from sibling to sibling but was more focused on the mounted cow head that hung on the wall over the side table. It was Curtis the Cow. Curtis had been put up when I was a kid and Perry

had named it. He'd named the other animals, too, but I
didn't remember any others.

"...three years ago, I transitioned to the trampoline
when my coach felt that I couldn't make the Olympic squad
for gymnastics. Beam was where I excelled. I have excellent
balance. And flexibility."

After giving Jack another wink, Briana grabbed her
hamburger and took a healthy bite.

"...then I reminded my congregation that gluttony was a
sin," Perry spouted while Briana's mouth was full. He
reached for the baked beans and scooped a pile onto his
plate beside his second burger, two eaten cobs of corn and
three pickles. "We must all be cautious in our indulgences."

"At first, I was doing pike jumps but now I'm doing full-
in full-out, double back somersault with full twist in the
first somersault and another full twist in the second somersault which I think will get me to the next Olympic trials. I
could show you after dinner if you like." Briana took a swig
from her can of soda. Her high ponytail bounced to a beat
she only heard through an ear pod she had tucked into her
left ear. She spoke so fast her backup career could be an
auctioneer.

"The second week of the volunteer weed removal
program has been a success," Perry shared. "We've pulled
in those in need from the homeless shelter to assist and
offer water and snacks after the three-hour highway
cleanup." He shoveled in a huge bite of beans.

While they took us on two very different ego trips, Jack
sat quiet. He somehow ate a burger—with many sips of
accompanying iced tea to get it down—and a bunch of chips.

His plate was clean. All the while, Dad had made it through his second pour from his pitcher, only sloshing a little over the side. Mom kept eyeing Jack with suspicion.

"All I asked was for the potato salad," Mom muttered when Briana and Perry took bites of their burgers at the same time.

This again?

"You told me about the dinner less than three hours ago. When I was at work," I replied.

"You could have picked up some at the store like I asked."

I could've, but having Jack show up at work had fried my brain. The good news? Jack wasn't a stalker. Not a chance in hell.

No stalker would subject themselves to this dinner. They'd have given up and moved onto someone else.

No, he was here for a different reason, and it wasn't to hack me into bits with an ax.

Had he been serious, thinking I was sexy and fun and that he had thoughts about railing me over the back of a couch? I really, really wanted that. It had to be true, because again, this nightmare.

"I hate when we serve chips for dinner," Mom continued bitterly. "This memory problem isn't still lingering from your surgery, is it?"

I could feel my cheeks practically catch fire as Jack's head whipped my way and his eyes burned into the side of my face. The last thing I wanted to do was to have Jack think even less of me. Bookworm. Overweight. Librarian. Crazy family. Defective brain.

I bit my lip, knowing an outburst would do nothing but have Dad drink more, Mom dig her heels into her potato salad snit, and have my brother think I was slothful–one of the deadly sins along with lustful.

"No issues," I said, flicking my gaze at Jack for a second and offering him a fake smile that quickly slipped away.

"Listen to your mother next time, Hannah," Dad added, waving his drink hand in the air, sloshing some liquid onto the table.

I was so frustrated and embarrassed. Angry, too. Brittany had come a few times for dinner, but had bailed on the concept, telling me she'd rather have a pap smear.

"It was my fault," Jack admitted. His hand settled on my thigh, but static electricity had him yanking his palm away for a second. His eyes widened in surprise, then gave my leg a gentle squeeze. "The missing potato salad."

He winked, one that was far sexier than the ones Briana was giving him across the table. I felt his touch, but I also felt the reassurance that came with it.

Why was he throwing himself under the bus for me? Why did I find that so incredibly hot?

Everyone was quiet–miracle of miracles–waiting for him to say more, although Perry reached for another ear of corn.

"I turned her head," Jack admitted. He removed his hand from my leg and set it along the back of my chair. It was a more visible sign of solidarity. The hair on the back of my neck rose in response. What was it about my body reacting to him? "Obviously."

Or ego. God, he was worse than all of them.

"She doesn't need her head turned. She's already got

her head in the clouds with those books she reads," Mom said with a haughty sniff. "And she thinks people will come to a bookstore that caters to... *that* if she opens one."

Oh my God, I wanted to die of mortification. Jack knew all about my reading habits, knew one of the stories... intimately.

"You mean fiction?" Jack asked.

Perry huffed, a gluttonous forkful of beans just shy of his mouth. "*Fiction* is dangerous. Wild imaginings. Impossible dreams. And when the content is pornographic..."

"'He shall lie all night between my breasts–'" Jack murmured.

"See? Pornography!" Perry said, pointing at Jack.

Briana eye fucked my date and murmured, "He can lie all night between my breasts."

"Stop your smoting," Jack replied, holding his hand up. "That's in the Bible. Song of Solomon, I believe."

Perry opened his mouth, then snapped it shut.

I bit my lip, never having seen him shut down like that before. I wasn't sure if I should be impressed or scared Jack was out Bible versing my church-leading brother. I couldn't remember a time when anyone put Perry in his place.

"You a man of the Lord, Jack?" Dad asked. "You a preacher?"

"That would explain the suit," Mom added, eyeing Jack critically.

I picked up my tea, took a sip.

"Mortician."

I spit it out in a spray across half the table.

My family started talking at once.

I slapped my hands down on the table, making the burger platter jump. Stood.

"He said mortician, not murderer!" I shouted.

My family was rude and awful. I'd handled it fine when it was only me. Used to it. Expected it even. But they were doing this in front of a man. Sure, he was a stranger, but I brought him. Liked him.

They could fuck with me, but not Jack.

I ran for the powder room off the hall. I grabbed the knob, pulled and ripped the door right off the hinges.

"What the hell?" I muttered, staring at the door. I leaned it against the wall at a slant, then went into the powder room, letting the door fall shut behind me.

Five seconds later, Jack joined me. I whipped around away from the sink. Thank God I hadn't pulled my pants down to pee.

"What's the deal with the door?" he asked, studying how it had come off the hinges.

I shrugged. I was somehow ridiculously strong all of a sudden? I'd hefted that book box and now this? He wouldn't believe it–because I didn't–so I said, "Termites?"

He shifted his attention from the broken door to me. The ceiling was sloped since the room was tucked beneath the stairs. It was definitely a one-person space and it forced Jack to stand close to me. Very, *very* close. If I took a deep breath, my breasts would bump his suit. I felt the familiar charge being this close to him. Was this normal when attraction was *this* potent?

I recognized his male scent from the airplane. It wasn't potent cologne, but something dark and manly. It didn't make me sneeze like irritating scents did. In fact, it made me want to lean in and sniff him, which would make me weirder than Perry and Briana combined.

"Please tell me you're not a mortician," I said before he could comment on my family. The suits and the Bible verses made it a possibility. I had nothing against the profession, but... yeah, dead bodies.

"Please tell me you're adopted," he countered.

I flung my hands in the air and chuckled, although it was more from mortification than humor. "I told you!"

"And what's the story with all the dead animals?" He tipped his chin toward the squirrel on the wall above the mirror. It was standing on its hind legs on a wooden base, front little arms raised as if to attack. It'd been there for as long as I could remember and never noticed it anymore.

"My dad's a taxidermist," I explained. "When people don't claim their projects, he puts them up around the house. Fun, right?"

He frowned, studied me. I wasn't sure if he was eyeing me closely to see if I might turn crazy like my family. The chances were high. "What's this surgery you had and why did it affect your memory?"

Oh. That.

I waved it off. I wasn't going to tell him I had a brain tumor while we stood in my parents' powder room. "I had a little problem with my brain a few months ago."

His eyes widened, then roved over my face. "Jesus. Are you okay?"

I felt his concern in the same electrical charge between us.

Now that I had gamma knife radiation to zap a brain tumor, yes. Instead of saying that aloud and have him decide to take my sister up on her undressing offer, I nodded.

He sighed, ran a hand along the back of his neck. "I need to get the hell out of here."

Oh.

I knew it. Of course, he was leaving.

My heart dropped. I didn't blame him one bit. In fact, he made it a lot longer than I anticipated. Who wanted to be with a woman who had crazy running rampant in her gene pool, as well as brain tumors? I didn't know how excited I was about him until now, when it was over.

Over? What a silly thought. It hadn't even begun. At least he was honest and hadn't cheated on me.

"Right," I said, glancing at the wood floor. I didn't want to look at his gorgeous face any more than I had to. Not when he was leaving, and I'd never see him again. "I understand. Um... go ahead and I'll tell my family you left because you got called out for a dead body or something."

His body tensed, which had me looking up. He was frowning, his look almost startled. "What? A dead body? Why would you say that?"

"Mortician," I reminded.

He sighed, almost relieved. "No. No dead body." He pulled it his cell from his pocket, read the display. He must've had it set to vibrate. The change was slight, but I noticed the way his face closed off. It was as if he'd become a different person. As if he'd showed me a certain side of himself. "I have to go."

I nodded. He'd already said that.

"Do you have your phone on you?" he asked.

I shook my head. It was in my purse on the kitchen counter.

"What's your number?"

I told him and he typed it into his cell with his dexterous thumbs. The phone chimed again. He took a second to read whatever the next text was, then his dark eyes met mine. Held. "I'll call you."

Then he was gone.

13

JACK

I almost had a fucking coronary in the bathroom when Hannah had offered a dead body as an excuse for me leaving the dinner. She had no idea how on-target she'd been. It'd taken her prompt that I'd told her family I was a mortician for me to chill out.

It wasn't only the words, but how calmly she'd said it. As if she hadn't cared that I dealt in dead bodies all the time. That, to her, it was no big deal.

But it wasn't true. If she knew the truth, she wouldn't laugh, she'd be horrified.

Most people... *normal* people, were horrified when someone died.

Hannah was normal. A good girl.

My cell had vibrated in my pocket more than once while we were eating. Since that meal had been a shitshow, I'd ignored the calls. Then I got another while I was in the tiny bathroom with Hannah. Three in the matter of minutes had me annoyed.

Hadn't whoever the fuck it was known I was busy?

I hadn't wanted to look and find out, finally having Hannah right where I wanted. Cornered between me and a sink. The sink wasn't part of the plan. A wall or a bed were better options, but I was always able to revisit and revise any situation. We'd been alone. In a *very* small space. I wasn't even sure I could stand and piss without hitting my head on the sloping ceiling but if I'd have found a way to fuck her.

It hadn't been Dax calling to tell me he needed me along for a job. It'd been a Vegas area code, which meant Sal Reggiano. I was smart enough to know the powerful man needed a call back, with Joey Brains or some other assistant doing the work. Even when I had been inches from my girl.

Whatever the mob boss had to say wasn't for Hannah's ears. Or her family's.

The calls were a cold-shower-like reminder–more than the scolding from Dax–that I was being stupid being with Hannah. I'd been at her parents' house having dinner!

Dax was going to shit a brick when I told him. We didn't do stuff like family get-togethers. Holidays. Leftovers. Football tailgating.

Hell, I wasn't the man who hung out with people whose biggest concerns in life were forgotten potato salad. Sure, Hannah had an ice-queen mother, a lush father who stuffed dead animals—so fucking ironic, a pompous brother, and a skanky sister who'd tried to play footsie with me under the table before I kicked her in the shin and shut that shit down. They were harmless. The self-involved were easy to manage because they didn't see anything but themselves.

They especially didn't see Hannah.

Her family's kind of crazy was normal. Not the kind like me and Dax who roughed up or killed people for money. Okay, Hannah's family was really fucking crazy.

Still, I was a bad option for her. No matter how much I'd wanted to lower my head the few inches between us in the bathroom and kiss her, I couldn't. Not with a mob boss blowing up my cell.

I couldn't have missed the flash of hurt in Hannah's eyes when I told her I had to leave. She seemed to have a talent for hiding her emotions, but I could see it. She thought I was *leaving* leaving. That I was walking away. Permanently.

I'd put that hurt there.

Perversely, I was pleased because it meant she felt something for me. I couldn't have hurt her if she hadn't had interest or like or... felt something when she was with me.

I felt the same way. There was way more than interest and a shit ton of like. Hope? I had no idea what the fuck that was. All I knew was that her resigned expression to someone else bailing on her started to melt the ice around my heart.

That was a big problem because when one had a heart, killing became really fucking hard. Big Mike had lost his wife–Dax's mom–before I came into the picture. He always talked about how she had been the love of his life and a drunk driver had taken her out on the way to work. She'd been a nurse. Loved helping people. When she was gone, he said she took his heart with her and filled the void with the need for justice. To rid the world of drunks who had no license because they had seventeen DUIs. The police hadn't been able to do anything but follow the sad, weak laws. But Big Mike hadn't been held to them. He told us it made killing and roughing people up easy when you didn't feel. And when the people he took out deserved it. The world was a better—and safer—place without that specific drunk and all the drug dealers, sex offenders, and other scum he came across after. He shared this no nonsense, no feeling approach to life with us.

I hadn't been interested or pulled to someone until Hannah. It made no sense. Why now? Why her? She was tame and normal and... extraordinary. From what I could tell, she'd been through a lot. Alone, or at least with a crazy cast of helpers.

Besides Dax, I was alone, and I'd been okay with it. Hannah was the kind of person who loved people. Interaction. Seeing them happy. *That* was what made her good.

I wasn't good. I was successful based on the Maserati I was driving and the penthouse I owned. But taking calls from mob bosses was a pain in the ass, not a sign of success. I didn't want Sal Reggiano or anyone else to interrupt my time with my girl. But he had.

I didn't want to be the one who bailed on her. I wanted to be the one who stuck.

An hour later, I was back at my apartment. The ride down the mountains from Coal Springs was faster, the drive downhill the whole way and after rush hour.

I sent a text to Nitro.

> Find out everything you can about a guy
> named Kevin who lives in Coal Springs.
> Late 20s, early 30s. Dated the town
> librarian.

It wasn't much for him to work with, but Nitro would get the info on the ex. I'd take care of that asshole. Later.

Taking care of current business, I dialed the number that had called me during my time with Hannah. Knowing I had to deal with a mob boss, I'd skipped calling him back from my SUV. It wasn't that I respected him all that much, but my clients weren't to be underestimated. They wanted someone dead and paid good money to see it happen. They weren't high school football coaches or plumbers.

I was a bad guy, but these guys were *bad*. They'd have shot Hannah's family one after the other for being annoying shits, then kept right on eating their well-done burgers.

I stood in my kitchen while the call rang, looking out the windows at the expansive view of the Rocky Mountains. The sun had already set, but twilight lingered.

"You haven't completed your job for me."

Shit. It wasn't Joey Brains. It was Sal Reggiano himself. He was talking about Turkleman. And he was doing it over the phone. It was probably a burner, but it meant he *really* wanted this guy dead.

Because of Hannah, I'd forgotten about the job. Entirely.

"It's a three-game series with the Yankees," I said, getting my head on straight. I'd had Nitro collect on the guy when I took the job. While I didn't follow baseball and had no intention of killing the guy at a ballpark, I at least knew how long he'd be in town. Which meant I had two more days with the guy in Denver. Two more days to finish the task.

"What's the holdup?" he continued. "Eyebrows and Joey Brains are in town."

Meaning they could off Turkleman instead. If he'd wanted them to do it, I wouldn't have been given the task in the first place. It was an empty threat. Except why was he wasting his time calling me about some hit unless it was really important to him? I needed Nitro to dig further.

"I always complete a job," I told him, clenching my teeth.

"Don't disappoint."

He hung up.

Fuck, I hated my work sometimes.

14

HANNAH

The next afternoon on my lunch break, Brittany and I were walking down Main Street, weaving around the influx of tourists. We'd finished our meal at our usual cafe–me a grilled cheese and soup and Brittany the chicken salad on croissant–and now had coffees in hand that we'd picked up from our favorite shop a block behind us.

It was our standing Wednesday lunch date.

"I can't believe he showed up at the library! The guy from the plane." She shook her head, then smiled and offered someone a quick hello. Because of our jobs, we ran into people we knew all over town. If I ever wanted to pick up condoms or get a surprise party gift, I had to order them online. "That's insane... and it's happening to you. I told you! This is unbelievable!"

It was that. Completely unbelievable.

"Mrs. Metcalf was all for me going out with him."

"Mrs. Metcalf is a smart woman," Brittany countered, then took a sip of her drink.

"She doesn't care that he could be a murderer."

"If he's as handsome as you say, *I* don't care either."

I gave her a look, although my vagina was in agreement with them.

"He went to your parents' house," Brittany continued. "That says a lot. God, I would have suffered through one of your family dinners to witness it."

"He left," I reminded. "He got a call and bolted in the middle of dinner."

"After he told off your brother and fucked with your parents first. A mortician? Seriously?"

I'd given her a full recap over our lunch. She'd listened to the tale with the same eagerness as the little kids who came to Storytime.

"I have no idea what he does for a living. He could have been serious," I reminded.

I scoped out the window display at the baby boutique as we went by.

She sliced her hand through the air. "If he's as hot as you say, there's no way he's a mortician."

I laughed, stopped walking and crossed my arms over my chest. "Are you saying morticians are all unattractive? I could say the same for dentists. You deal with halitosis and weak gums."

She glared and patted her perfectly styled hair. "I'm saying his personality doesn't match someone who embalms bodies for a living."

She had a point. He seemed worldly and bold and dark and mysterious and not in a creepy, hearse-driving way. He smelled good, too, not like formaldehyde.

"He said he was going to call." I started meandering down the sidewalk again.

"Then he'll call."

I shook my head. I didn't have the same optimism as her. Her parents weren't crazy and either ignored her or were constantly disappointed. When they came to visit, she and her mom—and me—went shoe shopping and got facials. She didn't have a boyfriend who'd dumped her when she found out she had a brain tumor. Not that Brittany hadn't had shitty moments in her life. I wasn't stupid enough to think I cornered the market on rough times. She didn't have plain bad luck like me. It'd been a *rough* year; having the tumor symptoms for a few months without knowing why, then being diagnosed, then the treatment. Physically. Mentally. I was jaded. Doubtful. Skittish. Scared, too. "No. It was his excuse to leave. Everyone was on their worst behavior. God, I was so mad!"

My voice was shrill and raised, upset even now, the next day.

"If he met Perry and didn't throw his drink on him to see if he melted or burst into flames, then he'll call."

"Briana offered up her breasts for him to rest upon." I frowned, glaring at the outdoor gear in the next shop's window display. Hair on the back of my neck rose remembering. I was getting used to the sensation since it seemed to happen with increasing frequency.

Brittany stopped and turned to me, eyes wide in surprise. Dressed for a day of cavity filling and root canal drilling, she wore red capri pants and a multicolored sleeveless blouse. Both, against her dark skin, were striking. While Coal Springs was at eight thousand feet, it was still a warm day. "Say what?"

I waved my hand, not remembering the Bible quote exactly. Jack's ability to spout verses on the fly was something I wanted to know more about. I wouldn't call it a talent, but it sure had come in handy. "She pretty much offered herself up to my date."

"She's twenty-four, lives in your parents' basement and jumps on a trampoline for a living. If this guy is into that, then he's totally not the one for you."

We walked on to the next store, which was a vacant space, the 'for lease' sign in the window. It was where I wanted my romance bookstore to go. We stopped in front of the dusty window to peek at an empty room with a counter and shelving along the walls. It used to be a knitting shop, but the owner's husband had passed away and she'd relocated to Utah to be closer to her children. It'd been vacant since the beginning of the year.

Brittany and I walked past it every week. I wasn't sure if it was cruel or me being hopeful. Before my radiation, it'd been to make plans about what I was going to do, talk leasing agreements, and what color to paint the walls. We'd been excited together. After the radiation, I didn't talk about it at all. Getting the call that I had a brain tumor had scared me shitless. Soon after, I'd had to go through the gamma knife radiosurgery and recover. While that had stalled things, my dream had been put on hold due to hospital bills. They'd stripped away all my savings, the money I'd put aside for the new venture. I'd had health insurance through the ordeal, but it hadn't covered everything. And no bank was going to give me a loan when I still had medical debts. I rented my apartment and had an old car that wasn't worth much. I had no collateral.

I sighed, glad the prime spot had yet to be taken. I could picture exactly how I would arrange the books. Colorful displays in the window, Contemporary down the left wall, new releases front and center. There'd be comfortable pink chairs and couches for readers to sit.

I used to cry when we walked by, the missed opportunity and feeling of loss too keen. I'd been so close, then it all fell apart. No new business. No boyfriend. No money. A newfound panic about life and death. Over the few months since the radiation, I became resigned. Even more quiet and subdued than ever. It had felt as if the world was out to get me, and it was safer on my couch with a nose in a book. Heroine's might struggle in a romance, but there was a guaranteed happily ever after. I needed one of those right about now.

"It'll be yours soon enough," Brittany said, wrapping an arm around my shoulders and giving me a squeeze. "And it'll be amazing."

I could only nod, feeling forlorn.

I'd had a few months to come to terms with the delay of my dreams, Kevin's behavior, and the size of my bank account. Today, though, it wasn't any of those things that made me so disappointed. I was sad about an ex-stalker. How insane was that?

15

JACK

"What the hell are you doing with your phone?" Dax asked.

His put-out tone had me glancing away from my screen. "Trying to figure out what to say when I text Hannah."

He leaned his hip against the desk, crossed his arms, which made him look like Edward Scissorhands with the garden shears he held. "You're holding a man's arm down so I can cut his finger off. Is now the right time?"

We were in the back office of Jimmy McFee's bar. He owed Dax's client a shit ton of money after betting in an underground high stakes poker game and lost. A lot. Since he hadn't paid up, Dax was taking payment with his pinky finger.

Today, Dax had been tasked with offering the guy a payment plan that included body parts. I glanced down at the man in question, sitting awkwardly–and very nervously–in his chair. I had his wrist pinned to the desk, a pile of invoices and receipts beneath. Sweat dripped down his face as if he was in a sauna. Imminent amputation of a digit did that to a person.

"Take all the fucking time you want," Jimmy said, curling his fingers on his pinned hand into a fist.

My grip was firm while Dax tauntingly opened and closed the blades of the shears. Neither of us gardened, but yard work wasn't the only use for the tool.

I was helping because it was pretty hard to cut a guy's finger off when he was moving around. No one took the time to consider what was involved, but it was a two-person task.

As for Hannah, I wanted to call her instead of text, but she was at work. The library wasn't a hubbub of activity, but I didn't want to disturb her while on the job. A text made more sense and I sure as hell wasn't waiting until after five when the library closed to reach out to her. But what did I say? *I'm sorry about last night. I got a call from a mob boss and had to leave? I can't stop thinking of you?* I leaned further onto the desk, pinning Jimmy's wrist more firmly in place. He grunted in discomfort and probably panic.

I'd be losing my shit if I was soon going to be nick-named Jimmy Nine Fingers.

"You're one to talk, Jimmy," Dax said. "Taking too long is what got you into this mess."

"Don't fuck with me," I snapped. "I don't want to wait too long to get back to her." The words were more feral growl than general conversation.

Dax held up his hands in defense, which was ironic since he was holding a pair of shears. "That dinner sounded like getting shot in the foot would be less painful."

I'd given him a highlight reel of what went down the night before.

"I'm not interested in her family," I told him over Jimmy's head. "I'm interested in Hannah."

"Sure, but right now?" he countered.

"What's the emoji again for fucking?" I asked, ignoring him. My thumb scrolled through the options. Would Hannah like that or was it too much, too soon? She'd admitted she wanted to be railed. I'd admitted I wanted to rail her. Hmm. Was there a railroad track emoji? That would work. Or would she have no clue what it meant?

Both men stared at me.

"Emoji for fucking? I have no idea. I'm not a college coed," Dax grumbled, seriously annoyed.

"There isn't an emoji for it," Jimmy offered. He seemed to be sweating a little less now that Dax wasn't making snipping sounds with the shears. "You need to use the OK hand sign and a pointer finger together. Or the eggplant and water droplets. Or a peach."

"What's the water droplets for? Jizz?" Dax winced. "I'm guessing, Jimmy, that you're single because I don't think any woman's going to want that emoji in a text."

"Jesus, not jizz." Jimmy shook his head. "It's to indicate a wet pussy. Or that she squirts."

Squirts? That hadn't come up in the book Hannah and I had read on the plane, but I wasn't ruling it out in others in the series. I wondered if Hannah had ever squirted before.

Bad thought. No. I didn't want to think of her with another guy, especially one who got her to do that. It made me fucking furious. If anyone was going to make her come so hard she squirted, it was going to be me.

Challenge accepted.

"Fine, no water drops. What would you say to a woman you're interested in?" I asked Jimmy.

"Seriously?" Dax sighed, running his free hand down his face and sighed. "Interested? Next, it'll be dinner and a movie. Kissing and making out and second base bullshit. We're cutting a man's finger off and you're talking like a fucking teenager."

I didn't disagree. I needed help and not the kind from a mental health professional. I'd never had to talk to a woman before. Sex had always been transactional, light on the conversation. Nothing more. I was a decent looking guy. I had money. I'd never had to do more than crook my finger to have a few hours of fun. Often enough, I never even got the woman's name. She never went to my apartment. Rarely went to hers.

Did it make me an asshole? Not when expectations were set up front. There were women who were only interested in a quick fuck, who didn't want personal history to go along with a skilled dick.

Hannah was different. The pull I had to her was unexplainable. The air between us was literally electrified. Why her? It made no sense, but I didn't give a shit. I wanted to fuck the hell out of her, no question, but I wanted more than that. I wanted *her*. I never imagined the whole picket fence thing before, but if Hannah was standing behind that fence, I was game. Thus, the stupid-ass texting questions.

"My advice?" Dax offered. "Skip the fucking emojis. Like I said, you're not a coed."

Jimmy swallowed hard, his eyes bouncing between me and Dax like a ball at a tennis match. "I have three ex-wives, so I'm not the best one to ask." He looked a little more afraid. "I don't want you circling back to me if it doesn't work out."

"How about this?" I asked Jimmy, leaning in and meeting his anxious gaze. "You help me come up with something good to text my new girl and I'll keep my friend Dax here from taking that finger today. I can't guarantee he won't return though."

Dax groaned and dropped the shears on the desk with a clatter.

I thought I saw tears in Jimmy's eyes. Dax's too since he wasn't going to complete the job he'd been hired to do.

"Deal."

16

HANNAH

Hi

I got the text and wondered who it was from, then shrugged it off as spam. Scammers were getting better and better these days with their creative texting to get someone to reply. I'd fallen for the I'm-your-friend scam once and received so many texts about winning an electric drill set, I'd wanted to switch phone numbers.

So I blocked it and went back to work. At a tap at the front door, I looked up laminating a book at the workstation in the back room. Dan, the mailman, held two boxes stacked one on top of the other and gave me a little finger wave from his grip at the bottom. I saw him every day on his route, and we'd gone to high school together.

I went around the desk and opened the door for him.

"Hey, Hannah. Take the top one, will you?"

The way he was struggling, they looked heavy. Before I could tell him I was a weakling, he leaned his upper body forward to tip the top box toward me.

I reached out automatically to catch it. "Whoa, okay, um... huh. I got it."

By the heft of it, the box was full of books. Peeking at the address label, it was from one of the book distributors we ordered from, and they packed well. No fluff only neatly arranged hardback books. Heavy ones, like my boxes from the romance convention.

Adjusting my hands on the bottom for a more comfortable grip, I handled it as if it was full of feathers.

"Wow, Hannah," Dan commented. "Taking up weightlifting?"

I raised the box up and down a few inches. Up. Down. Up. Down. Easy. Even easier than the box I carried up to my apartment. "Um, I guess."

"Then if that's not too bad, here's the other. Mind taking both?" One box was one thing, but two? "I'm behind and I've taken over a second route since someone's out sick. I need to get everything delivered because we've got our first birthing class tonight."

His wife, Marnie, was expecting their first child in the fall.

"No, wait, I don't think–"

He set it on the other one so I could barely see over the top edge. "Oh boy. Um..."

My arms hadn't ripped from their sockets.

My back wasn't breaking.

What the hell was going on?

"Got it?" he asked, checking to make sure I was good.

I met his worried gaze over the top edge of cardboard. He could've carried the boxes across the room and set them on the counter and I should have been upset he was bailing on me, lugging a heavy load. But it actually wasn't heavy, which was crazy. Dan was sweating with the exertion.

"Yeah, I guess I do," I said, surprising not only Dan, but myself.

I sure as hell didn't lift weights.

He waved and headed out, practically sprinting down the walk. I turned and went around the desk and into the back room, setting the boxes on the counter, then placed them side by side. I scoped the shipping labels, noted the weights. Thirty-eight pounds. Thirty-two pounds.

What the hell? Since when could I lift heavy boxes? Since when could I break my favorite mug with only a little squeeze of anger? Since when could I rip a bathroom door off its hinges? I raised my arm and bent it like I was trying to make a Popeye muscle. Gave the bicep a finger squeeze with my other hand. No change. Just my usual arm. A little muscle and a whole lot of flab.

Something was up and I had no clue what it was. I wasn't sure if I should be scared or not. Was this a tumor thing? I felt fine and being able to lift heavy things made things better, not worse. The doctors had said there would be some lingering side effects after my gamma knife radiation, and I'd had a few they listed, like headaches or sleepiness, but not one of them mentioned randomly growing ridiculously strong.

I needed to test this further. I spun around the room looking for something heavy. I went to the loaded down, squeaky wheeled cart that had been pushed to the inside of the doorway. The teenaged volunteers hadn't reshelved today, so it was loaded of books.

With my hands on my hips, I studied it and muttered, "There's no way I can lift this. I'm just losing my mind."

Still... I had to know. Squatting down, remembering the *lift with your back* concept, I set my hands on the smooth metal side walls of the cart, palms pressing in. Holding my breath, I expected to wrench a few muscles and sweat a little, breathing hard like I was the one in birthing class. No way the cart would raise an inch.

Except it did move. I lifted that thing right off the floor until I stood tall. Then I put it right down. Not because it was heavy, but because it wasn't.

Quoting Brittany, I said to the cart, "What the actual fuck?"

17

HANNAH

A few hours later, I was in the stacks shelving books, still freaking out about my new talent. With it being summer, it was a quiet afternoon. Smaller children were down for their afternoon naps. Big kids usually avoided the library until they were back in school in the fall. Mrs. Metcalf didn't work today so if someone needed help, they'd ring the little bell on the circulation desk. I pushed the cart I'd lifted like a circus freak to the end of one row, around the corner and down another.

I started whispering to myself. "So you can lift heavy things. There's nothing wrong with that. It's a good thing! Sure, everyone knows last week you couldn't lift a three-legged baby squirrel and now you can practically bench press a car. Okay, maybe that's an exaggeration, but every-thing's fine!"

A hand on the front of the cart stopped it. And me. And my thoughts.

I squeaked louder than the cart and put a hand to my chest.

"Oh my God, Jack. You scared me." I wasn't sure if my heart was beating so hard because he'd startled me or if I was pleased to see him. Either way, he was unexpected.

In another dark suit, this time with a blue tie, he looked as delicious as ever. Did he wear anything else? Did his closet have one long line of fancy clothes? He never did tell me if he was a mortician and I had to wonder.

He offered me a smile I hadn't seen the day before, not when we'd been with my parents. His eyes moved over me, my face, my outfit, then pierced into mine. "Sorry, gorgeous."

Gorgeous? I wasn't so sure about that. I was in a striped sundress I thought was cute and comfortable sandals since I stood most of the day, but nothing more than that.

"What are you doing here?" I wondered. He'd made it very clear the night before that he wasn't interested.

"You didn't respond to my text."

I frowned. "What text?" I wasn't all that popular, and it wasn't like my cell rang all the time. If he'd texted, I would have known. "Wait, did you send the 'hi' message?"

He nodded. "Everything I wanted to say wouldn't have come across well in a text, so I settled on the basics."

Hi was definitely basic.

"I thought it was spam and blocked the number. I didn't know it was you," I countered. "I... didn't expect you to call. I mean, not after the dinner."

"I said I'd call."

I nodded. "You did. But they're toss-away words. Things people say when they don't mean it."

"I meant it," he said, a little snap to his words. He ran a hand over the back of his neck. "I'm sorry I left in the middle of the meal. I had an important client call to take."

I looked at his chin. At the arch of his brow. At his very kissable mouth. "That's okay. I understand. You didn't have to come all the way from Denver though to tell me that. A short text would have been fine." He arched a brow, and I couldn't help but smile. "Okay, a little bit longer of a text than *hi.*"

He took a step closer, and I had to tilt my chin back to meet his eyes. "I came from Denver to do more than apologize."

I licked my lips. Suddenly, the air was thick, almost soupy with... God, lust.

"Oh?" I said, not sure what else to say. He looked good. He smelled good. He scrambled my brain.

It was quiet and sheltered between the stacks of books. Like we were in our own little world like on the airplane, only much quieter and without the fart smell.

He shook his head, then moved, not stopping until he had me backed against one of the stacks, his firm, muscly body pressed against mine. He was hard *everywhere.* "I came to do this."

And then he kissed me.

18

JACK

Fuck, yes. Kissing her was incredible. Electrifying. *This* was what I'd wanted to do on the plane. What I should've done the other day when I chickened the fuck out. Or in the bathroom the night before.

This? Us? It was happening. I might suck at texting, but now Hannah knew how I felt about her.

19

HANNAH

Oh my God.

His mouth was perfect. It wasn't a dainty peck or a simple first kiss. This was a KISS. His lips pretty much claimed mine with a static zap and when I moaned, his tongue plunged deep. Found mine. Ravaged.

His hands tangled in my hair, tugged gently, angling me as he wanted to deepen the kiss.

I gave over to his mouth, his touch, his control. After my radiation, I vowed to myself that I was going to live life to the fullest. At the time, I thought that meant eating dessert before dinner some days and cutting my hair the way I liked it, not the way a guy did. Not making out with an almost-stranger. Except...maybe my thinking had been too narrow since it was this amazing.

Was I insane? Was I thinking with my vagina? Probably both. Perry would say I was going to hell. Brittany would say I was headed to Pound Town. Mrs. Metcalf wanted me to marry the guy.

I heard his growl. The slight roll of his hips into my center.

He lifted his head. "You're thinking too much. I can practically hear your brain working."

I blinked my eyes open. When had they fallen shut? "Sorry, I–"

He shook his head. "It means I'm not doing it thoroughly enough."

His lips were glossy, cheeks ruddy.

"I can't get out of my head."

A little rougher tug on my hair had a gasp slip past my lips. The pain was slight, but it centered my focus on his eyes. On him.

"Better," he said, somehow finding what he was looking for on my face. Then he kissed me some more. A little rougher, with more pressure of his body against mine and a snug hold on my hair. I was at his mercy here.

My panties were ruined.

Eventually, I had no idea how long he kissed the hell out of me because my brain had definitely shut off, he pulled back, although only enough to murmur in my ear. "I want to cross every single item off your list and add some new ones."

My eyes were closed, again. I blinked them open. Met his heated ones. So hot, so fierce. He was more aroused than I was, which might actually have been impossible. "Wh–what list?"

Reaching down between us, he shifted his dick in his

pants. The action was so male, so virile. And I'd caused that.

My ovaries were fist pumping.

"The list from the plane." His breath fanned over my skin. "But we're going to do number six right now."

I looked left and right. Maybe I should have been more concerned about being seen long before now. We were at the very back of the long rows of shelves, in the W-Z part of the fiction section. Nowhere near the kids' area or the bathrooms. It was close to closing. No one was probably coming into the library, let alone venturing back this way.

His knuckles grazed my inner thigh, and I had no idea what he was talking about. Wait, when had his hand gotten under my skirt? Oh. OH.

"Nu–number six?" I swallowed when they brushed against my panties. I jolted at the contact, but he was pressed into me from torso to hips that I couldn't move.

That slight touch had me forgetting what he was talking about. And my name. And why I cared if he was a danger or not.

"So wet," he whispered.

I moaned.

"From your list on the plane. Number six was to do it somewhere public, where you might get caught. I don't have a condom and I don't want a quickie for the first time I fuck you, so here between the shelves where anyone might find us, you'll come on my fingers."

Oh my God. OH MY GOD.

Okay. This was the last time I would think it. He officially wasn't a stalker, if him doing dinner with my family wasn't enough. No man fingered a woman, then killed her. I never saw on the news about that happening in real life. Not in the crime documentaries that I loved to watch with Brittany. Not in any book I ever read. Fiction *or* nonfiction.

He nudged my panties to the side and stroked over me, finding me extremely wet. Like, world record arousal. He leaned his head down and softly groaned in my ear.

"Is that all for me?" he whispered.

Should I be embarrassed? Not when he asked like I was giving him a gift.

I nodded and bit my lip, rolling my hips into his touch, wanting more.

"I'd say the library is public and if you aren't a good girl and keep quiet, you *will* get caught. I admit, I don't want anyone else watching you come. I want that all for myself."

Then he plunged two fingers deep and I bit his shoulder to stifle a pleasure-laced moan.

He growled from the action, then worked me to the brink of orgasm with a speed that showed not only that I'd never been touched by a real man, but that he knew *exactly* what he was doing. "Fuck, you're tight. So good. You feel so fucking good. I can't wait for you to clench my dick this way."

He was a dirty talker. I hadn't taken that into account.

I hadn't taken *him* into account.

Potent. Overwhelming. Bold. Dark. A tad dangerous.

I loved it.

My hands gripped his arms through his suit jacket, his muscles rock hard. I lifted my head as the pleasure grew and grew. Met his dark eyes. Held them because while he had me pinned to the shelves and fingers inside me, his palm cupping my pussy, I was afraid I was going to fall. It was overwhelming and for a second, I was scared of how powerful it was. Maybe he saw a flare of panic in my gaze because he murmured, "I got you."

I let go.

I tipped my head back, bit my lip as I rode out the most incredible orgasm of my life.

"That's my good girl. Fucking gorgeous."

20

JACK

I liked this.

A quiet table in a pizza place in Coal Springs.

With Hannah.

The woman who I fingered a little while ago in the back of the library. Whose hot little pussy was perfection. Wet and snug and eager to be filled. Whose taste I licked off my hand like a popsicle.

While she was usually shy and reserved, when I got my hands on her she was so responsive. Uninhibited. The real Hannah came out to play.

And only for me.

After she locked up, we walked to her favorite restaurant, only a few blocks from the library. It wasn't a five-star establishment. It didn't even have tablecloths. Our sausage and jalapeno pizza sat on a little stand that took up most of the space between us and the paper plates, napkins, and our sodas.

"You keep looking around," she said, her voice laced with worry. "I know it's not fancy, but it's got great pizza."

The tables were bolted to the floor and were covered in wood grain linoleum. The metal chairs had red pleather seat cushions. The tile floor was a little sticky. The music being played was vintage 80s. There was an equally vintage Pac-Man arcade game in the corner next to the restrooms.

The scent of garlic permeated the air from the pizza the teenager who worked the counter had set between us. He called Hannah by her name and Hannah waved to the guy in the back making the pizzas. She knew people in this town.

Hannah tucked her hair behind her ear and reached for another slice. She'd already had two. I loved how she wasn't eating a fucking salad. No, she was putting away the slices as if cheese was a major food group. I found it amusing and endearing because she wasn't trying to be anything but herself. Every minute with her and I liked her more and more. That didn't even take into account how she came for me, almost as if she were surprised by how I could rouse that kind of pleasure from her body. I had to wonder if any guy had gotten her off before.

"Gorgeous, I don't want fancy."

"Says the man wearing a fancy suit and drives a fancy car," she countered. Her cheeks were flushed from her orgasm and, unlike at her parents' house the night before, her shoulders weren't up by her ears like earrings.

"I *have* fancy," I said. "Doesn't mean I *want* it."

The slice was by her lips, and she held it there. "You'd rather have a beat-up car?"

I wiped my mouth with a paper napkin I pulled from the metal holder on the table. "I sound like an asshole complaining about being financially secure. I'm not. What I mean is, my life's pretty hectic. Simple and not fancy is really appealing to me."

"Your job is hectic?"

I nodded. "Maybe it's time for a new job."

I'd never really considered that, until now. That maybe what I thought was normal–because no one else would think the life of a hitman was normal–wasn't any fun at all. I didn't have any hobbies. No friends besides Dax. The people I worked with, I killed. I knew the doorman of my building by name, but I was a big tipper at the holidays.

Hannah's normal was open, friendly. Simple.

"Hi, Hannah."

Hannah looked up at the woman who called to her. Her timing was fucking fantastic because I didn't have to lie to my girl about my work. She approached our table. The smile on her face made her seem pleased to see Hannah, but her shrewd, maneater gaze was squarely on me. She wore a white t-shirt, but no one paid any attention to it since her ass was practically hanging out of a pair of tiny Daisy Dukes. She was attractive. Any man with decent eyesight would agree, but in a desperate sort of way.

"Hey, Paige. How are you?" Hannah asked, her tone lacking any kind of enthusiasm.

"Good. It's been a long time."

Hannah nodded. "It has." I had to wonder if there was a reason for that.

"Who's your friend?"

"Jack," she replied, nothing more.

"Jack," Paige parroted, drawing the one syllable out. "What are you doing with Hannah?"

As in, *Hannah's fine and all, but I'm a much better option.*

"Eating pizza," I told her. *Making her come all over my hand.* Whatever the fuck Hannah and I did was none of this woman's business. Other than distracting Hannah from talking about my work, she was worthless to me.

Paige laughed, which made her tits jiggle a little too freely in her v-neck shirt. She was wearing a bra, but she could have paid more for extra support. "What do you do for a living, Jack?"

"He's a mortician," Hannah piped in.

Paige blinked, as if her brain couldn't process that answer. Her smile slipped. "Mor–mortician?"

I shrugged and picked up my drink. "What can I say? It's an underrated profession. Plenty of job security. Plus, I like wearing suits."

She took in the one I had on today, but her gaze was now more repulsed than interested, even if it was bespoke. Fine by me. I drew hard on the straw, taking a big swig of soda.

"Good seeing you, Paige," Hannah said. "I don't want to rush you off, but Jack's got to finish his meal and get back to those dead bodies. God, I hope he washed his hands after that last embalming."

I swallowed wrong and tried not to cough as Paige stormed off. I didn't have plans to murder anyone tonight, but the night was young enough to create a body count.

Hannah picked up her own drink and put the straw in

her mouth. I tried not to imagine her sucking and swallowing like that on something else.

"Jealous, gorgeous?" I asked. Why the fuck did the possibility of that make me hard?

She sucked in a little more soda, then set the glass down. "I don't know what you're talking about." The snooty way she had her nose in the air made me laugh. After a moment, she added, "She's interested in what's in your pants."

I shrugged, uncaring. "The only woman I want interested in my dick is you."

My dick *really* wanted to get to know Hannah better, but it wasn't in charge here. I had to play the long game with her.

With a sag to her shoulders, she seemed relieved. As if I really would go after Paige while having a meal with Hannah. Hell, or in general. I remembered that she'd said her ex had cheated on her, so the reaction was valid. But I didn't appreciate being lumped in with the guy. I'd have to prove myself to her and that would take time.

"I'm not sure if you think so little of me or so little of yourself." Either way, I didn't like it. "We're going to have to work on that."

She waved her hand as if the topic was worthless. "Deep seated issue."

Obviously.

"Paige was the head cheerleader way back when," she explained. "Got the guys."

I looked out the front window of the restaurant even though Paige was long gone. "She seems like the type who peaked in high school but hasn't realized it yet."

Hannah laughed and picked up her abandoned slice. "That's a really good observation. Accurate, too."

She grabbed the hot pepper flake shaker from the empty table beside us and shook some spice on her slice. After a few bites, she asked, "Are you *really* a mortician?"

I shoved a bite into my mouth and dropped my crust on my plate, which she reached across and snagged. I had to finish chewing to answer. "No."

Relief made her practically wilt in the chair.

"What's wrong with a mortician?" I wondered. There really was job security. It wasn't like they were going to run out of customers, especially if I kept working.

"Dead bodies." She picked up her red plastic cup again and had some more soda.

"Squeamish?" I asked, at a loss. It was my job to make dead bodies, like employees at McDonalds made hamburgers. They were the final product I was paid for.

With the shake of her head, her hair slid over her shoulder. Hair that I knew felt like strands of silk between my fingers. That I knew she liked having tugged.

Remembering her pizza, she took a bite, chewed.

"I got pretty close to dying a few months ago," she admitted. "I'm all for staying alive."

Oh shit. Her brain tumor. Panic made my stomach feel greasy and not from the mozzarella. I didn't know anything about brain tumors, but yeah, those things were usually fatal. I'd never have met her. I was saving the world by killing the people I did, but her loss would ruin it.

I doubted she would see the difference between the two.

I saw it clearly. It was quick, my feelings for her. My

protectiveness was fierce. I'd do anything to protect Hannah. To keep her safe. Not only because I was a selfish asshole and wanted her all to myself, but because she needed someone on her side. Someone to have her back. Hell, to hold her fucking hand. It didn't seem like she had much of that these days.

"Your brain tumor."

She nodded.

I talked all the time with Dax about death. Big Mike had made it simple: some people needed to be taken care of. Bad guys needed to be eliminated. It meant nothing to us. But sweet, innocent, very naughty Hannah dying? I clenched my teeth.

"Will you tell me about it?"

She sighed and set her slice down. Wiped her fingers on her napkin. "I was getting headaches. Then weakness in my arms and legs. My doctors weren't sure what it was, so I had an MRI and there it was." She tapped her head with her left hand.

"At dinner, your mother mentioned you had surgery."

She nodded. I doubted she knew she was shredding her napkin into little bits. I knew she wasn't meeting my eyes because this was tough for her. Fuck, she was strong. A fucking brain tumor. FUCK. I wanted to round the table and hug the hell out of her. Instead, I reached out and took her hand, the remainder of the napkin dropping.

Her gaze lifted to mine. How had I considered her innocent even moments earlier? She'd experienced so much, and I could see it in her eyes. She hid it well, but I noticed.

I was starting to *see* her.

"It's called gamma knife radiosurgery. It's actually radiation, not surgery, since they didn't cut into my head or anything, but she calls it that anyway."

I squeezed her fingers. She tried to pull them away, but I wasn't letting go. Not now, not ever. "You had radiation?"

She nodded. Oh fuck.

"Like for cancer?" I realized what I was feeling was panic. I didn't know anything about radiation treatments other than people who were really sick got them. Ignorant of me not to know more, but I was pretty much healthy, never had to go to a doctor–other than a few years ago when I broke my finger hand fighting with a German bomb maker–and never had to wonder.

Until now. Now, I wanted to know everything.

She shook her head. "No. Not cancer. It was a benign meningioma. But yes, it was a kind of radiation where they aim gamma rays at the tumor and blast it. It took a few hours, and I was awake but totally out of it."

She was offering a simplified version of what happened. Maybe it was because I was freaking out and wanted to make it out to be less than it was. Or maybe she didn't really want to talk about it much.

Even what she shared sounded like fucking hell. And had been rough, totally manhandled her earlier with my need to see her come. I'd shoved her up against a row of shelves and finger banged her. I could have hurt her.

I was a selfish asshole.

She was fragile. Precious. I had to be careful from now on.

I quirked my lips. "Sounds like you were a superhero fighting a villain."

She quirked hers right back. "I spent the night in the

hospital and went home. My friend Brittany, she lives across the hall, stayed with me a few nights, but other than a few headaches, that was pretty much it."

"What about your family?" I had a feeling I wasn't going to like what I heard.

"My sister was away at a trampolining training camp in Texas. My brother lives in the Springs but had a prayer chain going."

I had no idea what the fuck that was, but it didn't sound like it helped Hannah in any way whatsoever. It seemed like she had scientific breakthroughs on her side more than divine intervention.

"The night I was in the hospital, my parents came to visit. Since the radiation wasn't that big of a deal and I was back to work after a few days, they pretty much moved on."

I was picking up on a theme. Her parents were dicks. They didn't seem to even remember Hannah because she came across as uneventful, unlike her crazy siblings. Even her very serious ailment had an uneventful fix. *Not a big deal* was a lie. Maybe she used those words to devalue what happened to her. Maybe because she hadn't been cut open or had to stay in the hospital more than a night or that her recovery was fast that it really wasn't a *big deal.*

But it *was* a big fucking deal. It *was* eventful. It was just... quiet. Maybe if she'd had an alien burst out of her stomach, then her parents might care more.

I craved uneventful. Wished it for myself. Not a fucking brain tumor, but a quiet life.

"And now? Is it gone?" My voice was a whisper, almost afraid of asking the question because I was petrified of the answer. I didn't want her to *die.*

Totally fucking ironic.

I held my breath.

Her slim shoulders shrugged. "I'm fine. The tumor shrinks over time to nothing."

That was it? She was *fine?*

She set her free hand on top of mine. "You look panicked. Don't be. The panicking part of it is over."

I didn't like that answer. Not one fucking bit. Especially since that meant there was a stretch of time when she'd been freaking the fuck out. Probably alone.

I stood, not releasing my hold on her hand and went around the table to kneel beside her. Fuck the sticky floor. Cupping her cheeks, my eyes raked over her face. Her confused eyes, her pert nose, those kissable lips.

"I'm allowed to fucking panic when my girl says she had a fucking brain tumor." My thumbs caressed her soft cheeks.

She swallowed. Those dark eyes flickered with emotion. Interest even. Maybe, hope. "Your girl?"

Over pizza and 80s music, I started to fall for the one woman I needed to stay the fuck away from. But I wouldn't. Not a chance. Big Mike had been correct. The right woman was worth it. Except his wife had been killed. Hannah had been sick and almost died. I didn't even want to think about losing her. All I knew was that she was worth it.

"Damn straight. I'm sorry I wasn't there for you when you were going through all of it. But I'm here now."

21

HANNAH

Holy shit. HOLY SHIT.

"You don't know me," I whispered, looking at him through my lashes. It was almost as if he was too bright, too potent to look at straight on.

His palms were warm, his touch gentle. So different than his dominant touch earlier in the stacks. No static zap this time, but there was still something here, something extra potent between us. I hadn't felt it when I first met Kevin... or ever. I hadn't felt this way about anyone.

"I want to," he murmured. Someone came in to pick up a to-go order, but Jack didn't even look that way. "Do you want to know me?"

I felt really, really shy. Maybe cautious. My heart had been hurt this year in so many ways. I lost my health. I lost the business I dreamed of. I lost a boyfriend. I was getting all those things back, but in a different way than I expected.

The change was scary, but all of a sudden it became hopeful and exciting. I nodded, because it was exactly what I wanted. So much. I did want to know him. It wasn't because he gave me my first man-given orgasm either. And he'd done it like on my list! In the stacks at work! I'd settle into how naughty and amazing that was later.

"That's my good girl." His gaze was warm. A smile teased at his full lips. *Good girl?* I should yank off my panties and give them to him now. Oh yeah, I already had. "Then it's settled."

I couldn't help but smile back. He made it seem so simple. "Just like that? We met on a plane, Jack. This is crazy."

"Your family is crazy," he grumbled, glancing away for a moment, probably remembering the horrific dinner. But then his dark gaze was holding mine again. "You can't tell me you don't feel whatever this is between us."

"There's something here," I agreed.

He nodded and sighed, as if relieved that I was right there with him in this.

I was Jack's *girl*. I was his *good* girl. I wasn't sure what that meant, but it seemed getting fingered was part of it. I could still feel them deep inside me. I probably would for days because he hadn't been gentle, as if he couldn't control himself. Inside, I was grinning and jumping up and down. Tossing confetti.

I'd never felt this way with a guy before. I wasn't a nun, but I also wasn't Paige either. I knew of her conquests from high school and since it had been almost ten years, I had no doubt her list was much longer now.

Good thing Jack had no interest in being on it.

For once, talking about the tumor and the treatment of it hadn't made me want to climb in bed and throw my blanket over my head. Brittany was well aware that had been my coping strategy, losing myself in a panicked depression nothing but a '*the procedure went great, and you should make a full recovery*' from the doctor would cure.

Even then, it had taken me some time to grasp what had happened and even more time to realize not every headache meant the tumor was back. I still hadn't gotten my thoughts worked through completely on the whole thing and still had irrational–and sometimes rational–fear.

Jack's earnestness was heartwarming. He knew the truth and wasn't running. I felt... whole. Or like I wasn't alone. Brittany had been incredible, but she'd never looked at me the way Jack was now. Brittany was my BFF and Jack was my... lover?

I'd felt his hard dick when he'd pinned me against the shelves and found my g-spot like a pro. Hmm, I shouldn't think about *how* he was a pro at it. The petty jealousy I felt when Paige wanted to lick him like an ice cream cone was coming back.

He had a past. Only, I didn't know what it was.

Jack's cell chimed. He pulled it from his jacket pocket and read the screen.

His face morphed from the gruff but sweet Jack I was coming to know to a serious, hard facade. I saw it the night before in my parents' bathroom.

"Is everything okay?" I asked.

His eyes met mine as he shoved the cell away. He stood, tugged me to my feet. "We have to go."

I blinked as he threw some bills on the table, even

though he'd already paid when we ordered, and tugged me out of the restaurant. We hadn't finished our pizza and wasting the remainder by not taking it to-go.

"What's going on?" I asked, letting him lead me.

He squeezed my fingers. "Nothing, I was done with my pizza, weren't you?"

I was almost running to keep up. "Jack, you're hurting my hand."

That had him stopping, turning to face me and wrapping an arm around my waist. He scanned the sidewalk, even the road and to the other side. It was a busy time of day since restaurants dotted these few blocks with outdoor seating, taking advantage of the good weather.

"Shit," he murmured. "I'm sorry, gorgeous."

"What's going on?"

He gritted his teeth, then said, "Something came up with work."

"Again?"

He didn't answer because he seemed too in his head. "I'm going to take you back to your car."

I blinked at him. "What? You're leaving? After what we just talked about?" Had he changed his mind about sticking after all? What had the message been about? A wife asking when he'd be home for dinner? God, had I even asked if he was married?

He nodded, his mind clearly elsewhere, then finally looked at me. "Sorry. I told you my work was hectic."

"Are you married?" I asked bluntly.

He stared at me as if I'd spoken in tongues. "What? No."

"What is it that you do then? Do you own a restaurant or something?"

"Something," he muttered, not meeting my eyes.

He was giving me whiplash. Maybe he was lactose intolerant. We did have extra cheese on the pizza and maybe there wasn't cheese on the burgers the night before, but he'd had a lot of baked beans. I might be his girl, but if he had intestinal issues, that wasn't something discussed until much, much later in a relationship.

Relationship.

Was that what this was? I had no idea, but if he needed a bathroom and some privacy, he could say that. I was the last person to hold any body issues against someone.

I was so confused. He'd made me come on his fingers, then called me his girl. Now he was escorting me home.

"Jack, is it really work that's making you run off?"

He nodded. "Yes. Definitely yes. Nothing else would keep me away. Dinner. Tomorrow night?"

"I think we can say dinner is a bad time for you."

He sighed, knowing I was right. "Lunch then. Even better. I'll see you sooner."

I shook my head. "I have to work."

He bit out a swear word as if tearing off a piece of beef jerky. "Dinner. I promise I won't bail."

I studied him, the taut lines of his body. The way he was distracted by whatever was going on with his work, but still solely focused on me. Not anyone on the sidewalk who had to veer around us. Or the car whose radio was blasting driving by.

"I'm... I'm still your girl?" I asked, sounding ridiculously vulnerable. Brittany would whack me up the side of my head for that question. I needed to know. I didn't want to be strung along, especially by my emotions.

He wrapped his other arm around me and pulled me in for a hug. I felt his steely length pressing into my belly, then his lips on the top of my head.

"Hell, yes," he murmured. I felt his cell vibrate against my boob, where it was caught between us in his jacket pocket. He needed to go, and I was stopping him.

I tipped my chin up. "Okay to dinner, but what if I come to you?"

The only time I met him was here in Coal Springs. It wasn't fair he kept coming up here to see me. Plus, I wanted a peek into his life in Denver.

He stroked my hair back from my face, his face softening, as if only for me. "You'll come down?"

I nodded. I would come down out of the mountains for him.

A dark, predatory gleam took over. "Then bring a bag. You'll stay the night. Oh, and unblock my number, gorgeous."

22

JACK

After I walked Hannah back to her car in the library parking lot, I kissed the hell out of her. Right there in public, although the lot was empty since it was after hours. Fuck, I needed her mouth. Her sweetness. To feel that she was as needy for me as I was for her.

There was no question she doubted me. I'd been called away both times we were together, and both over dinner.

So I kissed her until she was clinging and sagging against me, her hands curled around the lapels of my suit jacket. I wanted to get under her skirt again. Hell, I wanted to rip the skirt right off and fuck the hell out of her over the hood of her car. But she needed gentle, not caveman, I reminded myself. She'd had a fucking brain tumor. I needed to control myself.

Instead of giving in to what we both wanted, I told her I'd text her my address as she got in her car. It wasn't what I wanted, but I knew her panties were wet from her earlier orgasm. The one I gave her.

In my rush to get back to Denver, I broke most state and federal traffic laws. "Call Dax," I said to my car's computer, which was synced to my cell.

"Did Jimmy earn his pinky finger?" he asked when he picked up, wondering if the text I sent had worked with Hannah.

"Sal Reggiano's a problem," I said, instead of telling him she blocked me. I was practically vibrating with fury. I'd been hired to do a job for him. I didn't actually work for him. I was a fucking contractor. I said when, not him.

But the bastard hadn't gotten that memo.

"What's going on?" All playfulness slipped from his tone.

I quickly glanced in the rearview mirror, then switched lanes around a slow-ass semi as I barreled down the mountain.

"He's having me followed."

"What? Right now?"

Another glance and all that was back there was a Subaru with a kayak on top. Probably not one of Sal's men. "Not right this second, although maybe. I'm on my way back to the city."

I couldn't pick out a tail on the steep and twisty highway, but that didn't mean there wasn't one.

"Why?"

"He texted me when I was with Hannah."

"Do I need to tell you being with this chick is bad?"

"You just did, asshole. Sal texted and asked why I was in Coal Springs. That's bad."

There was a pause. "Yeah, that's bad. Is Hannah with you?"

I wanted her to be. It was the only place I could keep her safe. Except, I was what was a danger to her. She'd been living her librarian life, trying to keep herself alive, before I came along and brought the mafia with me.

If Sal wasn't happy with me or my work ethic, it wasn't like he was going to write me a one-star review. He was going to kill everyone I cared about to make his point. That meant Dax, but he could take care of myself. That also now meant Hannah, and she *really* didn't want to die. But she couldn't take care of herself. In a normal person way, yes, but not in a dating-the-hitman-I've-got-bad-guys-after-me way.

"No. She's still in Coal Springs."

"I doubt Reggiano took a vacation to the Colorado Rockies for a chainsaw bear statue." Meaning Sal wasn't in Coal Springs watching me eat pizza with the town librarian. Dax was trying to be reassuring, but it wasn't helping.

"Either he sent men or pulled in Paul's goons to tail me." Using his son's men made sense.

"I bet neither and he had a tracker put on your car."

"Fuck!" I gripped the wheel, swerved into the right lane and took the fast-approaching exit.

The Subaru honked and I ignored it, pulling over on the dirt shoulder, halfway down the ramp. This was a no service exit with the steep slope of a mountain right at the edge. There was nothing in this area but pine trees, sheer rock and bighorn sheep. The sun had long set behind the peaks, and it was getting dark.

I climbed out, the call with Dax switching back to my cell.

"Why the fuck does he want to track me? My day involves picking up my dry cleaning, going to the gym and other boring shit." I bent at the waist and looked under the wheel well by the driver's door. Nothing.

"Until Hannah," Dax said, meaning I'd been to Coal Springs twice in two days, not offing Turkleman like I was supposed to. "It sounds like he doesn't like you stalling on the project you've been assigned." He wasn't going to say anything incriminating like murder on the phone. "Why haven't you finished that project yet? Oh yeah, Hannah."

I was already around the hood and looking under the wheel wells on the other side. And found the tracker on the back one. "Fuck. Found it."

I tugged the small tracker free, went back to the driver's side, climbed in and threw the device on the passenger seat. I wanted to smash it with my heel, but then they'd know I'd found it. It was better for them to follow me back to Denver and away from any connection to Hannah. In the distance, traffic whizzed by on the highway. When I shut the door, the road noise dropped off.

"Thank fuck I didn't take Hannah home." I ran a hand over my face, relieved. I'd wanted to be a gentleman, follow her home from the library, make sure she got in safe, but I'd needed to get back to Denver. Also, that would have meant I kissed her at her front door and that would have meant I'd have fucked her in her bed. I knew what she looked like when she came and I wanted to see it again, this time when she was riding my dick. Not much of a gentleman. But she wanted both sides of me, and I'd give them to her, but not when a mafia boss was pulling shit.

"Hannah's safer *away* from me until I figure shit out." I literally hadn't led Sal to her door, thank fuck.

"Kill the turkey and don't take any more jobs with the mob boss."

Captain Obvious.

"That's top of my list," I replied. "Plus keep my girl safe. For tonight, she's better off away from me, but I've got to stop running out during meals with her."

I didn't want her to doubt me. Or what I felt for her. She took priority and leaving her like I had *was* making her one. From her perspective, though, it probably didn't seem like it. But I had to deal with Sal and get that behind me. There was no way we could be together otherwise. It was too dangerous.

Maybe I was too dangerous for her. My job? Dangerous. Being with me? A risk.

But after her pussy clenched around my fingers and she bit my fucking shoulder...there was no going back.

My job had never been an issue before. Not once. I'd been taught to not have deep feelings for anyone. That it was dangerous. That it could *hurt.*

Sitting in my car off the side of the highway, I understood what Big Mike meant. I was frantic for Hannah. I wanted to make that brain tumor never happen. But I couldn't and that made me feel helpless. Probably like how Big Mike felt when his wife had been killed. Helpless.

Until he went vigilante and finished the guy who hit her with his pickup. I could go vigilante on Sal. On her parents.

On her ex. With anyone who did her wrong. Unlike Big Mike, I could keep Hannah alive.

I also saw what my life was like, empty and cold. I saw what I wanted. I wanted peace. Quiet. The simple life where bad guys didn't exist, or at least weren't my problem. I never expected to find that with a Coal Springs librarian. Maybe it was time to figure out what to be when I grew up.

"She's going to think you have the shits or something," Dax said, cutting into my thoughts.

I winced, because he was probably right. That would be more believable than me telling her the truth.

"She's offered to come down to see me tomorrow night."

"Is that wise?"

My dick said yes. My heart–shit, did I have one?– said yes.

"She'll need to stay with me. Ensure she's safe in my apartment until I know Sal's out of the picture."

"I'll come over," he ordered. "We'll figure out your plan to wrap up that project together."

He might think I'm stupid for wanting Hannah, but he was helping me keep her anyway.

23

HANNAH

Instead of going to my apartment, I went across the hall to Brittany's. Knocked on the door. She answered right away, a carton of Chinese food in her hand. Her feet were bare, but she still wore her business casual clothes from work.

"Lo mein?" she asked, stepping back to let me in, while she used chopsticks to fork more noodles into her mouth.

"No, thanks." I shut the door behind me. "I had pizza with Jack after he fingered me to orgasm in the V through Z fiction shelves."

A noodle fell from her mouth. She swallowed hard, then asked, "What?"

"But wait, there's more." She and I met for lunch the day before. Soooo much had happened in that short of time.

She went to her couch, dropped onto it and pointed at the other end, indicating I was to settle in for a long night of her grilling me. Her apartment was better decorated than mine. More stylish chic than my IKEA garage sale style. "That's not all?"

I shook my head. "There's also this."

Jack had made me forget I could lift heavy things.

Her coffee table was solid wood. Literally a two-foot-thick slice of a cottonwood tree. The top had been sanded and shellacked to a high gloss. It was rugged but was a fun contrast to the soft pink palette of her living room. It also took two burly movers, a dolly, a hefty tip, and a six pack of beer to get it moved in. Meaning, it was heavy.

If I was right, then I could lift it.

I squatted down like I was weightlifting in the Olympics, wrapped my hands around the bark covered sides, and picked that thing right up.

Two magazines and a scented candle slid off and onto the thick shag area rug.

As I settled it back onto the floor, I couldn't miss Brittany's stunned expression.

She cleared her throat. "I think we need some wine."

24

HANNAH

"The other day, I was there to help you carry a box of books up the stairs. Now you can lift that slab of tree without getting a hernia or slipping a disk?"

Brittany abandoned her Chinese for wine, the half-eaten carton of lo mein open on the counter, chopsticks sticking out. We both had glasses filled all the way to the brim.

"Yes. I can't believe that's what you're asking after and not the fingering-by-Jack part."

She waved her hand in a circle. "Don't you worry. We're gonna get to that. I'm saving the best for last."

"You think that's better than me being able to lift ridiculously heavy things all of a sudden?" Carefully, I took a sip off the top of my glass.

"If you don't think getting fingered to orgasm by the guy you have the hots for isn't better, then we have a problem."

I shook my head quickly. "No, it's way better. Although one's a little more explainable."

"Did you tell him about this" –she pointed at her coffee table and twirled her finger in a circle again– "talent?"

I gave her a *don't be crazy* look. "He met my family. Knows I had a brain tumor. I don't want to push it."

She plumped out her lower lip, tilted her head from side to side, considering. "Reasonable. So did you start that powerlifting class at the gym? Is that what this is about?"

I glanced down my nose at her with an *as-if* look. I had lots of looks I gave her, rotating through them depending on the seriousness or ridiculousness of her words.

"What? How else would you explain it other than you have newfound superpowers?"

"Superpowers?" I chuckled, thinking I hadn't had enough wine for that possibility. "That's a stretch."

"Is it? Spider Man's superpowers came on quickly after being bit by a spider."

"I wasn't bit by a spider," I countered. *This* was an example of her ridiculous words.

"Explain then."

I shrugged. "I have no idea. This... ability has come on since last week. First it was my favorite mug at work. I was talking to my mother, and I squeezed it too hard and the handle snapped off. No, wait. First was lifting my carry-on into the overhead on the plane. Then the box of books with you."

"The breaking the mug thing makes complete sense. I'm surprised you haven't broken shit sooner over her."

We could talk all night about the issues I had with my

mother, so I moved on. "Then, at my parents' house, I ripped the bathroom door right off the hinges."

Her mouth fell open. "Crazy, but again, it makes sense knowing what you went through during that dinner."

I didn't want to rehash that, so I pushed on. "Then Dan the mailman literally dropped two huge book boxes in my arms. They didn't rip off. That's when I started to see a pattern. So I picked up the rolling cart loaded with books as a test. Easy peasy. Then that." I pointed at her log table.

"You've become abnormally strong out of the blue."

"Pretty much. Yeah."

She tipped her head to the side, studying me. "Taking any new medicines?"

I shook my head. I was on meds because of the tumor and radiation, but nothing new.

"No spider bite. Swim in toxic waste?" She snapped her fingers. "Maybe I've been right all along and you really are adopted and you came from Paradise Island."

"Paradise Island?"

Brittany was a fan of comic books and one three-day blizzard, I'd been forced to read all about Wonder Woman, who was her favorite. Paradise Island was where she was born. Then we watched the movies.

"Funny." I had to laugh because I loved Brittany so much. She watched me powerlift her coffee table and was taking it in stride. I was the most boring friend ever, so perhaps she was finally glad I had some excitement in my life–which didn't involve dying.

The action made a little wine slosh over the brim and onto my fingers. I took a few big gulps to get the level down inside the glass as I wiped my fingers on my skirt.

Brittany took a swig herself, then shrugged. "She's stronger than the earth. That's you, Wonder Woman."

"Obviously, I love a good story more than most, but this isn't fiction, B." I shook my head. While I appreciated her lightheartedness, not everything was funny. "This is my life and there's something going on."

"Think you should go to the doctor?" she asked, her humor replaced quickly by concern. "I mean, it was only a few months ago you had a brain tumor. Maybe it's something to do with that."

It had crossed my mind, but I had avoided the irrational panic I felt sometimes when I had a headache, or I felt a twinge anywhere in my body. I shook my head. "I got a scan two weeks ago, remember? All good."

She sighed. "Right. All good. Not a spider bite. Not toxic chemicals. Maybe–"

"Radiation?" I tossed out. It was the only plausible explanation, and then it wasn't that plausible at all. Radiation treatments were done for all sorts of things, tens of thousands of times a day around the world. It was a serious thing, but it was common. I hadn't heard once, ever, of anyone getting superpowers–as Brittany put it–from the procedure.

She was thinking the same thing because she asked, "Did they mention crazy strength was a side effect?"

I shook my head. "Of course not. But it's not like I can call up the doctor's office and tell them about this."

"I'm sure they've heard it all."

"A psychiatrist, maybe."

"If you're not sick, then who cares?" She finished her

glass of wine, then shrugged. "I'm jealous that out of the two of us, you're the one who got superpowers."

"And got fingered in the library."

"Bitch," she replied with a grin. "Let me get more wine and you can tell me all about the good stuff."

25

JACK

"The only window of time you're going to be able to take care of Turkleman is at the restaurant," Dax said. He wasn't happy with his words, only honest.

I shook my head, even though we'd gone over the possibilities for hours. We were in my kitchen and Dax was opening and closing my fridge door as if something might magically appear in there to eat. I didn't cook and there wasn't more than yogurt and some old leftovers.

"I can't bail on Hannah at dinner for a third time."

He looked over his shoulder at me. "Then take her with you."

Pancake hopped up onto the counter and I set my hand on his head for a pet. "To a hit? Are you insane?"

He shut the door, finally, and turned my way. "It's a restaurant, not a skyscraper rooftop. Besides, it would justify you being there besides murder. An alibi. Just another couple on a date." Pancake started turning in circles, liking to get rubbed all over. Dax noticed and frowned. "Cats shouldn't be on the counter."

"This is Hannah. I can't risk it having her anywhere near a job. And you're well aware I don't cook. You won't get toxoplasmosis or tularemia or whatever it's called." Still, I picked up Pancake and set him on the floor. He walked off, tail high, like the snooty ass he was.

"She'll be in a restaurant full of people."

I sighed. I didn't like the idea. Not one fucking bit.

"I'll get him at the ball game later instead."

"Don't be stupid," he countered. "There are cameras everywhere and thousands of witnesses."

"Not in the can."

"At a ball game? While the men's bathrooms aren't anywhere near as crowded as the women's, have you ever gone into one at a sporting event and been alone while taking a piss? I wonder what the average beer consumption is at a baseball game."

He was not helping, only shooting down any option that didn't involve Hannah.

"We've gone over the options. Nitro shared his schedule and since you saved it to the last minute, this is all you've got."

Meaning I didn't take care of this before now when I had better opportunities because I had my head up my ass over Hannah. And my fingers in her pussy.

"I'll run him off the road."

He shook his head. "Not guaranteed we can make it happen or that he'll actually die."

"I—"

He held up his hand to stop me. "We've been through it. It has to be at the restaurant."

I looked up at the ceiling, knowing he was right. If I wanted Sal to stop putting trackers on my car and butting in where his nose didn't belong, I had to get Turkleman dead, and the only place was at the restaurant. "Fuck!"

26

JACK

As promised, I texted Hannah during the day with my address. I didn't take any of Jimmy Almost-Nine Fingers suggestions and did my own thing. Fortunately, it worked because she'd unblocked me and written back, telling me Mrs. Metcalf had volunteered to close the library for her, so she was able to arrive earlier than I anticipated.

This was a good thing because I was fucking eager to see my girl. It was a bad thing because it meant showing up at the restaurant earlier than I expected. More time where Hannah and an arms dealer were in the same establishment.

Per Nitro, Turkleman spent his day in his hotel suite working. He had guards at the door and probably more inside we couldn't see from tapping into the security cameras. It seemed illegal weapons traders had conference calls like every other businessman and they kept him busy until dinner. He had reservations at a popular Denver restaurant at five-fifteen to make it to the ballgame when it started at seven.

That meant my window to finish the job was about an hour.

And as I opened the door to the restaurant for her, that clock started.

"Um, am I dressed right for this place?" she whispered, leaning close. Her soft scent made my dick stir, which was a problem.

"You're perfect," I whispered in her ear, then kissed her temple.

I'd met Hannah in the garage of my building, the doorman having notified me that she was here. Instead of taking her upstairs to strip her out of her pretty blue dress and find out what kind of sexy panties she had on—which was what I wanted to do instead of going out to dinner and killing Turkleman—I had her leave her overnight bag in her car, led her to mine and drove to the restaurant.

I shared the fake last name I used for the reservation. I hadn't told my real one to Hannah and with a large group coming in the doors behind us, I doubted that she heard.

"My friend Dax recommended this place, although, he probably knows which fork to use better than me."

The place was high end, most likely with tiny, rabbit sized portions, lots of sauces and a wine and liquor menu longer than Cheesecake Factory's. Knowing her favorite restaurant was a hole in the wall pizza joint, I could see why Hannah felt out of place. No one but a snooty grandmother or a pompous arms dealer would find this place charming or relaxed.

As we followed the hostess to our table, my hand at the small of Hannah's back, I caught sight of Turkleman. His table was against the back wall, and he had two other men with him. Based on their size and similar suit choices as Joey Brains and Eyebrows, I took them for his guards.

I settled Hannah in the seat that gave Turkleman her back and when I sat across from her, I had a clear view of him eating oysters on the half shell. From Nitro's report and photos, he was sixty-one, bald, and had virile Mediterranean ancestors. If Telly Savalas and someone's Italian *nonni* got together, they'd have made this guy.

I barely glanced at the menu before I set it down. These kinds of restaurants always had steak.

I studied Hannah as she looked over the menu. Her hair was pulled up into a loose bun, with tendrils framing her face. Her dark eyes were enhanced with makeup and her lips were glossy and shiny in the soft light. She was so fucking pretty that it hurt. Why was she sitting with me? How had I even caught her interest? Sure, I'd gotten her off with my fingers, but I liked to think I was more of a catch than only sex-skilled.

A basket of homemade focaccia and a ramekin of butter were set between us.

Hannah set her menu down and looked my way.

"Tell me about Dax," she said, taking a slice of the salt topped bread, she used her knife to smear a healthy coating of butter onto it. She picked off a piece and put it in her mouth.

I watched as she licked a spot of butter off her thumb.

"What?" I asked, transfixed.

"Dax," she prompted, then stuffed the piece in her mouth. She moaned and chewed. "God, so good."

Fuck. I had a hard on from watching her eat bread and listening to her practically have an orgasm over dairy. I grabbed a piece for myself. I didn't skimp on the butter either and shoved half of it in my mouth. Over her shoulder, Turkleman was talking, gesticulating with his arms in a way that indicated he was talking about baseball or killing someone with a club.

"We met in elementary school," I said, after swallowing. The bread was fucking good. "His dad had a fighting gym and since my mom worked all the time, I hung out there. When we weren't off getting into trouble. We're still best friends."

"I can see you as a kid."

"Oh yeah?" I wondered.

She nodded. "I bet you were adorable in the child-sized suits."

I gave her a look that told her I wasn't amused, but I really was.

"Your mom raised you on her own?" she asked.

As I answered, she buttered another piece of bread. "My father walked out when I was eight. She didn't have much choice but to work two, sometimes three jobs. Because of that, I didn't see her much. Then she died. I lived with Dax and his dad, so I didn't go into the system."

The smile was gone from her face, but I didn't see pity in her eyes. She passed me the buttered bread slice. I took it from her, our fingers brushing. The static electricity was back with a little zap.

"So the suits are a new thing?"

I shrugged, took a bite. "Dress for the job you want, isn't that the saying?"

"You really are a mortician then."

I couldn't help but smile. "Nothing that exciting. Dax and I run a company that helps high end clients problem solve." That was my standard line. Most people nodded and didn't ask more. Not Hannah.

"What kinds of problems?" she asked.

Turkleman stood. He wore a white dress shirt and sports coat, no tie. From across the room, I could see the patch of dark chest hair peeking out of the open collar. He cut across the restaurant toward the bathrooms.

Now was my chance.

I looked to Hannah, offered her a small smile. "I have to use the restroom. Be right back."

She nodded. I stood, then headed off to kill a man, a slice of Hannah-buttered bread in my hand.

27

JACK

Fuck. Turkleman wasn't in the can. He was by the emergency exit at the end of the hallway on his cell. He gave me a casual glance, but his focus was on his call. He had no idea I was going to kill him. I was only another diner.

Except, I couldn't do the job in the hallway, not when anyone–man or woman–could appear. There was no choice but to enter one of the unisex bathrooms and wait the expected few minutes before I exited.

When I did, the hall was empty and the other unisex bathroom's door was slightly open, which meant he was gone.

"Fuck," I muttered, running a hand over the back of my neck. Time was running out.

I went back to the table where Hannah was talking with the waiter.

"There he is," she said, giving me her gorgeous, innocent smile. "Do you know what you want?"

Yeah, Turkleman dead and you in my bed.

As I slid into my seat, I asked her, "Did you order yet?"

She nodded. "I picked the salmon."

The waiter, dressed in black pants and white dress shirt, waited patiently.

"Steak, medium," I told him.

We handed off our menus and with a slight bow, he was gone.

Flicking my gaze over Hannah's shoulder again, I got confirmation that Turkleman was back in his seat, their waiter swooping in with their meals on a huge tray nestled on his shoulder.

I couldn't kill him while he was eating, so I focused on Hannah.

28

HANNAH

All at once, Jack turned his gaze on me. It was potent and almost mesmerizing. Tonight he wore–surprise!–a suit. Black over a black dress shirt with a black tie. With his equally dark hair and five o'clock shadow, he looked menacing. Except his eyes were warm and his look almost soft, just for me.

"Your mother mentioned you wanted to open a bookstore."

I licked my lips. His eyes followed the action.

I eyed the remainder of the bread in the basket but decided against it since I'd already felt like a pig eating two slices. God, it was good.

"Yes. Romance fiction is a billion-dollar industry. There's a voracious demand for" –I made air quotes with my fingers– "*those types of books,* as my mother calls them. I have a business plan, the layout of the store already planned."

"In Coal Springs?"

I nodded. "Yes. While small, it has a huge tourist industry eager to spend money. On Main Street, there's a vacant store."

"What's stopping you? Don't tell me it's your family that's holding you back or wanting you to open a potato salad food truck."

I rolled my eyes, then sobered. "No, it's not them. Or my mother's obsession with side dishes. The money I saved to open the place got redirected to my medical bills."

He frowned. "What about a small business loan?"

I studied the white tablecloth for a moment, then glanced up at Jack. "No collateral."

The last thing I wanted to do was have a depressing conversation or point out how broke I was, so I smiled. "It'll happen someday, regardless of my family's support."

"Have they always been like that?"

"What? Overbearing, insensitive, and plain crazy?"

He shrugged. "I was going to say self-involved and petty, but they are your family and don't want to hurt your feelings."

I smiled, because they were *really* self-involved. "I always liked to read. To get lost in a story. As you saw, Perry and Briana are... a lot. My parents' attention was always pulled to them. I was overlooked probably because I wasn't as needy."

"You had quiet independence."

I realized I was swirling the butter in the little dish with my bread knife, and I set it down.

"They don't see it that way. They see me as difficult."

He shook his head. "Which makes zero since because there's no question your brother's a cult leader and your sister–"

His words cut off and his gaze shifted slightly.

I frowned. "Jack?"

He stood. "I need to use the restroom."

29

JACK

This time, when Turkleman headed toward the restrooms, he actually went into a restroom. I knew because I caught up to him quick enough to see him enter one of them. I stuck my foot in the door before it could shut and be locked.

His gaze lifted to mine in surprise.

He tipped his head. "Take the other one."

"Not happening." I was motivated by more than money now. Sal wanted this fucker dead. After learning what he did for a living, I wanted him dead, too. The world would be better without him. Now, though, I was also motivated by Hannah. She was out there by herself and that was fucking wrong.

I pushed my way inside, not taking my eyes off Turkleman. His bald head glowed under the lights over the sink.

While I doubted he was prepared to use a weapon in the bathroom, I was still careful.

"What the fuck, man?"

I didn't answer, only reached out, grabbed him by the nape with one hand, his chin with the other and snapped his neck. He sagged in my hold.

There was a tentative knock on the door. "Jack? Are you okay?"

My head whipped toward the closed door.

Hannah. Shit.

Thank fuck I'd flipped the deadbolt, not that she would barge in on someone's privacy. It was one thing to see me taking a piss though. It was another seeing me with a dead guy.

"I'll be out in a sec," I called, panting.

My heart was jackhammering and not because I had a dead man in my arms. He was getting heavier by the second.

Fuck!

Okay, get this done and get Hannah the hell away from here.

I let Turkleman drop to the ground with a thud and got to work, squatting down to loosen the line beneath the sink. It immediately started spurting water on the floor. Then I whacked Turkeman's head against the hard tile so it looked like he slipped and fell.

An eagle-eyed detective wouldn't see past this shoddy effort, but it would cause misdirect for a stretch. Perhaps until Turkleman's name hit the system and the FBI or Interpol got wind of his death and take over. They'd know it was a hit and probably not care who did it.

Still, I needed Dax's and Nitro's help to ensure there were no security cameras back here and wiped clean if there were. Definitely not in the bathroom, but maybe in the hallway, especially now that Hannah would also be on any footage. I didn't take time to look for something subtle.

Pulling out my phone, I texted Dax.

> Clean up in aisle five.

He'd know what that meant and what to do. Taking one last look at the dead man and the water starting to spread across the floor, I sighed.

Fucking hell. I didn't need this bullshit in my life. I turned, exited the bathroom and shut the door behind me.

There stood Hannah, nervously waiting.

"Here." She thrust a little pink tablet toward me.

I stared at it, trying to switch gears from dead guy to my girl.

"What's that for?" I asked, lost.

"For your stomach. We've had dinner three nights in a row, and you've had to leave in the middle each time. Are you lactose intolerant? It's okay if you are."

In that moment, with my eyes on hers, seeing the concern in them for my intestinal wellbeing, I fell in love.

30

HANNAH

Instead of answering, he kissed me. Unlike the others, this one was actually sweet. Reverent, even. Before I had the chance to even process more than that, he retreated and took my hand. "I need to be inside you."

Um... what? Our meals were at our table and getting cold.

"But–"

"My butt is fine. It's my blue balls that are a problem. Think you can help me with them?"

Um... hell yes.

Okay, so we weren't finishing our dinner for the third night in a row. This time, while still leaving in the middle of it, I was going with him.

His eyes held mine, searching. Waiting.

I nodded, because he was asking for consent. Here in

the bathroom hallway, he was telling me he wanted to fuck me and me and my vagina were agreeing. Wholeheartedly.

It was possible he growled. "Let's go."

He took my hand and led me back to our table, then released his hold long enough to pull out his wallet and throw a few hundreds on the table where our untouched dinners were waiting for us. Yes, hundreds.

The waiter instantly appeared at our sides. "We'll take the meals to go."

When he took our plates and retreated to pack them up, Jack leaned down and whispered in my ear. "Once isn't going to be enough, gorgeous. You're going to need the nutrients."

Oh my.

31

JACK

I had Hannah tucked in my car and on the way back to my apartment in minutes. She was quiet, but fidgety. She wrung her hands in her lap. Crossed and uncrossed her legs. Was her pussy aching?

Reaching across the console, I set my big hand on top of hers. A spark of static electricity zapped us.

She gasped. "Why does that keep happening?"

I flicked my eyes toward her, then back on the road. "We're potent together. Now, panties."

She blinked. "What?"

I raised my hand, flicked my fingers. "Give me your panties."

"Here?" She glanced around at the dark downtown. There were people and other cars around, but no cared what happened in a random SUV. "Now?"

"Gorgeous, in the library I had my hand up your skirt

and my fingers buried deep in your pussy where anyone might see. You're shy now?"

She wanted it like in the romance books where the guy took charge. Where he knew what she needed even if she might not know herself. Knew how much to push to ensure she got what she needed.

She warred with herself for a moment, then shimmied, sliding her hands up her thighs, the hem of her blue dress going with it. Hell, yes. She was as naughty as I suspected.

I watched as those white panties came into view. Then she pushed them down, worked them over one sandaled foot, then another. She held them up and I was sure they were wet because the scent of her arousal filled the air.

A horn blared and I veered back into my lane.

Out of the corner of my eye, I saw the smirk playing around her full lips.

Fuck me, she was going to kill me. And not from blue balls.

I snatched the scrap of cotton from her and tucked them in my suit coat pocket–after I sniffed them. Best scent in the world. Then I focused on the road. And floored it.

32

HANNAH

Jack parked in his building's underground garage. He came around and helped me out of the very fancy SUV and, after retrieving my overnight bag from my own car, led me to the elevator.

Beneath the hem of my dress, I was bare. Going commando made it... airy. I only hoped I didn't have a wet spot on the back of my dress.

This was all blatant foreplay. Going bare for him. Him knowing I was bare. That my panties were in his pocket. It was an intimacy I never had with anyone before. And it was hot. Sexy, even. I *felt* sexy.

The elevator doors opened, and he led me in with a hand on the small of my back. As the car rose, he set the to-go bag of food and my overnight bag on the floor and pressed the stop button on the control panel.

Then he turned to me.

"Um, Jack–"

"I've got to taste you."

Taste me? Like the book. Oh my God. I was bare because he wanted to *taste* me in a stopped elevator car.

I looked around. Obviously, we were alone. The walls had wood paneling and there was a hip-height brass railing. Fancy, like his car. But I'd seen enough TV shows to know that the more posh the place, the more cameras. Everywhere. The thrill of possibly being caught wasn't the same as being recorded.

He dropped to his knees before me. I was now taller, and I set my hands on his shoulders. His gaze was heated, almost burning. His cheeks were ruddy and there was a wildness about him. His hands slid slowly up my calves, then higher. As they raised my dress, he told me, "This is my private elevator. No cameras."

And then he had his hands on my waist, my dress bunched and caught on his wrists.

I was bare down there and he was staring. I wasn't skinny. I had dimpled thighs and a slight pooch to my stomach. Lots of curves. All of that was enough to give me a complex, but he was looking at me *there*. I groomed, shaved and trimmed so I was neat and tidy, but lady parts were weird. What if he thought–

"Fucking gorgeous," he growled, then, as if he couldn't resist a second longer, lifted one of my legs and threw it over his shoulder, then put his mouth on me.

He gave me one long lick, then found my clit and flicked it. Then again.

"Oh fuck," I called, my head tilting back as I stared at the ceiling. It felt so good. His hot breath, the talented swirl of his tongue and... oh! He slid a thick finger into me and did some magical curl. "There!"

My hands tried to find purchase in his shoulders, but he was too muscled. My hands slid up to tangle in his short hair and hold him to me. I was so close to coming. Ridiculously close. If I had any brain cells functioning, I would recognize he was able to get me there even faster than the day before in the library. Tongue *and* fingers were better than fingers alone.

I went up on my tiptoes and rolled my hips into him. His grip tightened, holding me right where he wanted me.

Because he was eating me out like a starving man.

He *had* missed his dinner.

33

JACK

The sound of my name echoed off the walls of the elevator when she came. Fuck yes, she pretty much screamed it. Her fingers tugged at my hair, her leg pulling me into her pussy as she rode out her pleasure.

I kissed her inner thigh as I held her up while she recovered. Then I lowered her leg, rose and wiped my slick mouth and chin with the back of my hand. Fuck, she tasted good.

Reaching out, I slapped the button to get the elevator moving again. We didn't say anything, instead stared at each other as she tried to catch her breath. Her cheeks were flushed, eyes wild.

I couldn't help the smirk that played at my lips. She wasn't a virgin, but I loved showing her that sex was more than missionary in bed. It was looks. Tastes. Teasing.

The doors slid open, and I took her hand, pulled her to me and tossed her over my shoulder.

"Jack!" she cried, slapping my back.

I slapped her ass in return as I cut through my apartment to my bedroom and–

Wait!

Fuck, I had to be gentle. I'd been wild in the elevator, but not rough. I was getting more desperate to be inside her by the second, but there would be no throwing her on the bed.

Carefully, I lowered her from my shoulder and set her in the middle like the fucking precious treasure she was. The hem of her dress was askew, but it wasn't up around her waist still, which was a fucking shame.

That pussy. So pretty and tasted so good. Sweet. Sticky. Hot. Tight.

With her all mussed and well satisfied, she was perfect, and I couldn't damage her. It would kill me to hurt her even a little bit. I'd broken a man's neck not an hour earlier. I knew what I was capable of, but not with her.

Fucking finally. I had her exactly where I wanted her. But my fantasies had her naked, which was easily fixed. I needed to tame my cravings for her. To temper the fantasies about how I wanted to fuck her and make her mine. I couldn't be Colin to her Mia.

I knelt on the bed and crawled up and over her, cupping her face and kissing her sweetly. Her body was soft and warm beneath mine and I kept almost all my weight off of her. Needing more, I kissed along her jaw, down her neck and to the V of her dress, sampling the swells of her lush tits, then worked my way lower toward her pussy. I was an addict, and she was my drug.

"Jack?"

I popped my head up, gazed down at her.

"What are you doing?" she asked, eyes wide.

"I hope it's obvious after the elevator."

"Yes, but again?"

"Never had a guy eat your pussy?"

I was angry either way she might answer. Pissed she'd been with selfish losers or pissed that she'd had someone else satisfy her this way.

She shook her head, her dark hair splayed across my tan comforter.

Fuck. I got one of her firsts.

"What about you though?"

"I love pussy, gorgeous. I could stay down here for hours."

"I need..." Her words were more than a breath.

I let my breath fan her swollen folds. "What? What do you need, gorgeous?"

"You."

I couldn't help but smile. "Oh, you've got me."

She shook her head. "No, all of you. Not down there. I want what was in the book."

I sucked in a breath, pushed back so I knelt back on my heels straddling her thighs.

She looked incredible laid out in my bed. Just as I imagined. And I imagined a-fucking-lot. Yet– "I can't risk it."

A little frown creased her brow. "Risk what? I'm on birth control and I've been tested and I'm clean."

I set a hand on her thigh, gently stroked her soft skin. "That's good to know. I meant hurting you."

She bit her lip, eyed me up and down. "I don't think you're going to hurt me having sex. Unless you have a baby arm or something for a dick."

"Your pussy can take me," I assured her. "I'm worried about your head."

She sighed like a deflating balloon. "Oh, Jack. My head is fine. I don't need careful."

She took my hand and raised it up. Compared to mine, hers was so small. Soft. Not rough or rugged like mine. I had swollen knuckles from fighting. Scars.

"Maybe I want it rough."

I almost came in my boxers hearing those words come from her lips. Images of all the ways I could take her popped in my head. Hard. Filthy. Rough.

"What happened to my good girl?"

She smiled. "My inner bad girl wants to play."

34

HANNAH

Jack's gaze became dark and predatory at my words. Words I couldn't believe I said. He looked me over, every inch of me. As if he was making plans, maybe even a list of what he wanted to do.

"I've never had it like that, and I think I want it," I added, suddenly worried I'd gone too far. "But–"

His eyes met mine, probably hearing the worry in my voice. Not about having sex with him. No. I wanted that.

"But what?"

"But I'm not good at it. At sex. I'm sure you've had a lot of it, and I probably won't make it good for you."

"Stop talking," he snapped.

"Jack."

"Stop talking or I've got something I can put in your mouth to quiet you."

Oh my.

He closed his eyes and groaned, low and deep. "The fact that what I said turned you on shows that you're going to like it just fine."

"I didn't... you know, please the guy. Kevin thought I was... fat."

"You mean your cheating ex? The one who's going to die, or at least be maimed for life."

"Him and the guy from college."

His jaw clenched and I'd upset him. I tried to squirm out from underneath him, but he lowered his weight onto me, enough to keep me from moving.

"Lemme guess. You didn't come."

I licked my lip and shook my head. "See? That means there's something–"

"If you say something's wrong with you, I'm going to flip you over and spank your ass."

He studied my face for a second, then pushed off me. Before I knew what he planned, he'd flipped me, in a very unladylike manner, onto my stomach. His bed was huge and plush, the bedding as fancy and expensive as his SUV. I felt the cool air on my butt as he flipped the hem of my dress up.

A hand came down in a light swat on my upturned ass. The sound registered first, then the light sting. It didn't really hurt and quickly morphed into heat.

"Jack!" I kicked my feet, but he was on his knees straddling my thighs.

"There's nothing wrong with you, gorgeous."

Swat.

"You're not fat. Or overweight. Or any of those bullshit

words. Those dipshits weren't real men. A real man takes care of his woman."

Swat.

"Ow! By spanking her?"

"If that's what she needs. You said you wanted to be a bad girl. Well, bad girls like getting spanked. I bet your pussy's dripping to prove it."

His hand slid over my butt, then cupped me from behind. I startled, then moaned. I was wet still. No not still, but *more.*

His words, his actions, the spanking... I never knew. Read about and got turned on while doing it, but that had been in a book. This? Jack was *very* real.

"You came on my fingers in the library. You just came all over my face in my elevator. Your taste is on my fucking tongue."

"But that wasn't me satisfying you."

Tucking an arm about my waist, he hoisted my hips up so I was on my knees, my cheek still pressed against what felt like three million thread count bedding.

"Oh my God, Jack, what are you–" He put his mouth on me. "OH MY GOD."

I squirmed, definitely embarrassed that my butt was in the flipping air, and he not only saw everything, but licked it. Top to bottom, and by bottom, I meant *bottom.* "Jack!"

"Am I hurting you?" he asked, his breath fanning over my swollen flesh. Then his fingers slid over it. Traced it. Learned it.

"No."

"Am I too rough?"

He'd been manhandling me, but he maneuvered me

around easily enough and the spanking had been more of a scientific test of arousal and interest than discipline. And I asked for it because what I read of *rough* in romance books was something I craved.

Fiction and reality were two very different things when Jack was involved.

I squirmed because he was being too gentle now. His touch was so light I could barely stand it. I was so worked up from the elevator orgasm that I was close.

"No," I replied.

"Good."

"Shh. I'm not being rough."

"But you're–"

Perry was probably right. I was sinning hard core. And it felt so fucking good.

"In fact, I'm being very, *very* gentle."

I whimpered, wiggled my butt, telling him I wanted more without saying it. Because if I did, what kind of woman did that make me? I needed his fingers in me like at the library. I needed something else in me. Big and hard. He had to be both.

"You still want rough?" he asked, kissing the back of my thigh.

"You're not sticking anything in my butt without a shit ton of lube and a hell of a lot more foreplay."

I felt him smile against my skin. "Noted, but that wasn't what I was thinking."

"Yes, I still want it rough." I wanted *it* because he wasn't doing anything except petting my pussy. I'd thought I couldn't get any wetter, but I was practically dripping with need. I clenched in eagerness. "Yes, I want you to do unspeakably rude things to me."

"Then we need a safeword."

"A safeword?" What kind of rough did he have in mind?

"How about... trampoline?"

He was sweet and filthy. I couldn't help but laugh into the bedding.

"Okay?"

"Yes. Just.... do something!"

"Yes, ma'am."

35

JACK

I loved her pussy. With my hands on her thighs holding her open from behind, I licked and learned every swollen inch. What made her gasp. Startle. Moan. Drip. Then I got my fingers in her, knowing her secret sweet spot when she moaned my name with sultry abandon. That didn't even include that she'd thought about ass play and wanted it.

I looked forward to teasing her, edging the hell out of her until she was a sweaty, desperate mess.

But not now. Not when she needed to know I would always satisfy her. That I wasn't either one of her ex's. That she wasn't broken. Unappealing.

I'd never do anything to get her to say trampoline. Never push her too far. Never give her more than she could handle. Because what got her hot, got me hot.

I brought her to orgasm swiftly so she'd know she was

responsive–even though her being soaked wasn't proof enough. And *very* sexual.

As she collapsed on my bed in a sated, satisfied heap, I wiped my mouth once more with the back of my hand.

I could spend hours between her lush thighs. Days. The fact that she felt like she had to reciprocate meant she didn't understand this. Yes, I wanted to make her come more than I wanted my own release. And yes, I wanted to come really fucking bad. But I got immense satisfaction, and a shit ton of caveman pride, in feeling her shift and push into me for more. Her moans. The way her pussy fucking wept for more.

She wasn't unresponsive. She was hips up with my finger teasing her virgin ass. My handprint was a pretty shade of pink on her pale skin. She was so uninhibited. Begging. Moaning. Fucking perfect.

She wasn't shit at sex. I'd prove that to her one orgasm at a time and if I had to, I'd keep her in my bed until then. And I hadn't even taken my clothes off yet.

It was time for that to change.

36

HANNAH

When I opened my eyes after my second Jack-induced orgasm, he stood at the foot of the bed and taking his clothes off. I hadn't had a chance to see much of his bedroom before, but it was clear there'd been a designer involved. The walls, carpet, and bedding were various shades of tan and cream. The furniture was definitely not from IKEA. But I didn't care about the decor. I was stuck on Jack, undressing.

The suit jacket was shrugged off and dropped to the floor. Next, he loosened the tie, pulled it over his head, let it drop. Then started on his shirt, undoing the button at one wrist then the other. All the while, he was staring at me.

Me, sprawled on my stomach in a glorious heap, my dress bunched up around my waist. Eyes roving lazily over my body.

For me, this was a treat. An epic show, watching Jack take his clothes off.

A cat jumped on the bed, startling me. I hadn't expected Jack to have a pet, let alone a fluffy one that was technically cockblocking.

Jack sighed. "That's Pancake." He grabbed the cat and carried him to the hall and set him on the floor, then shut the door behind us.

"I can't believe you have a cat," I said, when he came back to the end of the bed.

"I can't believe you're in my bed," he said, undoing the buttons on his shirt. "I've imagined this, ever since the plane."

"You pictured me in your bed... on that flight?"

"Since you gave me the perfect view of your ass putting your carry on in the overhead bin."

My mouth dropped open in surprise, from his words and his body.

When it joined the jacket on the floor, I sat up and crawled to the foot of the bed. Going up onto my knees, he was right in front of me. His body was perfect. Well proportioned. Well-muscled. A smattering of hair between flat, dusky nipples. Lower, those chiseled abs. And lower still, God, it wasn't a romance novel tease. That deep V that disappeared into his pants.

But all of that wasn't what had me reaching for him, running my fingers over his heated skin. It was the tattoos. I'd seen a hint of one peeking out at the wrist on the plane. But now I knew how vast the art was. On his left arm was a full sleeve, colorful and complicated. It crept across his shoulder and around his ribs. On the right arm, there were more, but not as extensive.

"Keep looking at me that way, gorgeous, and see what happens."

His voice was dark like midnight, and I glanced up at him. "I can't appreciate you?"

"I haven't even gotten my pants off yet."

I dropped down onto my heels and set my hands in my lap. "Don't let me stop you."

He smirked and undid his belt, opened his pants and pushed them down. I must've missed him taking off his shoes and socks because he kicked the garment out of the way.

Jack in a suit was incredible. Jack in a pair of snug, black boxer briefs that did nothing to hide how hard he was, was insane. My mouth watered and my vagina did too at the sight.

Then he put his hands in the waistband and pushed the cotton down. Rose to his full height.

My eyes widened.

"Oh my God. You're *really* big."

He was bigger than either the guy from college or Kevin. And hard. And perfectly made. Thick and long, a dark pink color. Heavy balls hung below between two sturdy thighs. Balls were ugly, but somehow made Jack seem virile. Pre-cum oozed at the tip and I reached out to swipe at the pearly drop.

He hissed at the contact and his dick pulsed.

I wanted him. I wanted *it*. Now. I tugged at the tie on the side of my dress.

"I want to do that," he said.

I let my hands drop again. "Fine, but hurry."

He stepped closer and took over, getting me out of my dress quickly. Ever efficient, he undid the clasp on my bra as he did, so I was bare in a matter of seconds.

"Fuck, I knew you were perfect."

He cupped my breasts, his hands rough with callouses but the touch gentle. His thumbs slid back and forth over my nipples, and they went instantly hard.

"Jack," I breathed arching my back and pressing myself further into his hold. "Please."

Our eyes met for a brief second, then that spark between us finally ignited.

"Up on the bed."

I moved quickly as he went around the side of the bed, opened a drawer in the nightstand and retrieved and unopened box of condoms. With deft fingers, he opened it and pulled out a long strip, dropped it on the bed before tucking the box back in the drawer.

He tore one off, ripped the foil open and put it on as I breathed hard and tried not to squirm in anticipation.

Settling one knee on the bed, he crawled toward me, then dropped down onto his back beside me. Hands went to my waist and lifted me up and over him so I was on top.

"Oh."

One big hand settled on my hip, the other stroking his dick. Leisurely, slowly, as if he couldn't wait a second longer. "Be a good girl and ride me, gorgeous."

"I'm not sure if–"

"You can take it."

I wasn't afraid of a little D, but I doubted I'd be walking right tomorrow. But that was a tomorrow problem.

Shifting on my knees, I got so I was right over his hips. Rising up on my knees, I hovered over that broad, latex covered head.

"Hannah," he said, and my eyes met his.

I knew what he wanted. To see me as I took him inside. I lowered down onto him, stretched wide as I went. I had to lift and lower to get him into me, it was a tight fit.

His jaw was clenched, eyes flared. I licked my lips, knowing this would take a while.

I whimpered at the hard feel of him and then I was in the air and then on my back.

Jack was over me and then filled me with one rough, deep thrust.

"FUCK!" he shouted.

I moaned, like the sluttiest whore in existence as my inner walls clenched and rippled around him, trying to adjust.

He held himself still. Our breaths mingled.

My heels pressed into his thighs. My legs spread so wide.

"Jack, move. Please."

He must've seen something in my eyes to know I was okay, that I was desperate, because he did.

Hooking the back of my knee over his elbow, he started to fuck me. There was no other word for it. This wasn't making love. This was raw and sweaty and noisy and... amazing.

That electricity between us crackled and popped the closer I came to orgasm. Again. Three times!

He slowed long enough to lick his thumb and lower to his forearms to reach between us and rub my clit. Our bodies pressed fully together, and he took a nipple into his mouth as he fucked into me, making both of us come like it was his job.

And he took us both to Pound Town.

Number three on my list.

"Catch your breath," he said, kissing between my nipples. "We're just getting started."

37

JACK

While the coffee brewed, I grabbed my phone, checked the messages.

I leaned against the counter and felt Pancake weave in and out of my jean clad legs wanting attention. I'd never shut him out of my room before. I'd never had a woman in my apartment, let alone my bed before either. Now he was not amused at being neglected, the snooty bastard.

I didn't really have friends and Dax knew better than to fuck with me while I had Hannah all to myself. The only message that was there was from another Vegas number.

"Fuck," I muttered, pressing my thumb to the screen to open the message.

> I have another project.

Hannah was in my shower. Naked, well fucked and

washing my cum from her skin. We fucked twice, then slept, then fucked some more. This morning, I woke up with her good girl mouth on my dick. She hadn't been able to take all of me and had chosen for me to paint her tits with my cum instead of swallowing.

I didn't hold it against her. In fact, coating her skin felt like a claiming. It had been one of the hottest things I'd ever seen.

I looked forward to when we could forgo condoms and I could have it deep inside her. The thought of watching it drip out of her well-used pussy made me hard. Again.

Same went for the small bruises that were beginning to bloom on her hips, reminders for both of us of how I took her, how she wanted it. Needed it. To me, they were more claiming marks. Proof she was mine, that only I could satisfy her secret cravings and desires.

It made me want more of her and less of what Sal Reggiano wanted from me. He'd found out that Turkleman was dead, that I'd fulfilled my contract. I hadn't checked the news, but it was possible there was an article about it.

Except a second text, this one from Dax, reassured me everything was fine.

> The turkey was cooked just right. No leftovers.

Meaning no news reports. No investigation, or if there was one, it wouldn't lead anywhere.

I was done. Not only for Reggiano, but completely. I didn't need to kill for a living any longer. I sure as hell didn't need the money. After last night, I definitely could find more amusing ways to fill my time.

Dax and I did our jobs, didn't ask questions and didn't get involved in drama. That was what made us good. Made us dependable and professional.

It also made us untouchable and alone. Big Mike had taught us that was the way to be. I'd thought he was right. Until now.

I didn't want to be untouchable. Hell, I fucking loved when Hannah touched me. And I sure as hell didn't want to be alone, unless Hannah was with me, and we were alone together.

She offered me the life I didn't know I wanted. Peace. Quiet. Hell, I'd even move to Coal Springs and start shitting glitter.

The water in the bathroom shut off and I imagined Hannah stepping out of the shower and using a towel to dry off. All ready for me to get dirty all over again.

With my thumbs, I typed out my reply to Sal's message.

I quit.

Ever since fourth grade, Dax and I had been trained by his dad to take out the fucking trash. Retiring should've been harder than a text, but it was the easiest fucking thing.

Two words and I was free. I'd decline other work too, but this was the start. This was the beginning of saying no, of my new life with Hannah. I poured two mugfuls of coffee and carried them to my bedroom.

To start my new life in the best way possible. Naked with my girl.

38

HANNAH

"You read too fast," Jack said. "Slow down."

We were on his leather couch, the day after the Night My Vagina Broke. It would go down in infamy for me. When I was ninety, I'd remember it. For now, I was *feeling* it. I was sore and while he had the most incredible stamina in bed, he needed a break, too.

I didn't have to work today so he'd ordered in everything bagels and all the fixings; veggie cream cheese, capers, lox, and even sliced tomatoes. This didn't need to be cooked and yet he hadn't had any of it in his kitchen, proof that he really didn't use it.

Except for coffee. That he made and did a really good job of it.

Our plates in the dishwasher and refilled mugs on the aptly named coffee table beside us, I was tucked between

Jack's legs, my back to his front. We were reading from my e-reader which I always carried with me in my purse.

Jack had insisted we read a romance together. I had a feeling he intended to act out any sex scene that we came across. With this author, there were going to be quite a few before The End. My pussy silently whimpered at the idea of more Big D, but Jack was inventive and very creative so I knew he'd satisfy us both in other ways.

"You slow down when we get to the sex scenes," I muttered. I held the e-reader in one hand, the other on his jean-clad thigh. Yes, jeans. I figured he owned some, but this was a first. The fact that that was *all* he wore made me happy. In return, all I wore was one of his white dress shirts.

I was fed, well satisfied and cozy in Jack's arms.

"Research."

I giggled which made him tickle me. Which made me drop the e-reader onto the soft carpet beside the couch. Which made my hands free so when I rolled over, I could let them roam his bare chest.

"When did you start getting tattoos?" I asked, running my fingertip over a Celtic band on his bicep.

"Sixteen. Dax and I have matching ones."

I looked up at him through my lashes. "That's sweet."

He stroked my hair back. I'd showered and used his scented soap, but he didn't have any hair products because the jerk had naturally perfect hair, so mine looked a little wild and wavy. "Dax's dad, Big Mike, took us to get them after we–"

His eyes roved over my face.

"After you what?"

"After we both won our first fights. Big Mike owned a fighting gym."

"Is he gone now?" I asked.

"Florida. Retired."

"You said his dad took you in after your mom died."

He nodded. "Yeah. He's a good man."

"You took up boxing because of him?"

"MMA. Mixed martial arts. And yes. I was an angry teen, and he gave me an outlet. What about you?"

"What about me?"

"I feel confident you never wanted to take after your dad and stuff roadkill."

I rolled my eyes and had to laugh. "Not a chance."

"What about your mom?"

"She's an accountant. Too boring."

He smiled and it lit up his face. "I *really* like the books you read. If I do, then I'm sure the store you mentioned will be a huge success."

"Someday," I said, feeling the familiar twinge of disappointment.

"Tell me about it. I know you have it all figured out."

"Really?"

He shifted me so I was tucked between his side and the back of the couch. My top leg was thrown over his and my head was on his chest. I felt his heart thumping beneath my ear. I couldn't remember being so content. And I couldn't imagine ever going back to being alone.

"Really."

"Well, there's a vacant space on Main Street that's perfect. It already has some shelving and a cashier counter. It's on the same block with several popular restaurants and shops that cater to tourists. People read on their vacations and women–and you–enjoy escapist fiction like romance."

"The spicier the better," he added, giving me a squeeze.

"I'll offer all kinds. Spicy, sweet, all genres and make sure I'm as inclusive as possible."

"You've got it all worked out. I'm impressed."

I stayed quiet and he noticed. "What?" he prodded.

"Besides Brittany and Mrs. Metcalf, you're the only one who thinks it's a good idea."

"Maybe you've surrounded yourself with the wrong people."

"I can't ditch my family just because they're–"

"Crazy? Hurtful?"

I pursed my lips. They were those things.

"Family isn't always forged with blood. I should know."

Yeah, he should.

"I want to meet your friend Dax."

"Oh, gorgeous, he's dying to meet you. Soon. For now, I want to know if the heroine realizes she's fallen for the wrong twin."

"You know these books all end in happily ever afters, right?"

"I hope in more than just books."

39

HANNAH

It was always extra quiet in the library after Storytime finished. The void the group of toddlers left behind after they picked out books with their grownups was always pleasant. The hour-long program was its own form of birth control for me. It was a weekly prompt that I wasn't ready. So when the last finally left, I took my lunch break in the back room and read in peace and quiet.

Did he want kids? He'd had a brand-new box of condoms that we made a huge dent in, indicating I was a foregone conclusion, but also that he made birth control something he took responsibility for and made it a high priority.

Today, my mind was occupied with Jack. The day before, we spent the day together, reading and making out on the couch, until I had to leave to drive back to Coal

Springs. I had to work this morning and I hadn't brought extra clothes to stay with him a second night.

After only either eating out or from food deliveries from Denver restaurants, I wanted to make him dinner. It was something a girlfriend did. We'd never put labels on what we were, but he called me *his girl* and his *good girl,* so I felt messing up his kitchen might be okay with him. I'd never done it on a counter before, so maybe I could be his appetizer.

I couldn't help but grin at the thought.

I had a piece of notepaper on the desk beside my left-over salmon—the one from dinner the other night we never got to finishing, for *very* good reasons—that I was jotting down what I needed from the store. I wasn't the best cook, but I didn't have the money to eat out all the time.

Then it had me wondering about his stomach issues. Was he gluten free? Did he have lactose intolerance? I didn't want to make something that would bother him, so I would have to ask him. Lots of sex and reading about sex made me forget.

I grinned a little more.

Maybe tacos. I assumed he ate tacos. Who didn't? I could do corn tortillas and skip the cheese. I didn't want to make him the kind using the little seasoning packet and a jar of generic Americanized salsa, so I would go and find a cookbook in the non-fiction section and pore over a few recipe books for a more authentic option.

As I was wondering if Jack liked things spicy—in the kitchen, not the bedroom because I knew very well he liked it *caliente*—I heard someone behind me. Whipping around in my chair, I glanced through the glass window to the circulation desk to see who it was, but motion out of the corner of my eye had me turning further.

What the–

It was the man from the airplane. Not Jack. Not the one shaped like a beer keg with the BO. The other one. The farter. The one who'd helped me with my suitcase, called me doll and smelled like a bottle of cheap cologne.

In a suit, he looked respectable-ish, but it was the look in his eye that had my hair standing on end.

I stood, suddenly uncomfortable.

Because I'd been having my lunch, I hadn't paid attention to who else was in the library. It was possible we were all alone.

"Um, hi. Your friend Jack isn't here," I said, rubbing my hands together in front of me. Looking at him made me nervous. Wait. How had he found me? Had Jack told him? If he didn't, then how–

"Good."

Good? This was so not good.

I blinked, then moved to the right, away from him. He followed.

"Did you um, want me to give him a call?" I asked, making sure he knew I could have Jack on the phone in seconds. "Tell him you're here? Were you supposed to meet?"

We talked about a lot of things during our time together, but we still hadn't talked about his work. He'd distracted me with his dick. And his mouth. And with his hands. And with his very snuggly body on his couch. He never once brought up the men from the plane. I hadn't thought about them again to even ask.

"Listen, doll, let's not make this any more difficult than it has to be."

"Make what difficult?" I asked, but I wasn't sure if I wanted to know.

"I'll make this painless."

Blood rushed out of my head, and I began to shake. The hair on my arms rose. On my neck, too. The cloying scent of his cologne was filling the room, making me nauseated. I sneezed. Or maybe it was whatever it was he planned to do to me that would, I was sure, *not* be painless.

Reaching out, I grabbed the scissors off the table we used to laminate and cover books. A painful zap of static practically arched between the metal and my fingers. I held them in front of me. It wasn't the best weapon, but they were sharp.

"Cute." He grinned. I hadn't noticed the gold incisor when he was on the plane. He pulled a gun from behind his back, probably tucked in the back of his pants.

Oh, this was bad.

"What... what do you want?"

"You dead. I saw a cute chocolate shop on the way in, so I want to stop in and see if they have any caramels for after."

I knew the place. "They do have good caramels. I've even got a punch card for the place I'll give you if you don't kill me. I won't tell anyone."

He cocked his head. "About what?"

About what? I couldn't think clearly. "I don't know. Why do you want me dead?"

"Jack's taken a shining to you. You must be pretty

fucking hot in the sack even though you're a librarian and wear sensible shoes."

I glanced down at my sandals. They were comfortable, not strappy or sexy. Still, the guy was a dick for pointing that out. No question he was single.

"You're... you're going to shoot me?" I glanced through the glass window to the empty lobby area. "Someone's going to come in. This is a public space."

He rolled his eyes. "It's a library. Who the fuck comes to the library?"

He insulted my shoes and my job? I was scared, but I was also furious.

While the scissors weren't an ax, I tossed them like one. One of the bars in town had a hatchet tossing area and I'd gone once with Brittany. They hit his chest and the tip sunk in an inch or so, although the weight of them had them falling onto the floor.

"Ow, fuck!" he swore, putting his free hand over the small hole in his dress shirt that was beginning to trickle blood.

He set the gun down on the table beside my grocery list and came at me with a growl.

I swerved to the left, but he caught my shoulder and pulled me in front of him. More static, but I barely felt the tingle of it for how scared I was. His hands went to my throat and squeezed. Holy shit. I was going to die.

I was going to die.

My skin started to tingle, and I felt sparks of electricity through my palms where I tugged at his grip.

Why was there no one coming into the library? Why did I ever want peace and quiet?

Why was he doing this? What had I done? Jack! I needed Jack.

I wouldn't get to make him the tacos! I was so angry about dying like this. I survived a brain tumor only to be strangled? No way.

The small amount of air I could breathe was scented with bad cologne. Beneath his grasp, I sneezed. Then there was a sizzle.

And I was no longer in the library, but in international aisle of the grocery store staring at salsas.

40

HANNAH

My hand went to my neck. I could still feel the guy's hands, but they were gone. The cologne scent was gone. *He* was gone.

No, *I* was gone.

I spun in a circle on my sensible shoes. I wasn't in the library. I was in Herb's, the local grocery store. Muzak came from overhead speakers. What the actual fuck?

An older man went by, pushing a cart loaded with canned soup and cat food. He gave me a friendly, Coal Springs smile. Not the leer of the man from the plane.

I shivered and it wasn't from the store's AC.

Okay, I was safe. But I was also in the grocery store, not the library. It made no sense.

I breathed, I sneezed and I... teleported?

Heading past the taco fixings, I quickly made my way toward the exit.

There were two things flying through my head. I fucking teleported to the grocery store and I was almost killed by a friend of Jack's.

I had no idea how to know how the first happened, but I definitely knew the who'd know about the second. Jack.

I stopped by the coin return kiosk and the kiddie horse ride. Wait. If the man from the plane tried to kill me, what about Jack? Was he safe? Was the other guy, the one with the caterpillar unibrow, going after him?

I patted myself down with shaky hands. I had no phone. No keys. There was no way in hell I was going back to the library to retrieve either. Although, Mr. Cologne was probably as freaked out as I was. I doubted he had someone literally slip through his fingers and disappear like I had while he'd been attempting murder. Or anything else.

Still, I didn't want to connect with him and ask him after his half of the experience.

I needed to get to Jack.

The sliding doors of the grocery store opened, and I stepped outside.

All was normal. The sun was shining. Birds were actually chirping. People were coming and going like they hadn't recently been in mortal danger or bent the time/space continuum.

Brittany's dental office was a few blocks away and I speed walked in that direction, waving to a few people I knew as I went. Five minutes later, Amanda, the receptionist, pointed me to cubicle four where Brittany was working with a patient. He was tipped back in the chair, sunglasses on, dental dam in his mouth.

"Hey," I said, catching my breath.

Brittany and Mark, one of the hygienists, looked up. So did the patient.

"Hi, Mr. Brennaman," I said to him. He came into the library on Tuesdays to read the latest magazines. He sat in the reading nook and took his time while his wife was at Bridge Club.

"Is everything okay?" Brittany asked, her shrewd gaze raking over me. She had on blue surgical gloves, one of those bent mirrors on a stick in one hand, a big needle in the other. This wasn't the first time I'd been to her practice during the day, but it was a first interrupting her. I was a little shaky and a whole lot sweaty. "What happened to your neck?"

I put my hand to my throat. I could only imagine the red marks that my scoop neck tee didn't hide.

"Can I borrow your car?" I asked.

She frowned. "Um, sure. What's going on?"

I looked to Mark and Mr. Brennaman, who were both eyeing me and waiting to hear the latest news.

I stepped close, leaned down and whispered in her ear so only she could hear. "Someone tried to kill me in the library and to get away, I teleported to the grocery store. It seems I have another superpower. I need to go see Jack and make sure he isn't in danger as well."

She popped to her feet, implements raised. Her wheeled stool rolled backward in her haste. Dr. Todd walked by and she stopped him. "Can you please finish up numbing Mr. Brennaman for me?"

He was in his late thirties, reed thin, and did ultramarathons for fun. He glanced between the two of us. "Sure."

"I'll be right back," she told him.

Brittany set her tools on the tray, and I followed her down the hall to her office as she ripped off her gloves and tossed them into a trash can.

She shut the door behind her and leaned against it. "What do you mean you teleported?" Her voice was a whisper, even though we were alone.

I flung up my arms. "I have no idea!" I hissed. "One second I was being strangled, the next I was in the grocery store."

"Why the store?"

"*That's* your question? Not, why was I being strangled?"

"Good point. Are you okay? Your neck is all red. Jesus, that's scary as hell."

I nodded, touching the spot where the man had grabbed me. "It was one of the men traveling on the plane with Jack."

"What?" Her eyes widened. "He wants you dead?"

"Jack?" I shook my head. "I think someone wants *him* dead."

"Then why go after you?"

"He said Jack was taking too much interest in me."

"Why does that matter?"

"I have no idea, but I need to go to Jack and warn him."

"Are you sure? I mean, what if he sent the man? God, you could be dating a murderer!"

"I told you that all along!" I said, my voice rising. "You and Mrs. Metcalf didn't care."

"Right, well, clearly, we can make mistakes. But, Han, he can't want you dead. He went to your parents' house for dinner. He's literally been wooing you."

"We had sex. Lots and lots of really good, really naughty sex."

Her eyes lit up like I told her I was the Tooth Fairy.

"That's my girl." She thought for a moment. "Why would Jack do all that–and sleep with you–then want you dead? He could find someone to kill more conveniently located in Denver without all the fuss."

"Have you heard yourself?"

She shrugged. "It's true. If he was going to kill you, all I'm saying is he wouldn't introduce himself to your family. And shut down a source for really great sex."

"I got that. Now you're saying he's a good guy again?"

She sighed. Shrugged. "Yes. I'm Team Jack the Orgasm Giver. He put a spring in your step and a smile on your face these last few days. He's a keeper."

I nodded, itching to get to Jack. "Good, I have to go. Where are your keys?"

"Not so fast, Wonder Woman. What's this with teleporting? That's fucking insane."

"I don't know!"

"You went from the library to the–"

"Grocery store."

"That's weird. What did you do to make it happen? Did it hurt?"

"Did it *hurt*? No, it didn't hurt. The guy was strangling me. I was freaked and mad and... bam."

"That is so fucking cool," she said, grinning.

"It is if you're not being strangled by a bad guy, really are a superhero and know what the heck you're doing. Can we talk about this later? I need to go save Jack. Oh, God. Do you think the bad guy's still in the library?"

"Pfft." She waved her hand. "No way does he stick around after a woman disappears from his chokehold. I bet he's off to see his shrink right now."

"No one's working right now. The library's unlocked."

She went around her desk, pulled her purse from the drawer and grabbed her keys.

"Sweetie, it's the library," she said, handing them to me. "Everything is free. No one's going to steal books."

I exhaled. "Good point." I could deal with an unlocked library later. "Thanks for these."

I held up the keys and they jingled.

"Why don't you teleport to Denver and save on gas?"

"I ended up in the *grocery store*. Where would I end up if I did it again? And how do I even do it again?"

"Do you want me to strangle you to find out?"

"No!"

"Hey, Han? Remember when we were drinking lots of wine last week and I said you could save yourself?"

I nodded.

"This isn't exactly what I meant, but it's really cool."

Cool. I was almost murdered, and I could teleport to the grocery store. I didn't exactly think it was *cool*.

41

JACK

I pulled into my spot in the garage beneath my building, then climbed from my SUV.

I adjusted my suit jacket, then did the front button. This morning after Hannah left, I'd gone with Dax on a little money gathering job. But the guy had surprised us and had the cash he owed in hand. Dax seemed a little disappointed he didn't need to use the garden shears twice in one week. Since no amputation was required, it made for quick work. We'd grabbed lunch after delivering the loan payment.

Now I had a few hours to kill before I went to meet Hannah. She told me she wanted to cook me dinner. I had to decide if I wanted to feast on her before or after the meal. Maybe both.

A car came into the garage, tires squealing on the concrete. Instinctively, I reached behind my back for my gun. When the car slammed on the brakes, I saw who was behind the wheel and I let my jacket fall back in place.

Hannah. Something was up. Her eyes were frantic, and it wasn't her car. I also didn't take her for a NASCAR driving type.

She hopped out and I cut across the lot to get to her.

"What's wrong?" I asked, cupping her cheek, my gaze raking over her to make sure she was okay.

She swallowed hard, then licked her lips. "I, um, think someone might try to kill you."

I blinked at her. My sweet girl and the words she said didn't match.

"What?"

"She's right."

A man's voice came from behind Hannah. Eyebrows appeared from behind one of the concrete pillars. I tried to grab her and pull her behind me, but she shrugged out of my hold.

"You're not going to kill him," she practically snarled, reminding me of a little scrappy Terrier.

Eyebrows smiled and walked toward her. His demeanor was easy and casual, but I knew that was fake. There was only one reason he'd been lurking in my parking garage. For me.

"*You're* going to protect him?" Eyebrows asked her. A slow grin spread across his face. Obviously, he found humor in the possibility.

"Hannah," I warned, reaching for her but she shrugged me off. Again. She had no idea what kind of man Eyebrows was. All she'd seen of him was being kind of an asshole on the plane. He was so much more of one than that.

Eyebrows got within a few feet of her and grinned. "Bring it, little girl."

This time, I lunged to grab her, but before I could, she took hold of Eyebrows and lifted him in the air. His feet dangled a few inches off the ground. "Leave Jack alone."

Then she threw him to the side, where he landed hard on the concrete, rolling a few times. He pushed up, stunned, then staggered to his feet. A car came barreling into the garage and because Eyebrows was too out of it to move, hit him with the screech of his brakes.

Jesus.

It was Dax. Thank fuck. Eyebrows bounced off his bumper and hit the concrete once more, this time not getting up.

It took a few seconds to process what had happened.

Hannah. Eyebrows. Hannah tossing Eyebrows. Dax hitting Eyebrows.

By then, Dax was out of his car and standing over him.

I only had eyes for Hannah. She stood in her latest librarian outfit of black pants that showed off her ankles and a sleeveless white blouse. On her feet were the sandals she seemed to love. She looked adorable, as usual. Except–

WHAT THE FUCK WAS GOING ON? Since when did my girl toss mafia goons around? Since when did she expect one to *be* around?

I went to her, backed her into one of the concrete pillars and set my hands on either side of her head.

"Who sent you?"

She stared up at me wide eyed. "Sent me?"

"Who do you work for?"

"The library."

I laughed, but I wasn't amused. I was pissed. "Please, with skills like that? You're a fucking hitman and I want to know why you're after me. Did you plan it all along, the plane, everything?"

She blinked up at me as I was speaking in a foreign language. "What?"

"I know the moves of a killer when I see one."

I'd faced mafia kingpins. Drug dealers. Traffickers. Weapons runners. All kinds of shit. I knew how to protect myself, plan. Know the target and the client. How to hurt someone. How to kill.

But Hannah I hadn't seen coming. Holy shit. She was *good*. She got me lured in real fucking good. Dax had warned me I'd been blind where she was concerned. I'd been stupid and been thinking with my dick.

I'd even let her in my fucking heart.

Out of the corner of my eye, I saw Dax standing watch. He'd missed everything that had happened except for the part where he'd ensured Eyebrows was down permanently. "Jack, I don't think–" he began, but I cut him off.

"Fuck off, Dax," I snarled.

Hannah's eyes were frantic, and I could see her body shaking. "He was going to hurt you and I–"

"So you could do it instead? Shit, woman, you're good. I have to give you that. You had me fucking fooled."

She frowned, her gaze searching my face. "Jack? What are you talking about? What is this about a hitman?" She set her hand on her chest, those tits I'd licked and sucked. "I'm not a hitman."

I grinned at her. "Yeah, well, gorgeous. I am."

42

HANNAH

I stared at Jack, my brain not processing.

"What?" I whispered, not able to get the word to come out any louder. I eyed the guy on the ground, then Jack. I'd never seen him like this before. Angry. Wild. It was all directed at me and not in a sexy sort of way. Then somehow my synapses started to fire. "You're a *hitman?*"

A hitman killed people for a living. Oh my God. The guy I'd fallen for, who I'd had lots and lots of amazing sex with, was a murderer. Mrs. Metcalf and Brittany were going to feel really fucking bad when I told them.

"Who sent you? What's your angle?" he snarled. He set his hands on my shoulders, squeezed, pulling my attention back to him.

Dax, Jack had called him by name, the friend he'd mentioned, stepped closer and crossed his arms over his chest. He wore a crisp suit, like Jack. Was a suit a hitman's uniform? Obviously, Dax wasn't fazed by what was going on. He'd said they were business partners, so was he a killer, too? The answer was yes since he'd just hit someone with his car.

"My angle?" I sputtered. What was he talking about? "You think I kill people? Four months ago, I had a brain tumor and was *dying*. I'm all for keeping people alive, thanks."

"Jack, Paul Reggiano called," Dax said, cutting me off. "Gave me a heads up that his father wasn't satisfied with your work. Or that you quit. Would've been nice to hear about that."

Jack eyed me for another few seconds, then turned his head toward Dax. "Turkleman's dead. What can't he be satisfied about? Plus, I quit after the job."

"I told you not to stall," Dax scolded, although Jack didn't look the least bit contrite as they did a stare-off. "And since when did you *quit*?"

Jack tipped his head my way.

"Oh," Dax muttered.

"Reggiano sent Eyebrows to kill me." Jack looked back to me. "But who sent you?"

I blinked. Was it possible to have a heart attack from freaking out? It was pounding so hard I was surprised they couldn't hear it. "Jesus, are you even listening? Sent me? I drove myself from Coal Springs. I'm not a hitman!" I shouted. My hair raised on my arms in a familiar and now scary way. "I'm a librarian."

"I think Reggiano's too misogynistic to send a woman for a hit," Dax commented. I wasn't sure if I should be insulted or pleased he was defending me.

"No one would see her coming. I didn't," Jack stated.

I felt like I'd been the one tossed across the garage. He really thought I was a hitman. That everything we'd done since the plane had been planned.

"You're an idiot!" I yelled in his face.

He'd tracked me down.

He'd gone to my parents.

He'd seduced me.

He couldn't see any of that though.

"Then how did you know he'd be waiting down here for me?"

"Because the other one from the plane came to the library to kill me, you jackass!"

"What?" Jack's posture went ramrod straight.

I nodded.

The other man swore.

Jack murmured to Dax. "I need to get her out of here."

I ducked beneath his arm and moved away from him. I could've tossed him aside with my Wonder Woman powers, but what would that do besides validate his foolish thoughts. "I'm not going anywhere with you. I'm going home."

"It's not safe," Jack advised.

I arched a brow. "Oh, and I thought I was a hitman sent to kill you."

Dax chuckled and both Jack and I glared his way.

"Until I figure out who you're working for, you're sticking with me."

I crossed my arms over my chest, indignant. "Aren't you afraid I might kill you in your sleep?"

Dax all out laughed this time.

While Jack would be very disappointed when he found out I really did work for the city of Coal Springs as a boring librarian, he had a point about me being in danger. I hadn't killed the guy who'd come to the library to murder me, unlike the guy on the ground not twenty feet away. He hadn't finished his job. If he wasn't in a mental health facility because I teleported on him, he'd probably come back.

But I wasn't going anywhere with Jack. "I really like being alive, so I'll go with *him*. He seems to be able to keep me safe." I pointed to the body on the ground, then Dax. I didn't miss the smirk on his face.

They stayed quiet as I went around the front of the car, then stopped right before I fell over the awkwardly sprawled dead body. Shit. SHIT! Carefully, I stepped over him and climbed into Dax's car, slamming the door shut behind me.

Through the window, I saw the men talking. Then Jack went to the driver's door and climbed in.

"Wait. I'm going with Dax." I reached for the door handle to get out, but he flicked the locks. "Jack!"

He put the car in reverse, looked over his shoulder, and did a quick one-eighty in an empty parking spot. In seconds, we were out of the garage and weaving through traffic on a busy Denver street.

"I'm not going with you!"

"Looks like you are, gorgeous."

"Where are we going?"

"Somewhere safe," he said, teeth clenched. His grip on the steering wheel was white knuckled. His gaze shifted from the road ahead to the various mirrors. "Where you can tell me what the fuck is going on."

"Me? *ME*? I'm guessing you don't have a lactose intolerance problem after all."

I crossed my arms and fumed. I'd driven like a crazy woman to get to Denver as quick as possible to warn Jack. I'd been right to do so since the plane guy had been there to kill him, but still. He didn't say thanks and then rail me over the hood of his car as a reward. He didn't kiss me or even eye fuck me.

"Wait, you didn't have intestinal problems. What were you really doing at that restaurant? It wasn't to take me on a date, was it?"

He didn't say anything, only clenched his jaw.

"Wow. *Wow.*" I felt tears coming on and I blinked hard, willing them away. I was *not* crying over this. Over what I thought was a romantic dinner cut short. "And then after…"

After, we'd had sex. I'd given him my panties in his SUV.

"You had a spatter of blood on your shirt on the plane. Did you kill someone in Vegas?"

"Yes."

"Oh my God. Did you kill someone after leaving my parents' house? What about the pizza place? Man, business as a hitman must be fantastic.

"Don't be angry with me for keeping secrets," he said.

"Why not? You're a *hitman!*"

"And what are you? Don't tell me librarians can bench press mafia goons."

He accused me of being a hitman? It was laughable. Completely insane.

What wasn't funny was that he was one. Jesus. He'd *lied*. The entire time.

"I was almost killed at work by a guy with horrible cologne and a gold tooth who was *your* friend. Jesus, you should be thanking me for showing up, not kidnapping me." Static electricity sparked from my pants rubbing against the leather seat.

"He sure as hell isn't my friend and I'm not kidnapping you. We're going somewhere safe until I figure this shit out."

I had no idea where I was going and unless I teleported out of this car–which sounded really painful if I messed up and I had no idea how to even do it–I was at Jack's mercy. A fucking hitman.

43

JACK

Ten minutes, and a shit ton of heavy silence later, I pulled up behind Apex Fighting Gym and into a parking spot between a concrete wall and a dumpster. We were west of downtown in an industrial area. There'd been revitalization, but it wasn't residential. It got real quiet at night. Unless someone had a drone or tracker on Dax's car–which I'd check as soon as I got out–we were safe from Sal finding us.

Hannah glanced around. "Where are we?"

"Big Mike's place."

"Dax's dad? I thought you said he moved to Florida."

"He did. Someone else runs the gym now but Dax owns the building. And the apartment that used to be Big Mike's up there." I pointed through the front window to the second floor. I glanced around to make sure no one was around. "Let's go."

I climbed out, letting Hannah open her own door as I checked for a tracker. She wasn't the woman I thought, and I was pissed. I'd opened up to her. Completely. Even fallen for her. Took her to my place, fucked her in my bed. Read romance on my couch with her in my arms. Yet, she'd been playing me all along.

Finding none, I pointed to the metal stairs that ran diagonally up the back side of the building and waited for her to take the hint. She must've recognized she wasn't getting far on foot and started up them. I followed, eyeing her ass–because it was still a fucking piece of art.

"I can't figure out how you did it," I said.

"What?"

"Got that middle seat on the plane as me. Wait. Of course." It was so obvious. "Reggiano got you a seat, too. All of us in the same row. He sent you to spy on me? To make sure I was doing a good job? Eyebrows and Joey Brains weren't enough." Fuck.

"Who is Reggiano? He sounds like a kind of cheese."

"Like you don't know."

She gave me a look that would shrivel a lesser man's balls.

"He's Vegas mafia," I said finally.

"I don't know anyone in the Vegas mafia." She held up a hand and added for clarification, "*Any* mafia."

At the beat-up metal door, I typed a code into the state-of-the-art security lock beside it. It beeped once and I yanked the door open. Reaching in, I flipped on the light switch.

This place, right down to the scent of it, reminded me of my youth. Of pretty much living here after the age of sixteen with Dax and his dad. It was a huge loft space. High rectangular windows let in tons of light, but being high on the wall, you couldn't see out. There was one main room, a kitchen, family room, dining room combination, then three bedrooms and three bathrooms along the back.

The appliances, the cabinets, the furniture, all of it, hadn't been updated. Dax kept this place for when Big Mike came to town, or if we ever needed it. We paid Travis, the guy who ran the gym, to have his cleaning crew keep it spic and span and in fresh sheets and towels. I hadn't been here in over a year.

It was an instant reminder of the boy I'd been and the man I was now. How my mother had worked so hard for a better life for me. Pretty much worked herself into an early grave. How I ended up being a fucking killer. I'd looked up to Big Mike. Dax and I followed in his footsteps. From a money standpoint, it was a solid career. I had more money than I'd ever need.

But that was all I had. Until Hannah. I *thought* I had it all with her.

Turned out, I had nothing.

"We're going to stay here why?"

"Because it seems a client wants me dead."

"And me," she reminded.

I wasn't sure if I should believe her that Joey Brains had gone to the library and tried to kill her. Yet the idea of it, of that fucker getting his hands on her, made me start to sweat.

"You're a hitman. Go kill him." She pointed at the door, perfectly content seeing me leave. As if.

I went to her, circled around. "So ruthless for a librarian."

"You said he's a mafia kingpin." She turned to face me. "I'm guessing he's not building houses for the poor or reading to the elderly in his spare time. Based on what I see in movies, he probably deserves to be dead."

I frowned. "Definitely."

"Then what are you waiting for? Murder the guy."

I shook my head, tsked her. "It's not my place to do so. But I need to know why he wants me dead before I do anything."

"You can do that from here?" she asked, raising her arms to indicate the loft.

She didn't notice I was circling her toward the leather couch until it was too late. Until she bumped into the back of it. The other side faced the huge vintage TV and a wall full of DVDs.

"I can because you're going to give me the answers."

Her pulse thrummed at her neck and her gaze met mine, then away. She was nervous. And aroused. Maybe it was the couch and the past promises of being railed over the back of one.

"I don't know anything," she admitted.

"You know Joey Brains has a gold tooth."

"Yeah, because he was grinning at me as he tried to strangle me."

I eyed her neck, saw for the first time the bruising there, which made me pause. Fuck, was she telling the truth? Had he laid hands on my girl?

Yeah, my girl, because I was a pathetic, twisted fuck who thought it was hot as hell that she'd gotten one over on me. Saved my ass, even. Threw Eyebrows across the parking garage like she was in the WWF. If she was a hitman, too, then she knew the life. My dick was hard thinking about it.

Except, if Joey Brains got his hands around her neck, she'd be dead.

"And you got out of that how? No way you could stop that guy from killing you if he had his hands around your throat."

I wrapped an arm about her waist and spun her about so I had her hips pressed into the couch. The air sizzled around us and everywhere my hands skimmed, it felt electric.

"Are you *frisking* me?"

"Hell, yes." I didn't think she was armed, but I also hadn't thought she was an assassin either. Especially when I'd had my head between her thighs, and she was moaning my name.

"You planning on killing me? Run me over with a car?"

I let her go. Stepped back. "Jesus, fuck." I ran a hand over my neck. "I told you, with Mrs. Metcalf as witness, that I'd never, ever hurt you and that I'd protect you from anyone who did. But that doesn't mean I'm going to let *you* kill *me*."

"That's why I came to you, the fact that you said you'd never hurt me." She spun around, eyes narrowing, hands going to her hips. It wasn't from the Bible, so I didn't know the quote, but it was something about a woman's fury and being scorned. Hannah was furious and it seemed she thought I scorned her. "Except it turns out you're a Neanderthal and an idiot."

"You threw Eyebrows twenty feet!" I countered. "If you're not a hitman, then who *are* you?"

"You know who I am. I haven't lied about a thing. Unlike you."

"What did I lie to you about?"

"That you're a hitman!"

"I told you that on the plane when you first asked me what I did for a living."

"We were talking romance tropes. I didn't think you were serious!"

"That's your problem, not mine. You didn't tell me you took self-defense classes. What are you, a black belt in Judo?"

She shook her head.

"Karate?"

"No." The one syllable was drawn out on an exhale that would make a teenager proud.

"Explain what happened in the parking garage. Eyebrows had to weigh two-fifty."

She pursed her lips. "You wouldn't believe me."

"I think we're past that, gorgeous." I crossed my arms over my chest. "We're at the I-picked-up-some-things-at-the-adult-store phase of this relationship."

She blinked, then licked her lips. "You did? What did you get?"

I nodded. It didn't escape my notice that her mind veered.

For a second. "I'm not having sex with you, you liar," she snapped.

"I'm not the only liar, here, gorgeous. Joey Brains wasn't at the library. Tell the truth."

Her eyes lit with an anger that could probably singe. "The truth? Fine. *Fine!* You asked for it." She took a deep breath, let it out in an obvious attempt to calm down. Which didn't seem to be working. I had to admit, she was fucking gorgeous, all flushed and riled. So un-Hannah-like. Or, the only time I saw her this way was when *I* was the one to get her there. By my touch. My mouth. My dick. My words.

I watched as she went around the couch, squatted down and picked it up. Hefted the thing like it wasn't eight feet wide, made of leather and built back in the nineties for Big Mike, who was built like a tank. "Somehow in the past week, I've gotten stronger."

She set the couch back down.

I shrugged. "You want me to tell you I'm impressed? I was there when you threw Eyebrows across the parking garage, remember."

She stared, then huffed and went into the kitchen and to the fridge. I thought she was going to grab a soda that should be stored inside. "When I mean strong, I mean" – her arms went wide to either side of the appliance as if she was hugging it and picked it up so it was a foot off the floor– "really strong. It seems to happen best when I'm mad."

"What the fuck?" I said, stunned. That fridge had been built in the eighties. Made to last. Built of steel. I'd tried to move it once to clean behind it. It hadn't budged.

"My friend Brittany thinks I have a superpower," she commented, setting the fridge back in place.

I couldn't help but chuckle. "Yeah, right."

Maybe it was my tone or my attitude in general, but she

came over and poked me in the chest. Static electricity sparked between us. "You still don't believe me."

"That you have a superpower?" I chuckled. "Of course not."

"You're going to keep me here, not believing anything I say. Not about the guy from the plane trying to kill me, that I'm not a hitman or that I have newfound strength."

I shrugged. "Pretty much." I loved that she was worked up, because now she knew how it felt.

"So you did kidnap me."

I nodded. "Pretty much," I repeated.

She nodded right back, practically vibrating with anger. "You're a lying, egotistical, blind, self-involved, murdering piece of shit. Remember, asshole, that I'd been right there with you in this, even with the sex toys. That, unlike you, I was telling you the truth."

I reached for her and the air arced, literally a spark shot between us. Then she was gone. Disappeared.

I wiggled my fingers, my fingertips tingling.

"What the fuck?"

44

HANNAH

I'd felt the electricity in the air. The way my hairs rose on my arms and the nape of my neck. It was the same zap that had happened between us ever since we met on the plane. I'd thought it was static buildup with my hair, the dry Colorado air, even the potency of what we felt for each other.

But no. It seemed like it was the sign that I was building up power to teleport. I'd felt it whenever I was around Jack. Perhaps because he brought out every emotion–until now, everything but anger. The angrier I got, it seemed, the more powerful the force.

That was what I felt when Joey Brains–God, what an awful nickname–had showed up at the library. Then, the charge built to a point that when he strangled me, I'd teleported. It had been out of my control, but so was being strangled. It was as if so many emotions–fear, panic, anger, self-preservation, and more–came out at once.

This time, I hadn't caught on to the buildup until I was yelling at Jack, so fucking furious that the same electricity started to crackle around us. My hair rose. I got a little zap touching the fridge. Then Jack. More and more until I fueled it enough to actually make it happen.

I'd been mad, sure, but I'd wanted out of there, too. He'd kidnapped me. Jack wasn't just a hot guy any longer. He was a murderer and I'd needed out of that apartment in a way he couldn't catch me. I wouldn't have made it down the exterior stairs, let alone down the alley. But teleporting?

Ha. It was the perfect double middle fingers to Mr. Doubter.

He'd stop doubting me now. I smiled at the thought.

I figured out how I'd teleported, and I caught on how to stick the landing. Meaning, until now, I had no idea where I was going to end up. It seemed I *landed* wherever I'd been thinking about right before I teleported. With Joey Brains in the library, I'd been thinking about my grocery list and ended up in the grocery store. This time, I'd been thinking about the toys Jack had bought for us.

I wasn't standing in front of taco fixings. I was in the dildo section of an adult store.

A smiling clerk dressed in head-to-toe goth came down the aisle. "Sorry, didn't see you come in. Can I help you with something?"

"Can I use your phone?"

45

JACK

I blinked.

"What the fuck?"

I spun in a circle.

"WHAT THE FUCK?"

Hannah was gone. Like, poof.

One second, she was using every swear word in the English dictionary to tell me off and the next she disappeared. She'd been right in front of me. Poking me in the chest. Then... gone.

Was I losing my mind? I ran a hand over my face, then down the back of my neck. Jesus, did *I* have a brain tumor?

I could smell her. That soft scent that drove me fucking mad. She'd been here. I wasn't going crazy.

No, I was going crazy.

"Hannah!" I yelled, her name echoing off the brick walls.

I ran around the loft, opening bedroom doors, peeking behind shower curtains as if she were playing hide and go seek.

She wasn't here.

Next, I went to the door, flung it open. Dax's car was still parked below.

What was it called in *Star Trek*? Did someone beam her up? Wait. She hadn't just *teleported*, had she? She said her friend Brittany thought she had superpowers, but TELE-PORTING?

If that really was what she did, because it seemed crazy that that was the most plausible answer, then where did she go?

46

HANNAH

"Thanks for picking me up."

"From an adult store on Colfax? I want the story," Brittany said, an hour later when she picked me up in front of Pleasure Palace.

"Who's car is this?" I asked, scoping out the interior of the white minivan as I put my seatbelt on. In the back was a booster seat, a pool noodle and stray crackers.

"Dr. Todd's. You took my car, remember?" She pulled onto the road headed west. We'd have to go a few miles to get to the highway that took us up into the mountains and to Coal Springs.

Shit. It was in Jack's parking garage. *My* car was still at the library.

I should be freaking out. I *was* freaking out. "Right. I'm so sorry, B, but I didn't know who else to call."

"I'm your BFF. You're supposed to call me."

"So did you save Jack?"

"Yes. With my superpower."

She hummed something, probably a theme song for a superhero movie. Her finger even tapped on the steering wheel along with it. She wasn't thinking clearly when it came to my current situation.

"I tossed a bad guy across a parking lot, and he got run over," I said, trying to get her to see this wasn't one of those comic movies. I threw a real guy, and he got *really* dead. "Then Jack accused me of being a hitman sent to kill him."

A bark of laughter escaped as she stopped the car at a light. "You? A hitman? You put spiders in a cup and carry them outside instead of smooshing them like normal people."

I flung my hands up, then dropped them back in my lap. "Right? That's what I tried to tell him. Not the spider thing, but that he was fucking insane."

"Then what?" The light changed and she accelerated, looking both ways before crossing the intersection.

"Then he kidnapped me to his sorta-dad's old apartment in some industrial area, we got in a fight, and I teleported."

"Again?" As if I did it all the time.

I nodded.

A slow smile spread across her face. "That's so awesome, but why the Pleasure Palace? That's a little odd."

I shrugged, slid my fingers over the shoulder strap of the seatbelt. "I've only done it twice, but it seems I get sent to wherever I was thinking about right before it happened. The Pleasure Palace is the only adult store I know because they have those commercials on the radio."

She glanced my way, eyes wide. "You were thinking about an adult store while fighting with Jack? Very kinky."

"He said he'd stopped at one and picked out some things for us. I guess he piqued my interest."

"A guy who's secure enough in himself to pull toys into the bedroom is a–"

"Don't say keeper. There's one thing I haven't shared yet."

Her eyes bugged out. If I shocked her any more, they might fall out. "There's *more*?"

She slowed for another red light. Colfax had one at every block for what felt like miles. At this rate, we'd never get out of town.

"Yeah. Jack actually *is* a hitman."

She tipped her sunglasses down and eyed me like I may have started spouting in tongues like Perry said he could do. "What do you mean he's a hitman?"

"I mean he kills people for a living. That's his job."

"Are you serious?"

"I *teleported* to an *adult store*." I put an emphasis on both because teleporting was the thing of sci-fi movies and I might read sexy romances, but I'd never been in an adult store. I ordered online where it was nice and discreet. "Why would I lie about this?"

"Good point. Okay, he kills people for a living."

"Remember when I told you he could be a murderer, but you said it didn't matter since he suffered through dinner at my parents' house? Yeah, well, he really *is* a murderer."

"But he suffered through your parents' house," she

reminded with a shudder. "Name another murderer who'd do that."

"I don't know another murderer!"

Maybe Dax was one. Wait. So was Joey Brains. And Eyebrows. I seemed to know quite a few. I doubted any of them would last as long as Jack had.

I turned in my seat, bending my leg so I could face her. "Are you hearing yourself? He *kills* people. He actually murdered someone during our dinner date the other night. In the restroom while the waiter brought out my salmon and his steak. I went back to see if he was okay and gave him a Pepto Bismol thinking he had stomach issues."

She started to laugh, then bit her lip. "Sorry." A snort came out before she could calm herself. "Jesus, Hannah. You wanted a second lease on life. You got one."

I sighed, looked down at my fingers. I threw a man and he ended up dying. I was an accomplice killer. If I was into sports, I'd get the assist. "Be careful what you wish for, right?" We were quiet through one stop light. "I've been trying to keep myself alive, B, and he kills people. He doesn't have any regard for life or death."

She sobered. "Oh, sweetie. What are you going to do?"

"I can't stay with my parents."

"I'd rather be strangled by a mafia goon," she replied.

I'd experienced both and one was a much faster way to go.

"I can't stay with you," I added.

"Why not? I thought that was why I came to get you."

"Someone tried to kill me! I'm not putting you in danger."

"You're riding shotgun, girlfriend."

"I know. I was going to have you drop me off at a hotel or something, but I realize now I don't even have my purse."

Instead of continuing straight through the next light–finally, it was green–she used her blinker and turned onto a side street.

"I know where you have to go," she said.

I looked around. I was loosely familiar with Denver. Knew how to get to specific places like a mall, a sports arena or the airport, but it was pretty hard to get lost since the mountains went north to south on the west side of town. But I didn't know what street we were on. "Where?"

"Back to Jack."

"What?" I squawked. "Have you heard *anything* I said?"

She nodded. "Yes. Especially the part where he's a killer. He'll protect you, Hannah."

He would. He'd said he wouldn't hurt me, no matter how much he yelled and fumed and he'd done a lot of both.

"The bad guy who came to the library, he said he was there for me because I was a distraction for Jack."

"Which means this is a Jack problem. You only got caught up in it."

"So I should stay away from him, not go back to him."

She shook her head, as she turned once more so we were returning the way we came, one block parallel to Colfax. "I'm not saying you're not in danger, but this is Jack's problem to fix and part of that is making sure you stay safe. And alive."

"You've never even met him and you're taking me to him? A murderer?"

"If he kills people for a living, then he will protect you."

"That makes no sense," I argued.

"It makes complete sense," she countered.

It did, but I wasn't going to admit it.

I sighed. "I'm really mad at him, B. Hurt, too. He didn't believe me when I told him the truth."

"He saw you hulk smash a guy. It's pretty unbelievable. Remember, I drank a bottle of wine after you lifted my tree trunk coffee table. You have to give him a little leeway."

"You believe me," I reminded.

"Yeah, sweetie, I do. But you don't love me. You love him."

"I don't–" She set her dark hand on mine, shutting me up. Squeezed. "Yeah, you do. Remember though, you have the advantage."

"How's that?"

"You can do the whole teleport-away-from-him-thing again if he makes you even madder. No matter how big and burly or how talented his dick, he can't stop you."

They were valid points. All of them. Including his talented dick.

"Now tell me where his apartment is. I promised to get the minivan back before T-ball."

JACK

"I got rid of the body downstairs and had Nitro wipe the security feed of the garage. I have him working on Reggiano, too. What's this about Hannah being gone?" Dax called as he came out of the elevator.

After Hannah had... disappeared, I'd left the loft and, after circling the block a few times to make sure she wasn't walking to Coal Springs, gone back to my apartment. Going to Big Mike's place had been for Hannah, not wanting a traitor and a liar in my place, but there had been no reason for me to stay. She sure as shit didn't need to be kept safe.

I could protect myself. If Hannah hadn't jumped in and dealt with Eyebrows, I'd have shot the fucker. But she had and everything changed. Except... WHERE THE FUCK WAS SHE?

My mind was caught on that and dealing with Sal.

Since he wanted me dead, I was better off being on my own turf.

I had my gun at my back, a K-Bar in my boot, and an arsenal lined up on my kitchen counter. What I needed was information. So I'd called Nitro and he told me Dax already had him working on it.

It meaning whatever the fuck was going on. Reggiano. Hannah, all of it.

"She's gone," I repeated when he came into the kitchen. I didn't know any other way to word it without sounding mental or like Captain Kirk.

In his dark suit, he didn't look like he just dealt with a dead guy he hit with his car. That was what made us good. We took care of things without wrinkles or dirt. Only the occasional blood spatter. "Gone where? How?"

I wasn't going to tell him how, or where, because I didn't know myself. "Not sure," I said, which was a response for either of his questions.

He was waiting for me to elaborate, but I wasn't going to do it. He wouldn't believe me anyway.

"You don't really think that woman is a hitman," he said finally. Obviously, he didn't.

"She was on the plane." I raised one finger, then kept raising more as I continued. "She knew about Joey Brains' gold tooth. She knew about Eyebrows coming after me and then threw him twenty feet. She has skills."

He crossed his arms and stared at me.

"What?" I asked. "You don't agree?"

"Occam's Razor."

"What about it?"

"The simplest explanation is most likely the right one.

She randomly ended up seated in the same row as Eyebrows and Joey Brains because she was at a book signing. Did you see if there really was a signing?"

No. Because she'd–we'd–been reading a romance book on the plane that had a sticker for the library where she worked. Because she'd told me about the romance bookstore she wanted to open. Shit.

I grabbed my laptop from the kitchen's built-in desk and set it on the island. I pulled up a search engine and typed in Vegas and romance book signings.

"LoveNLust Romance Con," I said, reading from the web page. "Happened that weekend."

"If I remember correctly, you're the one who stalked her, showed up at her work *twice*. Not the other way around."

I frowned. I had.

"You think that hellish dinner with the family you told me about was pretend? That they were actors backing up her librarian front after you gave her, what, an hour to organize?"

I grunted at that misery. No way that had been staged. They definitely hadn't expected me.

"But wait, there's more," Dax continued. "You believe she works as a librarian as a cover? In that small town? Her annual salary's got to be less than the cost of my suit."

I knew how much he paid for the suit, and he was probably right.

He wasn't done pushing the fact that he thought I was stupid. "That she takes hits in her spare time?"

I sighed, realizing he wasn't asking me these questions because he agreed with me, but because he didn't.

"Dude, this is all bullshit," he said. "The woman you're crazy about is a small town librarian with a crazy family."

"Then explain how she knew about Eyebrows."

"Because, like she said, Joey Brains told her right before he tried to kill her."

"You know this officially?"

"You forgot that I showed up and hit Eyebrows with my car. And forgot to tell me you quit."

I glared.

He continued.

"I was talking to Paul Reggiano about a job, and he pretty much said that his father wasn't happy with you because you quit on him. I think the only way Sal lets people quit is being dead. I'm glad I got there when I did because I wasn't expecting him to act that quickly siccing Eyebrows on you. While hitting him with my car was an added perk, you owe me for a new front bumper."

That made me realize that Dax probably hadn't seen Hannah fling Eyebrows across the lot, only driving into the garage after he was already down. He'd have probably led with that if he had.

"That explains why Eyebrows came after me, but how did you learn Joey Brains went after Hannah?"

He pulled out his phone, dialed, then set it on the counter. "I had Nitro look into her," he said as it rang.

My first instinct was to pop him in the nose. I didn't want Nitro and Dax to know every detail about her, because the kinds of searches that we got on people were so thorough we knew when someone lost their first tooth.

"Yo." Nitro's voice came through the speaker.

"Tell Jack what you found out for me about the woman."

"There are cameras in the Coal Springs library," Nitro began, and my mind instantly went to the first time I'd touched her, how I'd gotten her to come all over my fingers in the back stacks.

"Exterior front entry, lobby only," he added.

Mentally, I sighed. I was all for a little exhibitionism, but not if it was recorded for city records. Or for Nitro to see. No one saw Hannah come but me.

"Joseph Cazamucci, aka Joey Brains, entered the library today at twelve thirty-seven. Confirmed it was him by facial recognition. He approached the circulation desk, stood there staring straight ahead for a few seconds, then went around the counter and disappeared from camera view."

I glanced at Dax. Shit.

"SHIT!"

Joey Brains really had gone after Hannah. She'd been telling the truth.

"He comes back around the counter four minutes later, looking freaked out," Nitro added, ignoring my outburst. "He's spinning in circles and peeking under furniture like he's lost a little kid, then runs out the front door."

"Is Hannah in any of the footage?" I asked.

"She arrives at nine fifty that morning and is seen pushing a cart an hour later. Once or twice at the circulation desk helping someone. None are in the system, or I cleared them as locals. But no sign of her leaving and no sign of her on the footage after twelve-fifteen. Not for the rest of the day."

Meaning Joey Brains stood at the circulation desk–like

the first time I'd stopped in–saw Hannah in the workroom and joined her in there. To kill her. He hadn't been successful, and she hadn't escaped out of the workroom–which only had one door–since her escape would have been seen on the footage.

It sounded like Joey Brains acted like I had when she'd disappeared from me at Big Mike's apartment. Meaning, she most likely went... poof with him, too.

Thank fuck or else she'd probably be dead.

SHIT!

"What else?" Dax asked Nitro.

I was too stunned, too angry, too fucking freaked out to speak.

"Hannah Highcliff was on the same flight as Jack. Her roundtrip basic economy ticket from Denver to Vegas was purchased with her credit card last December. She chose to take the airline assigned middle seat instead of paying extra to pick one herself. Plus..."

He was quiet but we could hear him clacking away at a keyboard.

"Her details. Hannah Highcliff. Middle child of Marcia and Robert Highcliff. Accountant and taxidermist."

"Taxidermist?" Dax repeated.

"There was a fucking cow head in the dining room staring at me while I ate a well-done burger. I told them I was a mortician. Since it's pretty much the same thing, we're going for beers to talk shop."

Not.

"Jesus," Dax muttered, shaking his head.

Nitro continued. "Her older brother, Perry, appears to be running a religious cult in the Springs. Sister Briana has no job and... is this correct? Jumps on a trampoline? That can't be right. Lemme keep–"

"That's correct," I said, remembering seeing her fly over the house. "She wants to be in the Olympics."

Dax only continued to shake his head.

"Okaaaay," Nitro replied. "She's also in a relationship with a Kevin Cortez of Coal Springs."

Kevin. *Kevin*. "Kevin, as in Hannah's ex?"

Dax's eyebrows shot up.

"The one and the same. I sent you his info already." I'd asked him to look into the ex last week after the dinner from hell but hadn't gotten to killing the guy yet. "Although the stuff with the sister was a new find. The used car lot he runs has security cameras. They show a lot. I'm charging you double for seeing even a few minutes of the two of them going at it in the backseat of one of the cars. Let me say that woman is flexible."

I cringed.

Dax grimaced. "I assume you're going to take care of him?"

Our eyes met. Dealing with scum all the time made us jaded, but this was one person I was looking forward to dealing with. "Oh yeah."

"You want me to send the footage?" Nitro asked.

"Not a chance. What about the medical records I asked about?" I prodded. "Hannah had a brain tumor. Had a special radiation for it."

"Medical records are sealed. I can get in, but it'll take some time. I figured you only wanted validation that she was telling the truth instead of the specific details of her health, so I pulled up the security cameras of all facilities within an hour of Coal Springs that did the gamma knife radiosurgery you mentioned. I got a hit on facial recognition for her arriving at a cancer center in Boulder. Several visits actually, back in... May and a few more since."

"Cancer? She said it wasn't cancer!" I panicked at the thought, running a hand over my face. Fuck me.

"The irony here is ridiculous," Dax muttered, although he wasn't laughing. Her being sick, whatever the condition, was not funny.

"The place does all kinds of radiation treatments, including the procedure you said she had. You want me to look further into it?"

Dax eyed me across the kitchen island. He'd started the inquiry, but it was my call if I wanted Nitro to dig deeper.

Anyone who lied about having a fucking brain tumor was mental. She wouldn't do that.

"No."

"So you agree now that your girl is exactly the woman you fell for?" Dax asked.

Except for her ability to lift a fridge and teleport, yeah. She was completely, totally my girl.

And I fucked it up. Big time. Epically. I leaned against the counter, dropping my elbows on the granite and resting my head in my hand.

She'd come to Denver with the intention to warn me but ended up *saving* me. She'd kept the guy who killed people for a living alive.

Joey Brains was alive and Reggiano hadn't gotten either of us dead. Which meant, this wasn't over, and Hannah was out there somewhere, unprotected.

"If he wants me dead because I quit, then it's pretty

simple. The reason for a mafia hit isn't usually very compli-cated. But see what you can dig up on Sal and Paul Reggiano anyway," I told Nitro. "Father and son. And let me know if facial recognition gets a hit on Hannah anywhere. I need to find her."

"To grovel," Dax said, smirking.

"Give me some time on the Reggianos," Nitro said. "But I can tell you right now where Hannah is."

I jolted upright, as if zapped with a fucking cattle prod. "What? Where?"

"Your parking garage."

48

HANNAH

The dead body was gone from the parking garage. Everything looked boring and normal. It was as if the whole assassin thing hadn't happened a few hours earlier. Although an assassin in my mind was a cross between James Bond and a ninja, not smelly, overweight mafiosi.

Brittany parked Dr. Todd's minivan in the visitor's spot, and I hesitantly climbed out. I'd probably have PTSD about the assault later, but I still took a few seconds now to look around and make sure there weren't any bad guys skulking behind concrete pillars.

Brittany didn't seem scared, although she hadn't dealt with not one, but two brushes with death today.

"That's his car," I said, pointing to the SUV.

"And that's mine that I want back one of these days." Brittany tipped her head toward her way-nicer-than-mine car that I borrowed in a visitor's spot. Its return wasn't high on my list right now.

I wanted Jack to be the man I'd fallen for over the past week, the one who seemed to crave me. Not the irrational man from earlier.

"Mr. Hitman drives a Maserati?" she asked.

I nodded.

"The best paying jobs aren't talked about with college counselors," she muttered.

She could find all this funny.

Me? Not so much. I was mad at Jack. Really mad.

And he'd put me in danger.

And he didn't believe me.

And... there were a lot of ands.

Yet, here I was, ready to return to him with the hope that he'd keep me safe.

I took a deep breath and made my way toward the bank of elevators when one of them dinged and the doors slid open.

Out came Jack and Dax.

Jack stopped for the briefest of moments, eyes intent on me. In a split second, he took me in from head to toe. The fierce look on his face had me swallowing because no matter how mad at him I might be, I wasn't immune. Then his long legs ate up the distance between us. "Don't you fucking disappear," he growled as his arms banded about me with a familiar crackle of static electricity. Then was kissing me.

I gasped and he took advantage, his tongue finding mine.

I wasn't sure if my feet were off the ground or if the kiss was that good.

Brittany and Dax began a conversation I barely noticed. Because... kissing.

"I'm Brittany, the best friend."

"I'm Dax, the other best friend. I, um, guess we're not needed here."

"Yeah, be sure to tell Jack that if he fucks up again, I'll anesthetize him and pull out all his teeth."

"Gruesome. I like it."

Jack, completely ignoring our friends and their chatter, angled his head and took the kiss deeper. Took *more*. It was completely unrestrained. Then heavy doors slid closed, and all was silent. How had we gotten to the elevator?

49

JACK

Once we made it to my apartment, I ensured the elevator remained locked so no one could call it, pretty much locking my front door. Eyebrows had known he couldn't get to me anywhere else in the building but the parking garage. Besides it being a twenty-floor climb, the emergency stairs were well secured. There was no way into my fortress in the sky.

Maybe I should have brought Hannah up here earlier after Eyebrows' attempt, but I'd wanted to take Hannah somewhere secret where I could interrogate her. Someplace neutral. Someplace impersonal. Fuck, *interrogate* Hannah. I wanted to punch myself.

Sal would need time to regroup. With Eyebrows dead, Sal's interest in my death was no longer a secret. Any attempts on my life wouldn't come as a surprise.

I'd be ready.

But I'd rather be taken out by any of his men than to let Hannah keep thinking I still didn't believe her. Maybe what she'd done, the disappearing act, was some kind of an act of faith, where I had to know what we shared was unconditional. That whatever she threw at me–figuratively, but also perhaps literally–I could handle and would stand by her side.

She'd stood by me, and I'd kidnapped her and *interrogated* her.

Accepting that she could up and disappear on me meant that while I was confident no one was going to get in, I couldn't guarantee that she wouldn't get out before I made things right.

So I broke the kiss and yanked at the hem of her shirt and pushed it up her torso.

"What are you doing?" she asked. Her arms went up to help, giving me unsaid consent.

"Making sure you won't do that disappearing act again." I flicked open the back of her bra.

Fuck, would I ever not get rock hard seeing her perfect tits? I wanted to lean down and suck one pink tip into my mouth.

"How is this going to stop it?" Her voice was breathless, and she wiggled her hips to help me get her pants down. I dropped to my knees to work them down to her ankles.

"I have a feeling if you wanted to, you could do it again. But I doubt you're going to want to end up somewhere naked."

She'd kicked one sandal off and stalled, the other one dangling from her toes. Stared at me, as if the idea never occurred to her.

She nodded. "You're right."

"Joey Brains tried to kill you." I stated it as fact, not a question. I believed her and I was telling her as much. "Are you okay?"

She nodded. "Yeah. I threw scissors at him. Got him good enough he might have needed a few stitches in his chest."

"That's a good girl."

She took a shaky breath. "That... that made him mad, and he started to strangle me."

Then she burst into tears.

He. Was. A. Dead. Man.

50

JACK

I pulled her down, so she was in my lap, holding her close as she cried.

Fuck, what a day she had. Hell, what a year.

I whispered how proud I was of her, how brave she'd been, how strong, as I stroked her bare back. It wasn't only for today's events, but her brain tumor and recovery, too. She'd been stripped of so much, not just a setback with her bookstore dream, but her confidence. Her own power. She might not see it, but she was getting it back.

Minutes went by as she clung and cried, but eventually, the jag ended.

"It's tough being tough," I murmured, kissing the top of her head.

She lifted her face to look at me and I wiped her tears with my thumb.

"Sometimes you don't have a choice," she said, her voice soft.

"Sometimes you don't," I agreed. "But you don't have to go it alone."

"I had Brittany, and my family a little bit."

She meant the diagnosis and treatment.

"You have me now, too. I was wrong, Hannah. I'm so fucking sorry. I should have believed you. You surprised me with your strength, and I shouldn't have been. I think... I think I didn't understand how you would do that for me."

I saw now why Dax thought I was such a dumbass, how he'd been shaking his head at me as I spewed total fucking nonsense.

Hannah had tried to protect me. To *protect* me. To protect *me.*

Dax had my back like that, but he was like a brother. No one else had. Until now.

"Do what?" she asked, her little frown showing her confusion.

"Step in front of me and protect me from Eyebrows. Big Mike, Dax's dad, always said love hurt too much to be worth it. That's probably one of the reasons why Dax and I never do relationships."

I hadn't really thought about it before now, but it made sense when it was shoved in my face.

"But I think Big Mike was wrong. It is worth it. The right person. Because going through life like I have... empty, hurts even more."

"Oh, Jack," she said, reaching up and cupping my cheek.

"You're the strongest person I know, gorgeous."

Her cheeks were pink and splotchy, but she gave me a small smile, taking in the words as truth.

"Feel up to telling me the rest now? About Joey Brains in the library?"

With a sigh, she said, "There's not much else. I disappeared on him, too."

Thank fuck. "Where did you go? Or end up. Or whatever it's called."

She sniffed and the last of her tears were gone. The cry had been cleansing for her. For me, it reminded me that while she really was fucking strong, she was also very, *very* fragile. She needed someone on her side. Someone who believed her. Believed *in* her, like that her bookstore would be a hit. Protected her.

"I have no idea what it's called," she said. "That, in the library, was the first time it happened. I ended up at the grocery store."

"The–where did you go when you were with me?" I wondered, hooking my fingers in the elastic of her panties. She shimmied to help me slide them down. My hands immediately cupped her perfect ass.

I wanted her naked and I wasn't stopping. We only took a small detour with the tears.

Her gaze shifted and I couldn't miss the blush that spread across her face and down over her tits. She bit her lip then mumbled something.

"Where?" I asked, shifting her so she straddled me instead of sitting sideways in my lap. When she didn't repeat herself, my fingers slipped between those sweet cheeks and found her little asshole which I knew she loved to have played with.

She gasped and squirmed and her eyes flew to mine. "Pleasure Palace."

The pad of my finger brushed gossamer soft over the tight ring, teasing her and tempting me. My dick throbbed to be set free–and to someday get inside that virgin hole.

"The adult store?" I was so, so confused, but I was also too fucking turned on to understand deep thought. With her legs parted, I could see her clit hard and needy. I could smell her. See her pussy lips glistening. She might hate me still, but her body knew who gave it orgasms.

"It seems I go wherever I was thinking about when I... teleport." Her eyes fell closed and her hands settled on my shoulders.

"Teleport?" Leaning down, I kissed the tip of one breast, then gave it a soft lick.

"I... oh God. I don't know what to call it. One moment I'm one place, the next I'm another. I guess it's also called apparition. I disapparated from the safe house with you and apparated at Pleasure Palace."

"You want to talk appropriate verbs while I'm playing with your ass?"

"You want to play with my ass while I'm mad at you?"

"I know you're mad, gorgeous. I'm mad at me, too. I'll say I'm sorry for-fucking-ever. Do you want to yell at me before or after I fuck you?"

Shifting, I tipped her down so she was on her back and I was between her thighs.

Moving lower, I gave her seam one long lick, her sweet, sticky taste blooming on my tongue like candy. Dax told me I needed to grovel. I was on my knees between her lush thighs and the best way I could show her she was my fucking queen was to eat her pussy.

"Jack," she moaned.

There was nothing better than her saying my name like that. Pre-cum spurted from my dick in response.

"Before or after?" I said, looking up her gorgeous body.

Her dark eyes held mine. Gone was the hurt and anger, replaced by arousal. Was I using sex to redirect her? Maybe. But this was also for me. I needed to make her feel good. Needed her to give herself to me, because that trust–maybe she didn't even know she gave it freely–was what made my dick hard and my heart full.

Her mouth curled into a sinful smile. "Stop talking and get back to work."

The riled words were accompanied by her firm hand on the back of my head pressing me into her center. I had a very important job to do.

51

HANNAH

I liked Jack going down on me. No, loved it. LOVED it. But a girl had a list and wanted variety. And sex with Jack was *all* about the variety.

"I want to be railed over the back of the couch," I admitted once I caught my breath and Jack was kissing his way up my body.

His head popped up, like a kid when someone said it was time to go get ice cream.

I bit my lip, then admitted, "This floor is pretty hard."

His gaze shifted from heated intent to concern.

With the grace of a panther... no, a hitman, he popped to his feet, pulled me to mine and tugged me into his living room and over to his couch.

I laughed, which was so much better than crying.

His eagerness, I knew, was because he wanted to rail me over the back of the couch as much as I wanted to get railed. But also, because he would probably do whatever I told him right about now.

He was contrite and apologetic. I believed him and his words. His truth. That I was different. That we were different and that was a surprise for him. That he could be more. That he, too, had value *to me*. It was the perfect time to get what I wanted from him. And I wanted what Mia and Colin had in the book he and I shared on the plane. I wanted to *live*. Without Perry's level of shame and judgment.

"You want it rough, don't you?" he asked.

His dark gaze raked over me. I was naked and he was in his suit.

"Yes."

"Then be a good girl and do as I say. Bend over the back."

"You can't fuck me in your clothes."

"You let me worry about that," he replied.

Meaning all I had to do was obey. Oh my.

I licked my lips and moved behind the couch and put my stomach to the top edge. Then leaned forward.

His hands were on my hips, lifting me up so I was folded over comfortably. I could only see the dark leather, feel how cool it was beneath my fingers. My toes barely touched the floor.

I couldn't see what he was doing, but I could hear. His belt clanged. His zipper hissed. A rustle of fabric. A hand on my hip.

"You good with me fucking you bare, gorgeous? You said you were on birth control. I'm clean. I'd never put you in harm like that."

No condom? The idea had my pussy clenching.

"I'm good," I said, a little awkwardly since I was pretty much talking to the back of the couch.

"There's no going back, Hannah. Once I see my cum dripping from your pussy, you're claimed. Mine."

Oh God, those words were similar to what Colin said to Mia, but I didn't think he was playing a role. He meant them. Jack to Hannah.

I squirmed as best I could. "Please, Jack."

And he gave it to me. Every hard, thick inch of his dick thrust into me at once. Then fucked me like it was his job. Good. Hard. Long. Deep. Until we came on hoarse cries. Until he saw his cum slip from my pussy and he said, "Mine."

52

JACK

There was nothing better for curbing anger than makeup sex. And apologizing.

We were on the couch–not over it–with Hannah sprawled on top of me. Naked. I intended to keep her that way, not because she could apparate like Harry Potter, but because there was nothing better than her bare. She was warm and soft and so fucking pliant. I'd only opened up my pants enough to get my dick out, too eager to fuck to take the time to strip down. My dick was tucked back in my boxers, but I hadn't done up my pants or belt.

It was this little slip of a woman who gave my conscience a shove off my twenty-story balcony and put it in freefall. Because she was the only person I didn't want to let down and fuck, had I let her down. Not from Sal wanting me dead. That was the easy part to deal with.

Her forgiving me showed more about her spirit than my

level of groveling. Because of that, our love would never be even. She wouldn't know it, but I'd always treasure her more. Need her more. Crave her.

I'd hoped to be the man she deserved by quitting, but I should have known I couldn't escape the life that easily.

"How come you don't stand up to your crazy ass family the way you took on a killer like you *were* a killer?"

She stiffened and made to sit up, but my arms banded about her and held her in place. After a few seconds, she sighed, then relaxed. "You're right. I don't know why I let my family walk all over me. I guess it's always been easier being invisible."

"Gorgeous, you could *never* be invisible. If you showed me the whole fridge deadlift thing before you tossed Eyebrows aside like garbage, I wouldn't have questioned."

"It's a newfound skill," she admitted. "Like the bathroom door at my parents' house. Pretty sure now it wasn't termites."

Right, the door had been off its hinges when I'd joined her in that tiny powder room. She'd escaped to there because she'd been mad at her family.

"I'd say the ability to teleport like the crew from *Star Trek* is even more impressive," I replied dryly. "Can you please tell me how my girl's got superpowers?"

She turned her head so she was looking at me, her chin on my bare chest. Her palm settled right above my heart.

"At first, I thought... well, I thought I was crazy. Then I questioned if it was because of my brain tumor."

Panic instantly filled me, remembering that Nitro had footage of her entering a local cancer center.

"Are you sick? Is it back?" I wanted to run my hands

over every inch of her to see if she was hurt but knew that wouldn't help.

I killed people for a living, but Hannah was the one person who I needed to not die. Big Mike had always said in our line of work, we should expect to live short lives. He was pushing seventy, so either Florida was good for his health, or he'd been wrong. Dax and I were hanging in there, but we knew the risks.

Hannah deserved to die in her sleep at one hundred. I couldn't resist, cupping her face, then stroking over her silky hair. To know she was real and well and whole.

"No. I had a checkup two weeks ago and it was gone." She absently ran her finger over my tattoos. "I haven't had any symptoms like before or any radiation side effects. I haven't felt off, and that's where my mind goes first thing."

I never really thought about her worrying if it would return. If it filled her thoughts. If she was scared.

"It's okay to be afraid," I told her.

Her mouth slipped into a flat line, and she jabbed my chest. "Don't mansplain to me about how I should feel after a brain tumor. And you're the last person who should be telling someone it's okay to be afraid about dying since you, you know, kill people. I'm sure all of them were afraid."

Shit... yeah. "You're right about the mansplaining. I'm sorry. What I meant was, you can be afraid because if you are I will be here, like this, to hold you. You won't be alone."

Her muscles softened and she relaxed back into me.

"As for me killing people, can we come back to it? I don't want a superpowers cliffhanger."

My literary device use had her smiling.

She sniffed and sounded very much like a prim librarian when she said, "Yes, but I'm not going to forget."

"I never imagined you would," I murmured, my voice soft. I hoped she would keep me in line for years... decades to come.

She sighed, then returned to the unfinished topic. "I don't go to the gym. The heaviest thing I lift is a book. Until this week. I know what you're going to say, that I should go get checked out again. I went in two weeks ago and everything was good, but it's not like I'm going to go in and tell my doctor I can now lift refrigerators."

"Or teleport," I added.

"Or teleport," she repeated.

I'd have to agree with her, except these *abilities* made no sense. Her doctor would agree and think she was insane, and Hannah was probably the sanest, level-headed person I knew.

I thought I was as well until Hannah went *poof* right in front of me. "It is a little unbelievable," I admitted.

"A little? Imagine being the one who can do it and ends up in an adult store. We're not crazy, right?" she asked.

I took a deep breath. "I have no fucking idea, but we both know it happened. Joey Brains, too, but he's called that because he's not all that smart. What do you think is the cause?"

"I don't really know, but the only thing I can think of is the radiation. Maybe something happened from that."

Radiation? I'd gone online and looked up the gamma knife radiosurgery she'd had. While it was considered non-invasive, it was fucking brutal with a metal frame they attached to Hannah's head, then beams of radiation all aimed at the tumor... fuck, I wanted to hurl thinking about her going through it.

"Like Spiderman?" I asked. "This is more fucked up than my thinking you were a hitman."

"I didn't get bit by a spider." She sighed. "I told you before that Brittany's the one, like you, who thinks I've got superpowers. There is no definitive answer, Jack. I have no idea why it's happening."

"As long as you don't hulk smash bad guys to protect me or teleport to an adult store again, then we're good. Speaking of..."

I shifted us so my leg settled between hers. My thigh pressed against her bare, cum-coated pussy.

"You're not distracting me with the sex toys you bought... yet." She gave me her stern librarian look which only made my dick stir. Even more so with the use of the word *yet*. "Your turn to talk. You're a hitman. That means you kill people, right?"

53

JACK

It was time to come clean. She'd seen what kind of people I dealt with firsthand.

"Yes. But only bad people. *Really* bad people."

"The night at my parents' house, you left to kill someone?"

I expected a horrified expression, perhaps even an attempt to climb off me with revulsion. I got neither. She was more curious and perhaps that was the librarian in her that wanted to know the full story.

I shook my head. "Sal Reggiano called. Three times over dinner. He's the mafia boss in Vegas who now wants us both dead. Last week, I was contracted by him to kill a guy and I hadn't gotten to it yet. Someone distracted me."

This time, she looked away, not the least bit sheepish. Perhaps pleased with herself to have taken up my attention enough to keep me from killing someone. Or I'd like to think that.

"The next night, at the pizza place?" she continued.

"Again Reggiano, the needy fucker." I sighed. "He texted and asked me why I was in Coal Springs. Turns out, he was having me tracked. I was angry because I was with you, and I needed you to stay a secret."

She looked down at my chest, but I didn't miss the instant hurt that my words brought about. "Why?"

Reaching out, I tipped her chin up. "Not because I'm ashamed of you, gorgeous. To keep you safe. Now that you know the truth, you can see why."

Her dark eyes searched mine as she nodded. As if she was still unsure if I told the truth.

"He knows how important you are to me, and he was hoping to use that–the text at the pizza place–to keep me in line. When he realized he couldn't, that's when he sent Joey Brains."

Her eyes widened. "You're in the mafia?" It seemed being a hitman was one thing to handle, being in the mafia another. "Do you have a nickname?"

"Hell, no. We're not in the mafia and no stupid nicknames. Dax and I are freelancers. We take on a variety of clients."

"Helping them with a variety of projects?"

I smirked, remembering the bullshit line I'd told her about what I did for a living.

"Dax is also a hitman?"

I shook my head. My hand went back to sliding up and down her bare back. "He's a fixer."

She frowned. "There's a difference?"

"He fixes problems and I make them go away."

She opened her mouth to say something but closed it. Her brain was working on what I said.

"Reggiano's only one of our clients," I added.

"They hire you to kill people and Dax to fix things." She simplified it down to one sentence.

"Bad people," I clarified, making sure she was well-aware there was a difference. "Only very bad people. I do research and make sure the world is better with them dead."

"And dinner the other night? You didn't have a stomachache?"

Shit. I was fucked no matter how I answered.

"The target was eating at the restaurant. I had to finish him there before he went to the ball game. It was my last and only chance."

"Finish him," she repeated, making me sound so callous about taking a life.

"He was an arms dealer, Hannah. He sold weapons to other bad people in bad places who kill innocent people."

She was quiet as she thought about that. My words, to me, justified my actions. But I'd pretty much grown up to think in black and white.

"So you did it... in the bathroom?"

I nodded.

"How?"

"You want to know how I killed him?"

She nodded.

I didn't want to tell her, to have her know the extent of

the things I've done, but I couldn't lie to her, or lie by omission. I needed to know she was with me because of exactly who I was. "I broke his neck."

"I didn't hear about a murder on the news."

"I broke the water line beneath the sink so the floor was wet. I hit his head against the floor so it made it look like he slipped and hurt himself."

"That's not very realistic," she replied. "I mean, Mrs. Metcalf is more of a mystery book reader than I am, but I think a detective would see through it."

My lips twitched. She wasn't running. Instead, she was making a joke. "Probably. But when the detective found out the guy was a well-known, very notorious and very bad weapons dealer, they'd have to hand off the case to the FBI and they wouldn't look into it further. They'd know it was a hit and not care."

"He was a weapons dealer?" She swallowed hard.

"Yes. The last job I did was to kill a trafficker. He sold women into sexual slavery. The guy before that doped racehorses. Mistreated them. Real bad. I don't do anything random or unintentional. I like to think of their deaths as penance for the far worse things they've done to others."

"You get away with it?" She rolled her eyes. "Obviously."

I ran a hand down her back and cupped her bare ass. "Gorgeous, I always get away with it."

She looked unsure. We'd both shared big things. BIG. I didn't know which was more nuts, finding out the woman I was in love with had superpowers or if she learned the guy–I hoped–she loved killed people for a living.

"I'm a bad guy, Hannah, but I'm a *good* bad guy. I really need you to see that."

She looked down, absently touched my tattoos again. "I almost died, Jack. I was actually dying. Staying alive is all I've thought about these past few months. I know firsthand how weak we can be."

"You are *not* weak," I said, my words threaded with steel. Because I was the one who was afraid. "You are so fucking brave."

"What I'm getting at is I value life, perhaps more than others because of what happened to me. You... don't."

I shook my head. "I value life. I do," I added, when she looked skeptical. "The people who I kill *hurt* people. Animals, too. They're cruel. *They* don't value life. By putting them six feet under, I'm saving so many and getting justice for those who couldn't be saved."

It'd never been more important to be understood. I'd never given a shit what people thought of me. Until Hannah. I wanted to be good for her.

"I quit," I added. "I told Reggiano I quit. That's why Joey Brains showed up at the library. He wanted to hurt me in the worst possible way."

"Is that why the guy was waiting for you in the parking garage?"

I nodded. "The men from the plane were Sal's men. They follow his orders. But I'm not taking any more jobs."

"Why?"

"I want the simple life. Quiet. No bad guys. Only me and my girl and a little romance bookstore."

She blinked at me as if I'd blown pixie dust in her face. "What? You'd walk away from it all for me?"

"I already have except for some loose ends." Like killing Sal. And Joey Brains.

Setting her hands on my chest, she pushed herself up. I admired her breasts and the rest of her gorgeous body, but she was retreating. Pulling away. I could tell from the look on her face, and the fact that she wasn't kissing me.

FUCK.

"I... I need to take a shower. To think."

54

HANNAH

I loved Jack's shower. The multiple shower heads, especially the one that replicated rain. The last time I used it, Jack had joined me. And I hadn't gotten very clean.

Now I was alone, letting the hot water pelt me from all sides. Steam billowed, making the glass foggy.

He was giving me room to think as I asked. I'd never had a man apologize to me. Dad always went with whatever Mom said. Perry was never wrong. Kevin's shitty behavior he blamed on me being a bad girlfriend.

Jack was subtly groveling. Being cautious that I'd leave him, which was probably why he was okay with me being in here. There were only towels in his huge bathroom. No clothes. He'd been right. I wasn't teleporting naked, or in a towel, anywhere. Although, I could think of my apartment, and I would end up there.

Maybe. I was risk averse in general, but even more so

when it came to ending up in the grocery store or some-where else without any clothes on.

I'd only done teleported twice and I wasn't sure if my hypothesis of *thinking it and going to it* was accurate. Regard-less of what Jack said, I wasn't *that* brave.

There was no instruction manual.

It was surprising and new to me, and I could only imagine Joey Brains' face after I disappeared on him. I could only imagine Jack's.

Perhaps both of them deserved a little slack when it came to believing and understanding. Not Joey Brains because he wanted me dead, but Jack, yes.

There was no precedent. People had probably been stunned when the telephone first worked. Or saw an airplane in the sky for the first time.

Jack thought he was interested in a mild-mannered librarian and ended up with something else entirely.

I thought I was a mild-mannered librarian and it was turning out I was something else entirely. Something more. I liked this new and improved version. A guy looked at me like I was the center of his world. I felt pretty. I had an unknown sexual prowess. I could defend myself, and Jack.

The superpowers would have come about whether I met Jack or not, but because of him, I felt good, old-fash-ioned regular feminine power. That I was worthy of more.

More attention. More understanding. More love.

How could a man who killed people bring out the best in me?

Was it possible that I brought out the best in him as well?

He said he quit.

For me.

That he was done as a hitman.

For me.

He wanted to have a quiet life.

With me.

He mentioned my bookstore which meant he'd live in Coal Springs.

The only reason Jack would relocate to a small, Hallmark town was...

Me.

I hadn't used any soap. Or shampoo. All I did was stand under the spray and think. But I couldn't wait another second. I turned off the dials and opened the glass door. As I stepped out onto the plush bathmat, I saw Jack's reflection in the mirror. He was leaning against the open doorway, the sunlight from the bedroom windows at his back. Still in his suit, he'd done up his pants. Looking at him, no one would know how virile and sexual he was. What he was packing in those pants.

"Are you done thinking?" he asked. Pancake came into the bathroom to see what was up, sniffed with his head and tail high like a snooty king, then tore off like the lunatic he was.

I nodded.

His body was tense. His face unsure. He–Mr. I-Kill-People-And-People-Want-To-Kill-Me was scared. Of me. Afraid of what I was going to say. I wasn't even sure if he was even breathing.

"If you're going to work in a romance bookstore, you're going to have to read more and get to know the tropes," I said. "You can't just *be* one."

A smile split his face and he crossed the bathroom in three strides; it was a big bathroom. His arms went around me, not concerned I was getting him all wet.

"What should we read tonight?" he asked. "Cowboys? Those shifters you mentioned that like to bite? Or is that vampires?"

I couldn't help but grin. "I was thinking BDSM."

His eyes flared with heat and interest.

"You want me to tie you up, gorgeous?"

"You said you have a lot of ties. And new toys."

"Then teleport to the bed, gorgeous."

55

JACK

She stared at me like I was crazy. Maybe I was. I had time to panic while she was in the shower. That she might wash the idea of an *us* down the drain and want to leave.

But my girl surprised me yet again. She wanted me. Dead bodies and all.

Since it was my job to keep her safe, we had to work on the one aspect of that I couldn't control. Her superpowers. Yeah, they were real. I admitted it. I believed it.

Her teleporting to the grocery store and a fucking adult store wasn't safe. Her ability to control disappearing from one place and ending up in another scared the shit out of me. I needed to know she could be on top of it, that it wasn't a response but an intention.

"What?"

"Teleport to the bed."

"Why? It's right over there," she said, pointing past me into the master bedroom.

"Do you know how it works?"

"Kinda."

"Do you know for sure you end up where you were thinking?"

"No."

"Then we need to practice."

"I'm not a witch casting spells."

I reached out, grabbed a fluffy towel, and started drying her. "Gorgeous, you kinda are."

"I am *not* a witch."

I smirked, amused she didn't seem to like that term. "I need to keep you safe, and I won't have you ending up somewhere random where I can't be there to protect you."

Perhaps my words were laced with a hint of desperation and possessiveness. I didn't give a shit. I took care of what was mine.

Her shoulders relaxed and she sighed. "Fine. But I need clothes for this."

56

HANNAH

Five minutes later–because Jack either really wanted me to practice or really wanted to tie me up–I was dressed and had Jack's cell in my hand. We agreed, for this practice, I wasn't teleporting anywhere without one. Just in case.

We decided to start small. We were in his bedroom, not fifteen feet from the bed. My destination.

"Okay, how do you think I should do this?" We stood together, somewhat awkwardly. It wasn't like either of us had ever done this before, me, at least, intentionally.

I eyed the bed. If I picked Jack up with my newfound strength, I could throw him the distance. That wasn't the superpower we were working on, and I didn't think that one needed any help.

"You said you have to be angry," he said.

I arched a brow. "We just got done with that. I don't want to fight with you anymore."

"You also said the static electricity was part of it."

I forgot about that.

"Yeah, but have you felt it lately?"

He shook his head. "You think it's gone?"

I shrugged. I had no clue.

"I don't," he replied. "Maybe all that electricity was foreplay."

"Charged foreplay?"

He ran a hand through his hair. "I have no fucking clue. It happened on the plane, the first time we met. Every time since. Until we had sex. All I know is that now that I've had you, I can't get enough. Maybe we do it too much to build it back up?"

"Are you serious?"

"I'm not holding off getting inside you to test it."

I totally agreed with him. I wasn't abstaining from the best sex of my life to see if we could conduct static electricity. "Um...no."

"So we're going with you being angry."

"I said I don't want to fight with you." *And* we were fighting.

He shrugged, probably thrilled I wasn't mad at him. "Then be angry about something else."

I frowned. "What should I be angry about?"

"Your parents. Your brother and sister."

He wrapped his arms around me in a snug embrace.

"Jack, what are you doing?"

"Your sister played footsie with me under the table at dinner."

I tried to push back to look up at him, but he held me too tight.

"She did what?" I asked.

"You saw how she winked at me. She wants me."

I struggled in his hold, not liking this conversation at all. "Of course she wants you. Every woman with working eyeballs wants you."

"Think of the bed, Hannah," he murmured.

"Now I'm thinking of Briana," I grumbled, but eyed it across the room.

"Then get angry and get to the bed so I can prove to you you're the only woman I want. I'm going to fuck you so good."

I saw what he was doing, besides melting my recently-put-on panties. He was giving me something to be mad about and it was working. I'd deal with Briana later, but I stayed on task. So I fought against Jack's hold. I could put my strength into turbo, but I knew Jack would release me go if I really wanted it.

Still, I said, "Let me go."

"No," he said, the one word dark and potent. "The bed, gorgeous. I won't fuck you until you get to the bed. That perfect pussy aches. Needs to be filled."

I fought against him, stared at the bed. Wanted to be there. Wanted to be filled by him. "Let me go, I'll walk there."

"No. Be a good girl and teleport to the bed." He leaned down and whispered in my ear. "I reward good girls."

I growled, my pussy aching and empty and he was keeping me from getting what I needed. Then there was Briana trying to stake a claim on my man. Jack needed to fuck *me* and only me. I wanted to be a good girl and I definitely wanted that reward.

His dick belonged to me. It belonged *in* me.

I had to get across the room, and it was mine.

So I shoved at Jack, mad that he was denying me and—

Ended up on the bed. I was standing on top of it, but it worked.

"Holy shit, it worked," I breathed, then grinned.

"Yeah, holy shit." He blinked, a little stunned I actually did it, and that he saw it happen and where I ended up this time. A slow smile crept across his face as he loosened his tie and approached.

I dropped to my knees on the soft surface.

"I'm going to tie you up, fuck you like the good girl you are, then we're going to do it all over again."

I reached for him, but he snagged my wrists, wrapped them with the tie.

Our eyes met. "You'll teleport to the couch. The counter. The shower. Until you have it down and you pass out from orgasms."

With his hold on the knotted tie, he yanked me to him for a kiss.

I loved incentive-based practice.

57

HANNAH

"When am I getting my car back?" Brittany asked, having called Jack's cell. It'd been two days since she handed me off to Jack for safekeeping. I texted her to tell her I was okay and she immediately called back.

"You left me with a hitman. That's what you're checking on?" I was in the kitchen refilling my mug with coffee. I was barefooted and in clothes I found in a workout bag on Brittany's backseat. I was shorter and heavier, but yoga pants were really forgiving. The pale purple t-shirt was a little tight, but the way Jack's eyes snagged on my chest after I put it on, I didn't mind. I didn't feel fat when I was with Jack.

"Fine. How's your vagina?"

I glanced at Jack who was asleep on the couch, Pancake resting on his chest.

I laughed and leaned against the counter. "What?"

"If you two haven't reenacted the sex scenes in every one of your favorite books yet, that's not the hottie I thought he was."

"It's better than the books."

She squealed and I had to pull the phone away from my ear. Her reaction had me smiling. "Thank you, sweet baby Jesus. Makeup sex is the best."

"B," I chided, but there was nothing but a tinge of embarrassment mixed in with affection.

"So how's your vagina?"

"Not lonely."

"I'm over here fanning myself. Think his friend, Dax, is single?"

"I don't think their job allows for tons of one-on-one interactions."

"You've had two days of one-on-one interactions," she countered. "I want some, too."

"I'm not sharing." I did feel a wee bit possessive when it came to Jack. Especially after learning about what Briana did. He hadn't said that to make me mad and teleport. She'd actually played footsie with him with me sitting right there.

"Fine. I'll be over here babysitting your books and collecting your mail. And driving your car. I used the spare key you gave me and picked it up."

"No problem."

"When do you think you'll be back?"

Jack and Dax had talked about dealing with Sal Reggiano, but I'd been distracted by orgasms and Jack's stunning body. With more than a smidge of feminine satisfaction, Jack had been distracted, too.

"No idea, but I have Mrs. Metcalf filling in for me. She was more than willing to volunteer when she found out I was spending the time with Jack."

"Be careful."

"I will."

"And sweetie, have fun. You deserve it."

58

HANNAH

An hour later, I was on the couch reading when a voice called from the entry. "Everyone decent?" Seconds later, Dax came into the living room.

"Hey," I said, setting my e-reader down. The action had Pancake hopping onto the back of the couch, walking across it, then jumping down to go off and do whatever moody cats did. "You're Dax, right?"

His brows rose in surprise.

"Oh, um, Jack called you by name in the parking garage."

He caught on and his face cleared.

"Jack's told me a lot about you," I added.

He smiled. Nodded. Since Jack said they went to school together, I knew they were the same age. Both were also very attractive. Where Jack was dark, Dax was fairer. His lighter brown hair was shorn close to his head. Shorter and stockier and he reminded me of a boxer. Chiseled muscles. Thick shoulders, lean waist. Cauliflower ear.

Dax wore a tan suit with a white dress shirt and gray tie. He looked crisp and professional and not anything like I imagined a fixer to look like.

I hadn't seen Jack wear anything but black–or jeans, or nothing–which was fine by me because he looked *mighty* fine in that color.

"This is yours, right?" He set my purse, which I hadn't realized he'd been holding, on the back of a couch.

"Oh! Yes."

"I went to the library and picked it up. Your cell is tucked inside. Probably needs to be charged though."

"Thank you so much. I can't believe you went to Coal Springs for me."

He replied, but it wasn't the answer I expected. "You're the woman who's got Jack by the short hairs." As if that explained why he drove two hours round trip to grab a purse of a woman he never met before.

"Okaay. The um... short hairs, I'm not sure about that." I shrugged, then glanced up at him slyly. "He does like me touching other parts of him though."

He laughed, deep and rich. "I like you." He had an easy-going manner that Jack did not. I could see how Dax could tame Jack's intensity. "Where's Jack?"

"Shower."

He lifted his chin in acknowledgement.

"Want to sit down?" I asked, playing nervous hostess. This wasn't my apartment and Dax wasn't my friend, so I wasn't sure what was right.

He waved his hand. "Nah, I stopped by to see if he wanted to tag along on a project."

"You mean your fixer work?"

Dax raised one brow, eyed me in a calculated way that I couldn't tell was suspicion or curiosity. "He told you about that?"

For a moment, I realized maybe I wasn't supposed to know that. Or maybe I wasn't supposed to let Dax know that I knew. Or–

Oh, what the hell. The cat was out of the bag.

"Did you forget he told me he was a hitman?"

"No, but I didn't expect him to share much. My mistake."

"To set the record straight" –I set my hand on my chest– "I'm not a hitman."

He grinned. "I knew that, but I wasn't blinded by that spectacular rack like someone else."

"Hey, cut that out," Jack said, coming into the room and setting a hand on my shoulder. He kissed my head before he continued, "That spectacular rack doesn't belong to you."

Wow. Today he was dressed down in jeans and an Air Force Academy t-shirt. His hair was damp, and he smelled clean and good.

"I can look," Dax countered.

Jack growled. "Don't make me kill you."

Dax set his hand on his chest, then grinned and winked at me. "What a way to go."

I couldn't help but smile at his completely inappropriate compliment. But when a girl's been told she's overweight by her mother, classmates, and even ex-boyfriends,

I'd take the words in the spirit they were given: to fuck with Jack and to make me smile.

"Get your own girl," Jack snapped.

"I need to make a pickup," Dax said, changing the subject. "Want to join me?"

"Nope, I'm here with Hannah."

"You should go," I told him, not wanting to keep him from boy-time or working.

His eyes met mine. "I'm not leaving you here alone."

"Then bring her along," Dax said.

Jack's eyebrows rose almost to his hairline. "What? To a pickup? Are you insane?"

"Hey, why can't I come?" I asked. "I can take care of myself." I gave Jack a pointed look, hoping he'd catch my meaning without saying it aloud. While I would call my teleporting clumsy at best, I was doing it. I'd made it to all around the apartment and had sex immediately after each time.

Jack seemed to get off–literally–on me being Wonder Woman.

"Yeah, she can take care of herself," Dax parroted.

Jack gave him a death glare. "How do you know that?"

"She snuck past you at Dad's place."

I crossed my arms over my chest, which had both men's gazes dropping to stare. "I snuck past you at Dax's dad's place," I repeated. What I didn't say was that I could now teleport more easily if I had to.

The death glare lifted from my boobs to my face. I smiled sweetly at him.

"I want to go," I said, setting my hand on his bare arm,

then looked over my shoulder at Dax. "I mean, you're not going to kill anyone, are you?"

"I leave the killing to your man," he told me.

The glare continued through Dax's words. In fact, I wasn't sure if Jack even blinked. "Where's the pickup?"

"Smitty's."

"You doing a little gardening? Jack asked.

I frowned. Now they were speaking in code.

Dax shrugged. "Maybe. If she's gonna stick around, she needs to know what she's in for."

"No, she doesn't," Jack snapped. "I quit, remember?"

I set my hand on my chest. "I'm right here, you know," I reminded. "Is this a bad guy?"

Dax chuckled. "Yeah, sweetheart, he's a bad guy."

"How bad?"

Dax and Jack shared a look. Dax remained silent until Jack nodded.

"We're paying him a visit for an overdue loan. But he cheated on his wife and bragged about it. With multiple women. Refuses to pay child support."

"A cheater?" I turned to Jack, slid my hand around to his chest and looked up at him. "I don't like that. Maybe I could, um... throw him around a little for you?"

Jack's dark brow winged up and his mouth twitched.

"I didn't say murder," I reminded. "Maybe a little karma though."

"You do Judo or something, sweetheart?"

I didn't answer Dax, just kept focused on Jack. His eyes went from stormy to amused in a matter of seconds. "All right, gorgeous," Jack said. "You can throw him around a little. But you'll do what I say and if there's any danger, you'll... disappear."

I nodded, knowing that Jack's protective nature wouldn't allow for anything less than me transporting out of there.

"This is gonna be fun," Dax said, heading for the elevators.

59

JACK

An hour later, we were in The Sip and Swallow, a shady dive bar in the seedier section of town. A back office was a consistent place where we did "business" since it never had witnesses, there was usually only one door in and out, and because every bar in town had one.

Dax had given Smitty a chance to fork over the cash he owed, but he only offered up half, which was still a big fucking chunk of change. Instead of pulling out the garden shears, Dax had introduced him to Hannah, who'd been standing quietly beside me.

The guy was dumber than Joey Brains because not only did he ogle my girl's rack in that fucking too-tight t-shirt that should only be worn at home with me, but he'd also insulted her intelligence, her gender, and even her mother, although the last probably hadn't bothered her.

She wrung her hands and unconsciously tucked

herself against my side. This–not only collecting a debt, but also this bar–was not her turf. Not her lifestyle. Not her job. But she wanted to be here. Hell, she needed this. I could teach the guy a lesson for being a misogynistic lowlife, but that wouldn't help Hannah. After the number her ex did on her, she needed to kick some ass. To put a stupid fucker in his place. It wasn't Kevin the Cheater, but Smitty would be a good replacement. She had to do this herself.

Leaning down, I'd whispered a reminder. "Cheater."

That has worked in the same way as shaking the bag of kibble did for Pancake. She perked right up, got an evil– and slightly scary–gleam in her eye right before she grabbed the fucker by the front of his stained AC/DC shirt and hoisted him in the air.

"Hey! What the fuck?" he called while flailing.

He wasn't a big guy, probably weighing in at a buck fifty, but he was scrappy. He'd have beaten Hannah in a fight– both figuratively and literally–but she had the element of surprise. And a superpower. In her tee and yoga pants, she looked like she just picked up an acai berry fruit smoothie after yoga class. She might look like the girl next door, but my girl was so much more.

My dick got hard watching her.

"You sure she's not a hitman?" Dax leaned close and tipped his voice low. The look he had on his face was as skeptical as his words.

"Yup, not a hitman," I said.

Hannah looked more like Atlas lifting the earth than a mild-mannered librarian.

Smitty's hands were pulling on Hannah's grip, but

nothing was working. His feet flailed as they dangled six inches above the ground.

"Then *what the fuck?*" Dax breathed.

The room was small with a desk against one wall, an old metal filing cabinet against another, and a ratty couch along the third without the door. We stood close, ready to reach out and help like parents with a kid learning how to swim, but she sure didn't need us. She jumped right into the deep end.

"She might be a fixer though," I added, watching in awe. I had my gun in the back of my pants if he had to be put down.

"I heard you've got an ex-wife," Hannah told him. Her chin was tipped back to look him in the eye since she held him so high in the air. One armed. Without breaking a sweat or losing her breath.

"What the–" Dax breathed.

Fuck, that was my girl.

Smitty didn't answer, only glared and clawed, too insulted by being manhandled by a woman to realize–yet– he was in trouble.

"When a woman's talking to you, be respectful, asshole," I said.

"Yes!" he yelled. "Yes, I have an ex-wife."

"Why'd you get divorced?" Hannah asked. "Cheated?"

"No."

With a flick of her wrist, Hannah threw him against the wall with a hard thud. He slid down to the floor like in the movies.

"Whoa," Dax murmured, wide eyed.

Smitty winced, a hand on his chest as he tried to

catch his breath. Cool as a fucking cucumber, Hannah walked over, leaned down and grabbed him again. He went right back up in the air, reminding me of a flag in the breeze.

"She eat her Wheaties this morning?" Dax asked, not tearing his eyes off my girl.

"Cheated?" Hannah repeated, giving him a little jiggle.

I may have heard his teeth clack together.

"Yes!"

"I don't like cheaters."

"She got fat with each kid," he replied. He was definitely dumber than Joey Brains.

Hannah cocked her head, not liking that answer. Hell, *I* didn't like that answer.

"Dude, I'm PMSing and I'm *really* cranky? You know how women get, all emotional and a little crazy."

Dax snorted and I grinned.

"Please, I'm sorry," he pleaded.

Now Smitty knew he was fucked, although too stupid to know how since he'd never been tossed around by a woman.

"Probably not as sorry as your ex feels about meeting you."

"Don't kill him, gorgeous," I said, unable to keep the teasing smirk from my face. "At least not yet."

She turned, which made Smitty swing about and have his feet hit the file cabinet. "What do you want me to do with him then? Although, I'm wearing Brittany's clothes, and she won't be thrilled if I get blood on them."

Smitty, still dangling, made a pitiful sound, then started to cry. She winked at me.

I groaned, shifted my dick in my pants. She noticed and I winked right back.

Dax leaned toward me. "This is so much more fun than the garden shears."

I nodded because I hadn't had this much fun in a while either. At least since this morning when I'd had Hannah on her knees sucking my dick.

"How much back child support do you owe her, Smitty?" Dax asked.

The sum came out on hiccupping sob.

Dax held up the money Smitty'd forked over earlier. "I'm taking this to your ex. You're back to square one with your loan amount. I'll be back next week to collect. In full."

"Ooo, can I come?" Hannah asked, then tossed the guy onto the ancient couch, which groaned, cracked, then collapsed in the center.

Smitty held his hands up to protect himself. "No! No, I'll have the money."

Hannah came to me. Her eyes sparkled with life. Her cheeks were flushed. She looked... alive. I cupped her face. "You good?"

I had to make sure. Smitty was a slimy fucker and she'd touched him. I wanted to make sure it was only skin deep.

"Oh yeah."

"Time to go, gorgeous." I leaned down, whispered in her ear. "I have to fuck you."

She shook her head, then whispered right back, "I think I might have to fuck *you.*"

60

HANNAH

My pussy was tight around the top of Jack's dick. I straddled him as I lifted and lowered so only the top few inches were being stroked. It was meant to tease Jack, but the flared head rubbed over my favorite spot, and I was close to coming.

My hands pressed into his taut pecs as I looked down at him. His hands were over his head, knotted together and then to the headboard with one of his ties. I loved for him to be in charge, but this time, I'd wanted him at my mercy. After letting me go to the bar and toss the cheater around, I was as aroused as Jack. I needed to have sex and I wanted it on my terms. Maybe it was because I'd felt powerful dealing with that guy.

I'd made a cheater pay. Literally.

He wasn't Kevin, but it gave me some kind of closure.

That I wasn't the woman he'd made me think I was. That he was a low-life asshole, and I could do better.

I had. With Jack.

Just like letting me deal with the bar owner, he was letting me take charge in bed, too. It was empowering, but there was no question Jack was the one who said when and how.

He knew I needed this, and I would satisfy him as he did me. With a voracious need to please.

Unlike Jack, I made it past the elevator before I sucked him. In fact, I got him naked, in bed and tied to the head-board. Only then did I get him swearing and begging and telling me he needed to be inside me. Only then did I stop and climb on, riding him like the cowgirl I was not.

Sweat coated his skin, his jaw was clenched, eyes wild.

"You feel so good," I said, tipping my head back. I could come for Jack, but this angle, with me being in charge, I needed a little help to get there.

I set my fingers to his lips. "Suck."

He opened and his tongue slid over the pads of my fingertips, laving and wetting them. My pussy clenched remembering that tongue in action. Pulling them free, I slid them down my body and over my clit.

Jack grunted, low and deep, his eyes watching where we were joined. "Trampoline." He gritted out the safeword. "Fuck, woman, have mercy."

Sliding his feet up, he bent his knees and thrust up so he filled me all the way.

"Jack!" I cried out. Just like that, I came with the feel of him so, so deep and my clit being rubbed.

"FUCCCKKK."

I felt the hot spurts of his own release, pleased with myself knowing I satisfied him so well.

With him still inside me, I sprawled on his chest where I could hear his frantic heartbeat.

My cell rang from the bedside table. Without thinking–because my brain cells had been fried–I reached out and answered.

"Hello?"

"You've got some talents, Miss Highcliff."

I frowned. "Who is this?"

"Sal Reggiano."

My pussy clenched. My whole body did, at the name.

I sat up and glanced at Jack. Mouthed who it was. His eyes flared and he tugged at the tie that bound his wrists.

Reaching out with one hand, I undid the knot. It had been too easy, which meant that Jack could have freed himself at any time but chose to remain at my mercy. He was giving me so many opportunities for building my self-confidence. It was working.

I was talking to a mafia boss. Naked. With Jack's dick buried inside me.

That was a new one for me.

As soon as he was able, he snatched the phone from me and pressed the speaker button.

"What do you want, Mr. Reggiano?" I asked. If my mother had wanted Jack to call her and my dad Mr. and Mrs. Highcliff for being a dinner guest, I assumed Sal Reggiano wanted the same courtesy, regardless of whether the respect was deserved.

"You."

Jack wrapped an arm about me and lifted me off him. I

settled beside him on the bed, his cum starting to slip from me. He probably felt as skeeved out as I did having sex and then hearing the man wanted me. Gross.

"Joey Brains told me about you." His voice was deep and raspy as if he was a chain smoker.

I met Jack's gaze. "Oh?"

"How you disappeared on him. I didn't believe him, obviously. The man's dumber than a box of rocks. But no way would a woman get away from him."

"If you want me, then I guess it's a good thing he didn't succeed."

"Don't worry, I don't want you dead anymore."

Jack's jaw was clenched so tight, he'd have to see Brittany to fix cracked molars.

"I also saw what you did with Eyebrows."

I tried to understand how that was possible considering Eyebrows was dead, but he meant security footage. There had to be cameras in the parking garage.

"I didn't believe that either, but Smitty sure had a lot to say."

Jack closed his eyes and was probably praying to the false God Perry preached about. Maybe going with Jack and Dax to visit Smitty the Cheater had been a bad idea.

"Oh?" I asked, filling in the silence.

"While he might be behind on a loan for a shark, who do you think that person works for?"

I bit my lip, eyed Jack. He nodded. "You?"

"Through my son, Paul. He's finding his place there in Denver."

I cleared my throat. "You, um, must be proud."

"You'll come work for me. Use your impressive talents. No one's going to expect a woman like you to be a fixer."

I didn't know what to say to that. For a thrilling moment–like any woman would–I felt exceedingly proud of myself that the head of the Vegas mafia wanted me to be a fixer for him.

It was absolutely ludicrous.

Except he was serious.

"You're the perfect supervillain."

I licked my lips, stared into Jack's dark eyes as I asked. "What about Jack?"

"Jack? He couldn't even kill a man in a restaurant without making a mess. I admit, he's smart. He's keeping you around because of your superpowers."

I sucked in a breath at the word usage.

"You don't think he'd be interested in you otherwise, do you?"

Jack's gaze hardened. Sal Reggiano's words rang with a possibility. One that I would have believed even a week earlier. Now, though, I knew they were false. Lies. Because Jack had wanted me on the plane from Vegas, when I was a nerdy, over-weight woman who'd attended a romance book signing. One who couldn't keep a man. Who couldn't satisfy one.

I was the same person, but I saw myself differently now.

Jack didn't want to stand in front of me, he wanted to stand *beside* me. Because I was strong. And brave. And powerful all by myself.

Being able to powerlift a fridge sure didn't hurt though.

Jack remained silent through all this. I was sure he had a reason why, but I couldn't use brain power to figure out why. I was trying to be verbal and answer wisely for Sal Reggiano.

"That's not a very nice thing to say."

"Nice?" He barked out a laugh. "I don't need to be nice. People do what I tell them or die."

"I've already got a job as a librarian," I reminded. "I'm happy and set with it, thanks."

"I don't think you heard what I said. You do what I say or die."

An ultimatum. From a mafia boss.

I gulped. Brittany would clap gleefully, then shit a brick.

"You want me for my... talents. You're all bluster because I'm no good to you if I'm dead."

"True. I do need you alive, but I can kill your family. Your parents' home is so quaint. They have a surprising variety of dead animals on the walls. Even I have to admit it's a little creepy."

My eyes widened as I stared at Jack. Sal Reggiano knew about my parents. Knew about the inside of their house.

"Are you also a good shot, Hannah Highcliff? Are you a hunter, too? Your talents keep growing."

"My parents have nothing to do with this," I said.

"No, parents never do. You're new to the mafia so I'll give you your first lesson. If you don't do what I want, when I want, how I want, I kill everyone you love."

"Um... okay." I didn't know of any other answer.

"Good. I'll see you in one hour."

"What?" I frowned. "Where?"

"Your parents' house, of course. Oh, your mother says to bring the potato salad."

61

JACK

Hannah had never talked with a guy like Reggiano before. She might've thrown Smitty around, but he'd been harmless to her with me and Dax feet away and ready to step in. He was an asshole, especially to his ex, but he wasn't anywhere near the level of dangerous and ruthless as a mafia boss.

All things considered she was taking the phone call pretty well. Maybe it was the orgasm.

"You okay, gorgeous?" I asked, stroking a hand over her hair.

She stared at her phone. Nodded. I pulled her onto my lap. Maybe not the best idea since we were naked, and I felt my cum that had slipped from her coat my thigh. Now I was hard again.

Surprise, surprise.

She nodded woodenly.

"You sure we have to save them?" I wondered.

Her head popped up and she stared at me wide eyed. It was really fucking hard to hold a straight face. Then she laughed.

"I don't know what Sal Reggiano looks like, but I can see him sitting in my parents' living room right now listening to my mother talk about side dishes and Briana trying to flirt with him. He may run off before an hour."

I grinned. "You really are ruthless."

She shrugged and I kissed that bare shoulder.

"What are we going to do, Jack?" Her voice was soft. Scared. Not the tone I liked to hear from my adventurous, brave girl.

"Besides save your clueless family from being executed by a mafia boss?"

Her mouth turned up in a tiny smile. "Yeah. Besides that."

"I've got a few ideas." Leaning to the side, I grabbed my cell from the nightstand and dialed a number.

"Are you going to kill him?" she asked.

I wanted to. Sal wanted me dead, and he was threatening Hannah. I wouldn't lose sleep over it. But a rogue hitman going after a mafia boss? I was as good as dead. No, Sal Reggiano had to be killed in a very specific way.

"If we do this right, someone will do it for me," I said, then the call connected. "Paul. I think we have a mutual problem."

62

HANNAH

"When I said I had a few ideas, one of them wasn't having Hannah walk into her parents' house, collect Sal Reggiano and walk back out," Jack grumbled.

He was driving way too fast along I-70 toward Coal Springs. I was in the back seat of his SUV. Dax was in the passenger seat up front.

"I should go with her," he added. His gaze flicked to mine in the rearview mirror.

We'd picked up Dax and filled him in, going back and forth with ideas. All of them were based on the fact that Paul needed to deal with his father, not Jack. Mafia took care of mafia, he said.

That was the plan that was agreed upon—at least by democracy and not consensus. Jack wanted to go in with a gun in each hand and shoot the guy. I had a feeling that was founded in his need to protect me versus being wise.

"We went over this," I said. "I'd rather my family think you're a mortician" –Dex snorted at that– "than a hitman. Weapons would be a giveaway."

"He might be armed," Jack countered.

We considered that and Sal Reggiano probably would be, but most likely wouldn't be waving a gun around or holding my family hostage. At least that they were aware of.

"Reggiano won't want to shoot up a house in Coal Springs. Nothing says bad PR than killing a family in a town that's a hell of a lot like Mayberry."

That was sad but reassuring. I didn't like my family, but I didn't want them dead.

"I'll... disappear if there's an issue." I flicked my gaze at Dax.

"You sure you want to do that in front of your family?" Jack asked.

I shrugged, but Jack didn't notice since his eyes were on the road. "They think I'm invisible anyway. If I disappear on them, they'll think I wasn't there to begin with."

That sounded really sad, but true.

"When are you going to fill me in on this disappearing thing?" Dax used air quotes as he turned his head and gave me a look. I met Jack's gaze again in the rearview mirror. He nodded.

"I have superpowers." I said it as simply as if I said I had extra-long femurs or fake eyelashes.

"Like the lasso of truth?"

My lips twitched in amusement at his reference to Wonder Woman's crime fighting tools. "No."

"How about those bullet deflecting bracelets? Those would actually come in handy for this little outing."

"No shooting at my girl!" Jack practically shouted.

I agreed, but still grinned. "Those are accessories, not superpowers."

"I'm guessing one of them is lifting Smitty off the ground and tossing him around."

I nodded.

"And the other?"

Being strong was reasonable. Plausible. But the other? Hard to grasp. Still, I said, "Teleportation."

"Get outta here." He grinned like a boy who got a BB gun for his birthday.

"No!" Jack called. "Don't get out of here. Stay right there."

Jack was beyond nervous and protective right now. I loved it. I loved him.

Adjusting the seat belt, I leaned forward from my spot behind him and wrapped my arms around the seat and his shoulders. Kissed the side of his head before sitting back.

"Can you show me how to do it?" Dax asked.

"I barely know how *I* do it," I countered.

"How do you do it?"

"I get angry. Riled up."

"You've had this your whole life?"

"No. Just recently. Like in the past week."

"Then what caused it?"

"I'm not sure, but the only thing I can come up with is my radiation treatment."

"Like Spiderman!" he almost shouted.

"I wasn't bit by a spider!" I said, going over the same conversation once more. I wasn't sure if it was a guy thing, this superhero obsession.

"Well, I'm jealous," he muttered. "I want superpowers."

"If it means having a brain tumor to get them, trust me, you don't want 'em."

He stayed quiet, although I wasn't sure if it was because he agreed with me or because he didn't. To him, a brain tumor may be worth the superpowers. Then again, he'd never had one or known the rough stuff that went with it to make an informed decision.

"You don't believe me, do you?" I asked him, not offended. I probably wouldn't believe me either. Jack hadn't.

He shook his head. "Nope. Sorry. But I'll believe it when I see it."

"No teleporting in the car!" Jack called out.

I wasn't going to do it since we were going eighty and I had no idea what the "landing" would be like, so I changed the subject. "You said Paul Reggiano's going to take care of his father."

"Yes," Jack said.

"Take care as in, he's going to kill him."

"Yes."

"Because–"

"Because Paul wants to take over. Mafia doesn't mess with women and kids. When he threatened you, he crossed that line. Going after you isn't enough to take him out because these guys do a lot of bad shit, but it's enough for me to ask Paul for help. I've done work for him, and it would be disrespectful to me for him to let this slide."

"It's his father though."

"Trust me, they don't like each other," Jack replied, and Dax nodded in agreement.

"This is the excuse Paul's been waiting for then?" I wondered.

Jack tipped his head and shared a look with Dax.

"Paul's learned that his father thinks you can hulk smash people and teleport."

"Who'd he learn this from?"

"Me," Jack said. "But probably also from his father directly. Joey Brains told Sal what happened in the library and the parking garage security feeds showed him how you threw Eyebrows around. Even with that first-hand knowledge, Paul thinks his dad might be losing it. Another reason to take him out."

"I don't want Sal Reggiano to die because of mental illness when he's actually completely sane."

"Is he?" Dax asked. "The guy's filled the Vegas desert with dead bodies. He's not a choir boy. He needs to die."

I glanced at Jack.

"Remember I said we're the *good* bad guys?"

"Oh, I like that," Dax replied.

"This is one of those times," Jack continued. "The earth will be a better place with him gone."

I pursed my lips and considered. Could I go on with life knowing I had part in a man's demise?

"How about this?" Jack prodded. "It's you or him, gorgeous. He either wants you as a hitman or he'll kill you. And your family. And me."

"And probably me, too," Dax added.

"Him or me?" I repeated.

There was no other choice. "Then I go in alone and bring him out to Paul."

"Fuck," Jack muttered.

63

JACK

We parked down the street, about three houses from the Highcliff place, as planned. Dax and I watched Hannah walk down the sidewalk toward her parents' house, then turn up the walk. He even set his hand on my chest to keep me from going after her.

A bunch of kids were having a lemonade stand across the street from where we parked, so while we waited, we forked over twenty bucks to the little entrepreneurs and had a drink.

"Needs a little vodka," Dax said, leaning against the SUV and eyeing the contents of his plastic cup.

The stand turned out to be helpful because we looked like we were two men enjoying a summer treat instead of waiting for two hitmen and super-girl.

"Where the hell is Paul?" I asked, glancing at my watch for the tenth time. "He was supposed to be here. I don't like the idea of Hannah alone with her family let alone with a fucking mafia boss."

Dax's cell chimed. He pulled it from his suit jacket. "Your timing is impressive. That's Paul. There was an accident on the highway. He's stuck for now."

My eyes bugged out.

He'd only been fifteen minutes behind us and there'd been an accident. Typical.

"Fuck," I said, making sure I kept my voice low now that there was a clump of kids around the lemonade stand. Some had walked, some arrived on bikes. It was like a little gang. All were completely clueless about what was going on down the street.

"Hannah's going to come out of the house with Sal without Paul to collect him." I realized my voice went up and I leaned in and hissed, "She can't go off with a mafia guy!"

Dax tossed back the remainder of his drink. "Chill. We'll go down and see what's going on. Be backup until Paul shows up."

I'd been overruled about the plan where Hannah was to go in, chat up her family and walk out with Sal, letting them think he got his way. Since the man *always* got his way, it wouldn't be out of place. Paul would be there at the curb to greet his father and take him out for ice cream or a bullet to his brain. We'd given Paul the excuse he needed to end his father's reign, and life, and we'd get rid of the hits put out on me and Hannah. I could quit without having to look over my back or keep Hannah hidden in a secret bat cave.

"Chill? Remind me to annoy the shit out of you when your woman's in fucking danger."

I had a bad feeling about this plan. Had from the start. It was falling apart as I predicted. It was time for Plan B, although that was winging it.

64

HANNAH

I couldn't remember being this nervous and scared. Not even when Joey Brains was trying to strangle me. Perhaps it was because I hadn't had any advance notice from him. I knew Sal Reggiano was in my parents' house. I knew he wanted me to be his little superpowered soldier.

Two weeks ago, I'd have laughed at anyone who told me the situation I was in. No way would I have ever imagined this. I couldn't have even found this in a book.

I was weak. I was scared. I was alone.

Was.

Now I had strength. Yes, I was scared, but I wasn't scared of my own shadow. Of living. Of being seen. And I wasn't alone. I had Jack. Brittany, too. Maybe even my family in their own ridiculous way. Although I needed to have a little chat with Briana before I liked her again.

I could do this.

I took one last deep breath and pushed the front door open. "Hi!" I called.

"Banana, we're in here," Dad called from the living room, although all I had to do was turn my head to the right to see everyone.

We never sat in this room unless we had guests. Everything was always immaculate as it was never used. The fireplace in the center was cold and above the mantel was a huge, mounted elk head, the antlers sticking out almost four feet on either side.

"Where's the potato salad?" Mom asked, rising from the couch.

I focused on Sal Reggiano, sitting in the very uncomfortable wooden rocker. He was in his sixties, with gray hair that was thinning at the top. He had a tan that matched sunny Las Vegas. His suit was navy with pin stripes, and he had a gold handkerchief tucked into the breast pocket.

It was his gray eyes that were riveting. I hadn't seen such coldness. Such... malcontent. He was evil. It was a good thing Perry wasn't here because Sal might burst into flames or turn to dust if he started speaking in tongues.

Dad sat in the armchair beside him. Both he and Sal had drinks in hand. From the dark color and the ice in the highball glasses, it was scotch on the rocks.

Briana was sitting cross legged tucked into the other corner of the couch, one of the decorative throw pillows in her lap. Dressed in another stretchy workout outfit, I assumed Mom had pulled her off the trampoline to help entertain.

"The best one to wow the judges is the Back Cody," Briana said as she waved her hand. "An easy skill, but with the one and quarter somersault from front landing over to feet landing... I of course perform it with a straight three quarter back S and S. And then–"

Now I knew why Sal looked ready to kill. Briana wouldn't shut up. I wondered how long she'd been talking.

"Well?" Mom prodded, letting Briana continue to prattle on. She was in khakis and a red polo shirt, ready to either take up a job at the big box store or as an elf's helper for the Santa in the Summer event going on at city hall.

"No potato salad," I said, not taking my gaze off of the older man. I hadn't forgotten it. I had better things to worry about. "I'm not staying. Neither is Mr. Reggiano."

"What? We're having a nice drink!" Dad called.

"I haven't told him about the Half-In, Back-Out yet," Briana said, her voice having more pout than her lower lip. "Or I can show him."

"You can't leave, you just arrived. You didn't even tell me you were coming and bringing a guest," Mom said at the same time.

"It's frustrating when someone doesn't remember you, isn't it?" That was snarky as hell, but I didn't care. I needed Sal out of my parents' house and NOW.

I tipped my head toward the front door for Sal to get his numb ass out of that chair and outside. His son, Paul, had to be here by now.

Sal slowly rose, then pulled a gun from a holster under his arm. It was so cliché, but it was also very real.

Instead of panicking like normal people, my family piped up all at once.

"Whoa." Dad saw the gun but was probably too sloshed

to panic. Plus, Sal had shared a drink with him, so he probably thought they were best buds.

"What the fuck?" Briana, with her bouncing skills, flipped over the back of the couch and peeked over the edge.

"What kinds of friends do you have in that book world of yours?" Mom only crossed her arms and looked down her nose at me, completely unfazed about the weapon. Her disappointment in me went very deep.

"Yeah, Han," Briana said from her hiding spot. "Before he pulled out the gun, I thought this guy was a little old for you. Whatever happened to Mr. Hottie?"

"The mortician?" Dad chimed in.

"Are you a mortician, too? I mean you also wear a suit," Briana added. While hiding, she was completely unaffected by the weapon. My parents weren't bothered either. What the hell was wrong with them?

"I'm going with you. No need for the gun," I said to Mr. Reggiano. Fuck. Now what did I do? We never took the gun into account. Maybe we should've. No maybe about it.

I couldn't teleport out of the house like Jack wanted me to do. Sal would kill my family.

"Mortician?" Sal questioned. Then he grinned. He had better dental work than Joey Brains because his teeth were free of gold fillings and very straight. "Yes, you could say I'm a mortician. Perhaps, Hannah, your family might be interested in my services."

Meaning they'd be dead.

"I said I'm going with you," I repeated.

"Where is the other mortician?" Dad asked. "I meant to

ask him after his cremation services for the animal innards on my projects."

I frowned. Sal looked to my dad like he was insane. Or drunk.

"Ew, Dad," Briana said, making a gagging face. "Gross."

"Yes, dear, what happened to that other mortician?" Mom asked.

I met Sal's gaze and said clearly, "We broke up."

"I think, dear, that this one might be a little old for you?" Mom asked, leaning in closely but not tempering her voice.

Great, now she insulted the man with the gun.

"We broke up because Mr. Reggiano's a better man. I like what he has to offer. The perks are what clinched it for me." By perks, I meant Jack would stay alive.

"Why does a mortician need a gun?" Mom asked.

65

JACK

"He's got a fucking gun," I snapped.

Dax set a hand on my chest once more, holding me back. We were behind a big-ass tree in the Highcliff front yard, peeking around it like the Hardy Boys. We could see through the front bay window and into the living room. Sal was standing by the fireplace aiming a gun at Hannah. Her mother stood beside her. I didn't see the others in the family, but I assumed at least her dad and sister were there.

"You can't go in and shoot up the place," Dax warned.

"As long as Hannah ducks, I don't really care what kind of collateral damage there is."

"Her family's that bad?"

Even though I was going to lose my shit, I had to laugh. "Worse."

"If we kill Sal ourselves, we're dead. The entire mafia will come after us." We already talked about this, but it was a stark reminder. He turned his head and met my gaze. "We have to wait for Paul. He has to be the one to do it. It shows his strength to the entire organization and gives him the respect he needs to lead."

"I know, but Sal's pointing a gun at Hannah!" I stuck my arm out toward the house. "I need my rifle. I'll put a bullet in his brain from here."

"No kill shots. There's a fucking lemonade stand right over there. You can't shoot a rifle in front of little kids." He sighed. "We'll go in and save her. But no killing."

Fuck. FUCK!

I stared at the house again.

"Fine," I said, gritting my teeth. "We can't kill Sal. But we can maim and contain, right? He definitely deserves to be maimed for holding my girl at gunpoint."

Dax made a face as he considered. "We can do that. We can't walk through the front door though, otherwise he'll have his gun trained on us. Or he'll shoot us as example to keep Hannah in line."

It'd work better than shooting her family, I figured.

"Think they've got a shed out back with garden shears?" Dax asked. "He doesn't need all ten fingers for Paul to take him off and dump his body in a concrete foundation."

Backyard. Backyard. I glanced at the house.

"There's gotta be a back door we can sneak in."

BACKYARD. I glanced at the roof. Yes!

"I've got a better idea."

66

HANNAH

"He has a gun because he's a bad guy," I said to my mother, answering her question about morticians and weapons.

"Why are you dating a bad guy?" she asked, her eyes wide.

"I'm not dating him!" I tossed my hands up. "I'm going to work for him."

"Embalming? I thought you wanted to open a bookstore."

"I'm not *embalming* anyone." I shuddered at the thought.

"At least working for this man should give you job security. Especially since the retail space you wanted is no longer available."

"What?" My chest clenched. The space had been taken? It was my space!

"It was a silly idea. At least this man can give you job security."

"A man? You think I will have a better career because a *man* gave it to me?"

She pursed her lips. That was what she thought.

"Mom, the man you want me to work for has a *gun* and he's aiming it at me. At all of us. He's a *bad guy*. Why would you say that's better than me starting my own business?"

"Do you hunt?" Dad asked Sal. "I think that's the wrong kind of gun for big game. Especially if you're looking to make a trophy of it. Too much splatter. If you get one, let me know. I can taxidermy it for you." He actually pulled out a business card from his pocket and held it out to the mafia boss.

"Who wants punch?"

I spun about. What the fuck? Perry? He was holding a tray with glasses filled with a red drink. Had he been in the kitchen all this time?

"I'm trying out a new kind of juice for the Sunday service. It's a special retreat this weekend. Thought maybe your new *friend* might want some. Even sinners like you get thirsty."

Sal made a funny sound, and I turned back to him. I wasn't sure if he was having a heart attack or what, but he looked really pained.

My family could do that to someone.

"Perry, he's holding a gun," I said, not believing I had to remind them of that dangerous fact. "Now might not be the time."

"I didn't miss it," he replied with a shrug. "This is an open carry state."

Oh. My. God.

Where the fuck was Paul? If he didn't get here soon, I was going to teleport like Jack wanted and leave my family to whatever fate Sal had planned.

67

JACK

"You've got to be shitting me."

"What?" I said, pressing my palm into the trampoline mat to test its bounce.

"You want to jump on a trampoline to get onto the roof? This isn't middle school gym class. We'll never get that high on this thing."

I grinned, pushing myself up and throwing a leg over to climb onto it. "Oh yeah, we will. It launches you about twenty-five feet."

Dax stared at the apparatus with more interest and less skepticism. Then he looked at the house and back as if he was doing geometry in his head.

I'd seen Briana fly through the air. If she could clear the house, we could. Dax and I weighed at least fifty pounds more. I hadn't done well in Physics in high school, but even

I knew more weight meant more bounce. We'd get on the roof.

"I'm in, but what are we going to do when we get up there?" he asked.

I spared another glance at the house. The kitchen looked out over the backyard, so unless Sal decided, probably for the first time in his life, to enter one, then he probably wouldn't see us. The neighbors were probably used to Briana flying through the air, so men in suits wouldn't faze them.

"That balcony. I'm guessing it's off the master bedroom." On the second story was a covered porch. I assumed there were views of the mountains from up there. "We can swing down to it easily enough."

"I'm not Spiderman. She's inside," he said, referring to Hannah and her superpowers.

I frowned. "She can't climb walls."

"Yeah, well, she's got a gun on her and she's not teleporting either, like she promised."

When we got out of this, I was spanking her ass for not following the plan, and not for fun.

"Text Paul again and find out where the fuck he is," I said, pressing into the mat with my weight so I bounced a foot or so up and down. Ensuring my gun was well secured, I gave it a little more pressure and my feet lifted off. Then more.

Higher and higher I went. My arms went in circles, and I felt like a bird learning to fly for the first time. It wasn't as easy as it looked. The chances of me missing the roof and breaking my leg–and other parts of my body–were pretty high.

"Holy shit, that's a serious trampoline," Dax said, his head going up and down as he followed me.

After about ten seconds, I was literally flying through the air. I saw the lemonade stand on the corner and probably New Mexico in the distance.

I had to help Hannah and I'd do whatever that required. I gave one more hard bounce, this time toward the side of the mat and I launched myself right over the Highcliff roof, then onto it. I landed with a thump and a tumble. I'd never make it to the Olympics, that was for fucking sure. All I wanted to do was get to my girl.

68

HANNAH

There was a thump overhead.

Everyone's gazes tipped toward the ceiling.

"Stupid squirrels," Dad muttered. "Can I borrow that gun? I need to finish them off."

"You are not making any more stuffed squirrels," Mom ordered my dad. "All our friends already got them for the holidays."

That thump sounded like a big-ass squirrel.

Perry set the tray on the coffee table. No one touched the drinks.

Briana remained behind the couch.

"I said I would work for you," I said to Mr. Reggiano. "I said Jack was out of the picture. I think we can leave my family to their punch."

Sal eyed the punch warily.

Another thump came from above.

"Marcia," Dad whined.

"If we're done here, I have to work on my sermon," Perry said, grabbing a glass and walking out.

Sal sputtered, clearly stunned no one was scared of him or his gun.

Briana finally popped up from behind the couch. "Yeah, I've got to work on my routine. You sure know how to pick 'em, Han." She eyed Sal as if giving him one last consideration for flirting, then must've decided he wasn't worth it, or perhaps thirty years too old, and followed Perry out of the room.

"Jesus Christ. Are you adopted?" Sal asked.

69

JACK

Dax gave me a look as he swung down beside me onto the upstairs balcony.

"This is more fun than I've had in a while." He grinned as he caught his breath.

"Let's get my girl," I said. "Get Sal ready for Paul."

Maybe because this was fucking Mayberry, or because the weather was really good, only a screen kept us from entering the master bedroom. The sliding door was open. There were two twin beds, perfectly made. Over the bedside table between them, hung a mounted bear's head.

"What the hell?" Dax whispered, eyeing it. The mouth was open in a snarl, with big teeth and fake drool. "That'd give me nightmares."

"So would waking up beside Hannah's mother," I muttered.

Dax checked his phone. "Paul said he's almost here."

Good. About fucking time. I skirted around the beds. "Let's go."

I pulled out my gun. Dax did the same, then followed.

HANNAH

With a flick of his wrist, Sal pointed the gun toward the front door. With the other hand, he tossed back the remainder of his scotch. "Let's go. I can't stay here any longer."

"You're not going to kill them?" I asked, making sure he would spare my family before I agreed to go with him.

"I'd be doing you a favor if I did," he muttered.

I heard a creak from the stairs. I knew every sound those steps made, having grown up in the house. Flicking my gaze in that direction, I saw... Jack. What? How had he gotten upstairs?

The thumps. How had they gotten on the roof? Oh my God. They used the trampoline.

"Why are you smiling?" Sal asked. "Is it because you're leaving?"

"Yup, that's it," I said, nodding. "You're going to need to

put the gun away to go outside. There are kids out there. A lemonade stand."

He eyed me as if he didn't trust me.

"I thought mafia guys didn't mess with kids." I poked at his sense of honor, and he tucked the gun in the back of his pants.

"Why did he have a gun out in the first place?" Mom asked. "It makes no sense."

"Because he's a bad guy!" I shouted. Jack moved down another step and I saw Dax's legs behind him. "Mom, he's a *bad* man."

"Then why are you going with him?"

"So you don't die!"

"Why would he kill us? We're perfectly respectable people. We've done nothing wrong."

The mother-daughter argument had Sal distracted. I used it to my advantage. "Because–" I began. With the gun tucked away, I flung myself at him and grabbed him by the biceps. With one lift and toss, he flew toward the stairs. He went hurtling through the air and landed on the wood floor with a heavy thud, then slid a few feet.

Jack jumped the last few steps, flipped Sal over onto his back, straddled him and then punched him like he was in an MMA cage fight. Dax let him have a few hits, then made him stop.

Mom cried out in surprise.

Dad called out. "It's the mortician!"

Perry hurried into the room. Took in the scene and shook his head. "Three men, Hannah? So much sin."

I went to my brother, patted him on the shoulder. "Only one, Per. I'm sinning so much with only one."

He sputtered as if I'd admitted to tossing a bag of puppies into a creek.

"Enough of your bullshit," I said to him. "I know about the woman in Denver you see on Wednesday nights. The money you're funneling from your followers."

Mom gasped. "How do you know about all that?"

"Because, Mom, I see things. I'm not invisible. I might have my head in a book, but I pay attention. Unlike you."

"What are you–"

"I'm opening a bookstore, Mom. I'm selling *those* books. It's been my dream and I'm going to make it happen one of these days. It's not the Olympics and it's not a cult. I'm in love with a hitman and–"

"I thought he was a mortician," Dad said, blinking at me in complete confusion.

"What does that make you then?" Mom asked me.

Jack and Dax hoisted a beat-up Sal to his feet. Mom was more concerned about what I would become if I stuck with Jack than the fact that blood was dripping onto her floor.

I couldn't help the smile that spread across my face. "A hitman's girlfriend."

The guys dragged Sal between them, each of them having one of his arms. Jack stopped in front of me. "You got it wrong, gorgeous. I'm super-girl's boyfriend."

Then he let Sal go so Dax could deal with him and kissed me. Full-on, all tongue, lots of sin.

JACK

As planned, although a bit late, Paul showed up. Three blacked out SUVs were at the curb. He stood flanked by his goons. To locals on the street, they probably thought he was the President with a secret service detail instead of a mafia boss.

Dax *helped* Sal down the walk and two of Paul's men took him from him. He was too out of it from my beat down to do much more than whimper about morticians and half-twits and being adopted. He was shut into the backseat of the front vehicle, and all was quiet.

I had my arm flung around Hannah's shoulder as we stood in front of Paul.

"I see now why you retired," he said, eyeing her a little too appreciatively.

I wanted to punch him in the face for having any kind of thoughts about my girl, but we were at a balancing point.

I got out of the business and Paul took care of the one problem stopping me from doing so.

"We both get what we want," I said, tipping my head toward the SUV where Sal was.

Paul was in his late twenties. He looked like a younger version of his soon-to-be dead father. "He shipped me to Denver," he muttered. "The asshole."

"He was threatened by you," I told him.

Paul nodded. "He was right."

I slapped him on the shoulder. "You're returning to Vegas to take your rightful place."

Paul glanced around. Took in the quiet street. "And you're moving here."

Hannah looked up at me.

"Yeah. Hannah's starting a business and I'm going to help out."

Paul held out his hand. We shook.

He nodded to Hannah and told Dax he'd be in touch. While I might be retired, Dax wasn't. Paul had a lot of fixing that needed done.

He turned toward the middle car and one of his men opened the back door for him. "Let's stop at the lemonade stand on the way. I'm thirsty."

72

HANNAH

Jack drove to my apartment. Since Dax rode with us up from Denver, we were stuck with him. The looks Jack kept giving me were hard to miss. He wanted to fuck me and fuck me now.

It would have to wait.

Pulling out my keys as we walked down the hall, Brittany stuck her head out her door. "Hannah, I– Oh, hey."

"I don't think you've met Jack," I said, raising our joined hands in the air.

Brittany smiled. "Thanks for taking care of my girl."

I blushed, because knowing my best friend, she meant with his Big D."

"My pleasure," Jack replied, a smile pulling at his lips. Yeah, he caught her drift.

"Hey, Briana," Dax said. "Guess we should be thankful they're not kissing this time."

"Yet," Jack added.

"Um, sweetie, I have some bad news."

I glanced at Jack for a second. "Oh?" She looked sad and worried and contrite. Like whatever she was going to tell me I wasn't going to like. At all. "Are you okay? Your parents?"

She nodded. "Yes. I'm fine. They're fine. But, um, well, the vacant space for the bookshop was taken."

Oh. *Oh.* Right.

I looked at the industrial carpet, brushed it with my toe. "Yeah, my mom mentioned it when we were held at gunpoint by the mafia boss."

"What? *I missed it*?"

"We were at my parents' house."

She frowned. "Never mind."

I looked up and painted on a big ass smile. "Well, we're all healthy and alive, so that's something, right?"

"There are other spots in town. Better ones," she said, always rooting for me.

"It's not taken," Jack said.

Brittany looked at him, not convinced. "A patient told me that her aunt's hairdresser's son is the Realtor and that there's a contract on the entire building."

"I bought it," Jack admitted.

"What?" Brittany asked.

"WHAT?" I shouted.

"Oh hell, you really are moving to Coal Springs," Dax muttered.

Jack ignored all of us and said, "For you, gorgeous. I got in touch with the Realtor the other day. The space is yours. The dream is yours. It's time to make it happen."

Tears fell. Again. And I launched myself at Jack, kissing him.

"I guess we're not wanted. Again," Dax said, but I ignored him over the way Jack's tongue was pretty much mating with mine.

Jack's hands were on my ass, and I hopped up and wrapped my legs around him.

"Okay. Yeah. Want to go get some food?" Brittany asked him.

"And drinks after," Dax added. "I think they're going to be a while."

73

JACK

"I think we need a new place," I said, finally getting the chance to look around Hannah's apartment. We'd made it as far as her front door–the inside of it–before we got the needed bits of clothing off or open to have a hasty quickie.

I hoped Brittany and Dax had gone off for that dinner they'd talked about, otherwise they'd have heard the door banging from the... banging.

Hannah had gone into the bedroom to change, and I stood in the doorway to watch. Her closet was tiny, and not a walk-in. Her entire apartment was three rooms: living room/dining room/kitchen, bedroom, and bathroom. It was a newer building, well kept. Her space was bright and matched her feminine, soft demeanor. And the books. There were books everywhere. One whole wall of her living room was wall to wall shelves. There was a stack by her bed, on the bedside table. On top of the dresser.

This space couldn't belong to anyone else.

She pushed her head through a green t-shirt and pulled it down over her torso. "Why?"

"I'm not saying I'm a snob and need a big, fancy space, but Pancake is."

She bit her lip. "Oh really? What kind of place does *Pancake* like?"

"A house with a picket fence."

Her eyes widened. "Really?"

"Oh yeah. He's always wanted one."

Her eyes softened.

"And this space... is it for three?" she asked. "Or two?"

"I'm not giving up Pancake even if he is a snooty bastard."

I went to her, set my hands on her hips. I couldn't *not* touch her, even though I had her only minutes earlier. "The *we* I mentioned, it's you and me, gorgeous. Say yes."

"To living with you?"

I shook my head. "To a *life* with me."

My words had the wrong effect. She burst into tears.

"Oh shit. Okay, we don't have to live together."

She set her forehead against my chest, then shook it. "It's not that. You got me the bookstore. We only met two weeks ago."

I stroked her hair and forced her chin up so I could look in her watery eyes.

"As you can guess from my fancy suits, my fancy penthouse, my fancy SUV, and my extra fancy cat, I have a shit ton of money. It should be used for something good. And you're good, Hannah Highcliff... someday Hollister."

Her eyes widened. "Are you asking me to *marry* you?"

I shook my head. "You'll know when I'm asking, gorgeous. I guess what I'm doing, in a very bad way since I've never done it before, is to tell you I love you. Two weeks? I knew in two minutes."

She started to cry again.

"Crying like that's not good for a man's ego," I added, but I waited it out.

"You sound like a romance hero," I said on a sob.

He huffed out a laugh. "I'll be any trope you want as long as I'm yours."

"Oh my God, stop!" she wailed, then wiped her nose on my shirt. "But I don't have money saved yet for the initial book orders and the renovation costs and–"

"What part of *I have money* is confusing?" It was simple. She wanted the bookstore I'd give her the bookstore.

"I can't take your money!"

"Yes, you can."

"Jack."

"Hannah. If there's something you want, it's my job to give it to you."

"Sure, maybe a necklace or a weekend in Aspen, but not a *bookstore.*"

"Do you want a necklace or a weekend in Apsen?"

"No."

"Then you're getting a bookstore. And renovations. And books."

"I'm paying you back."

"Fine. I accept blowjobs and anal."

Her mouth dropped open. "Oh my God."

"I don't understand why you're upset. I should be the angry one."

"You? Why?"

"My girl didn't teleport like I told her to. I had to watch a mafia boss hold a gun to you. I jumped on a fucking trampoline to get to you."

"See? My hero." A watery laugh escaped. "I love you, too."

I sighed, pulled her into my arms. This, right here, holding her, was everything. I'd been craving simple, but all I wanted was this. "Thank fuck."

"You really want to live in Coal Springs with me? It's fast. Crazy fast."

I shrugged. "I think we know better than others that you never know what life is going to bring and you gotta take what you want."

"I'm boring," she said, as if that would deter me. It sounded like a perk.

"Good."

"I would rather read than go out."

"Me, too, it seems."

She arched a brow and pulled out the big guns. "You'll have to see my family."

I shrugged again. She seemed to think her words would deter me. "I think there's one thing that would solve everything with them."

She stared at me, trying to figure out probably how I knew the answer. "Oh? What's that?"

I grinned, kissed her soft lips, then said, "Make the fucking potato salad."

EPILOGUE #1

JACK

"Afternoon. Can I help you find something?"

Based on Nitro's report, this was Kevin, Hannah's used car salesman ex. I walked across the lot in his direction. Tucked between a few hotels and chain restaurants by the highway, it had been easy to find. The twenty-foot-tall blue, inflatable dancing cartoon character that bobbed and weaved also helped.

Hannah and Brittany were at the bookstore making plans and lists. I offered to pick up deli sandwiches for lunch, but decided to make a detour and finally–*fucking finally*–deal with her ex.

Don't kill him. Don't kill him. You can maim. Maim is good.

I sized Kevin up pretty quick. Latino. Black hair he got trimmed at the barber chain store at the mall right down from the place he picked up his no-press khakis and polo shirt. Above his lip was a mustache, although it was pretty patchy, even for a guy who I guessed to be around thirty.

As he eyed my SUV, his brain was probably churning as to why I'd want to buy a ten-year old station wagon or pickup truck.

"Kevin Cortez?"

He offered me a smile, as if we were new friends. "You found me. Looking for another vehicle?"

I walked over to a minivan that had seen better days. "Looking for something with a little extra space."

"Growing family?"

"Bodies."

He laughed, but it was totally fake. His gaze roved over me, suddenly warily.

"A friend of mine shared your name," I told him.

His chest puffed up, pleased as punch to have a friend. "Oh? Who should I thank?"

"Hannah Highcliff."

His smile slipped. "Nice girl."

Nice girl?

"Got your phone on you?" I asked, eyeing the car, not the man.

He nodded.

I waited, then when he didn't catch on that I wanted him to pull it out, I curled my fingers in a come here gesture.

He blinked, then pulled it from the back pocket of his pants.

"Pull up a map app," I told him.

He looked up from the screen. "You lost?"

"I'm not lost, but I think you are."

He frowned. "I know this area pretty well."

"Do a search for clitoris."

He huffed out a laugh, the kind that misogynistic pricks at bars made when they got together. "What?"

"You heard me."

He shook his head like I was crazy and typed it in. "Can't find it."

"Yeah, I figured. You still can't find a clit even with a fucking map."

He finally caught on and was pissed. "What the fuck, dude?"

I stepped close. Real close so I could smell his cheap cologne and desperation. "Leave town. You have twenty-four hours."

His Adam's apple bobbed as he swallowed. "What?"

"Get out of Colorado. As far from Hannah Highcliff as possible."

He shook his head. "No fucking way. If she didn't have a brain tumor, she'd still be a bad lay. Not like her sister."

Wrong fucking words. Before he could blink, my right fist shot out and jabbed him in the face. The crack of bone came right before Kevin spouted obscenities and covered his nose. Blood seeped between his fingers.

Ah, that felt good.

I stepped closer. He took a step back, realized he might have some balls after all, and held his ground. Reaching behind my back, I pulled out my gun and pivoted my wrist side to side to ensure I had his attention. "Twenty-four hours. If you haven't disappeared by then, kneecaps will be first. Want to know what'll be after that?"

His eyes widened and it was possible he pissed himself. I didn't look down to confirm. He shook his head, finally catching on that I was really fucking serious. I could shoot him, shove him in the minivan and get it over a nearby ravine. That was what I wanted to do, but I wasn't a hitman. I was a boyfriend.

Boyfriends didn't murder a girlfriend's ex.

He broke his nose.

And drove him out of town.

Fuck, yes.

EPILOGUE #2

HANNAH

I ripped open the shower curtain and waved the letter in the air. "Read this!"

Jack stood beneath the hot spray. He was all lathered up with soap. Muscly, tattooed, soapy. I wasn't immune.

"Coming in?" he asked. My shower was small, but we didn't need much room. "Gorgeous, my face is up here."

Yeah, I was staring at his dick, which was getting harder by the second.

"In a minute." I blinked out of my dick-dazzled fugue. "It's a form letter from the cancer center. It was in with the rest of the mail Brittany collected for me."

He ran a hand over his face, wiping the droplets away. He studied me, probably to gauge how freaked out I was. He ignored the water. The soap on his skin. Everything but me. "Read it to me."

I took a deep breath and tried to calm my racing heart. I'd already read it twice.

To whom it may concern:

We are writing to those who received radiation treatments at our facility between the dates of May 1st and May 7th. It has been determined that the treatments from the radiation machines in our facility, not limited to the linear accelerator, may have been affected by a maintenance issue. No impacts to procedures that occurred during that time are expected and no incidents during post-op appointments or follow up care have been reported. If you have any concerning issues or unusual side effects, please let us know immediately.

Sincerely,

Radiation Department, Cancer Center of the West

I looked up from the letter and waved it back and forth. "Our guess was right. It was the radiation. The superpowers. It has to be."

"Your follow up appointments said everything was fine?" He was focusing on a different part of the letter than I was. That maybe I didn't get the full dosage of radiation or that it didn't do the job.

I nodded. "All clear." I'd been panicked after the first read, but I had gone to a number of follow up appointments that all said the procedure worked as planned. "Maybe it's like those letters where your credit has been compromised. There's nothing I can do about the error, but the letter was sent to protect them from lawsuits."

"Maybe. Well, definitely. Are you planning on telling them about your new abilities?"

My eyes widened, then shook my head. "No way." I'd end up in a psych ward, most likely, or studied in an underground bunker somewhere. "But–" I bit my lip.

"But what?" He reached for the dial and turned off the water.

Absently, I handed him a towel and moved so he could step out of the tub and onto my bathmat. If it weren't for the letter, I'd be shamelessly groping him right now.

"Who else got treated and now has superpowers?" I wondered. "Am I the only one?"

He ran the towel over his face, then over his torso. "You think there might be others?"

I scanned the paper, then looked to Jack. Was I the only one who could teleport outside of books, TV, and film? Did they have some *other* superpower? If so, what was it? Invisibility? Speed? Who were they? Were they as curious and confused as me? Were they reading the same letter right now and wondering the same thing?

"Maybe. I don't know, but I'd love to find out."

———

Thanks for reading *Hannah and the Hitman*!
Ready for more laugh-out-loud romance? Binge read the entire small town, romcom series On A Manhunt next!
Start with Man Hunt!

What's worse than spilling coffee all over my billionaire boss? Accidentally emailing him my answers to a sex quiz.

That was me. I did that. I might be a genius, but that was really dumb.

I sneak into the office to delete it, but it's too late. He knows my naughtiest fantasies.

Instead of firing me, he wants to fulfill every one of them.

He's everything I didn't know I wanted: Older, fiercely protective and a possessive streak the size of Montana.

But can he really want someone like me with a past full of man struggles and a head full of math problems?

Find out the answer in this steamy small town romance where a nerdy heroine is outsmarted by a lumberjack-sized billionaire in a test of love. With all the books in the On A Manhunt series, it's always open season on men.

Read Man Hunt now!

JOIN THE WAGON TRAIN!

If you're on Facebook, please join my closed group, the Wagon Train! Don't miss out!

https://www.facebook.com/groups/vanessavalewagontrain/

GET A FREE BOOK!

Join my mailing list to be the first to know of new releases, free books, special prices and other author giveaways.

http://freeromanceread.com

ALSO BY VANESSA VALE

For the most up-to-date listing of my books:

vanessavalebooks.com

On A Manhunt

Man Hunt

Man Candy

Man Cave

Man Splain

Man Scape

Man Handle

Man Spread

The Billion Heirs

Scarred

Flawed

Broken

Alpha Mountain

Hero

Rebel

Warrior

Billionaire Ranch

North

Mountain Darkness

Mountain Delights

Mountain Desire

Mountain Danger

Grade-A Beefcakes

Sir Loin of Beef

T-Bone

Tri-Tip

Porterhouse

Skirt Steak

Small Town Romance

Montana Fire

Montana Ice

Montana Heat

Montana Wild

Montana Mine

Steele Ranch

Spurred

Wrangled

Tangled

Hitched

Lassoed

Bridgewater County

Ride Me Dirty

Claim Me Hard

Take Me Fast

Hold Me Close

Make Me Yours

Kiss Me Crazy

Mail Order Bride of Slate Springs

A Wanton Woman

A Wild Woman

A Wicked Woman

Bridgewater Ménage

Their Runaway Bride

Their Kidnapped Bride

Their Wayward Bride

Their Captivated Bride

Their Treasured Bride

Their Christmas Bride

Their Reluctant Bride

Their Stolen Bride

Their Brazen Bride

Their Rebellious Bride

Their Reckless Bride

Bridgewater Brides World

ABOUT VANESSA VALE

A USA Today bestseller, Vanessa Vale writes tempting romance with unapologetic bad boys who don't just fall in love, they fall hard. Her books have sold over one million copies. She lives in the American West where she's always finding inspiration for her next story.

vanessavaleauthor.com

- facebook.com/vanessavaleauthor
- instagram.com/vanessa_vale_author
- amazon.com/author/vanessavale
- bookbub.com/profile/vanessa-vale
- tiktok.com/@vanessavaleauthor